The Standing Hills

The Standing Hills
Caroline Stickland

St. Martin's Press
New York

Library of Congress Cataloging in Publication Data

Stickland, Caroline.
    The standing hills.

    I. Title.
PR6069.T485S7 1987   823'.914   86-26160
ISBN 0-312-00193-2

First published in Great Britain by Victor Gollancz Ltd.

10 9 8 7 6 5 4 3 2

To William

And standing hills, long to remain,
Shared their short-lived comrade's pain.

A. E. HOUSMAN

Chapter One

On Wednesday, 19th June 1860, the midday to Exeter pulled out of Waterloo exactly on time. As it rattled and jolted out of the station two young men in a first-class carriage regarded each other, as English travellers do, while pretending ignorance of each other's existence. Both opened their copy of *The Times*.

Had Fate decided to people this carriage with two who, though both young and both able to afford a first-class fare, were yet opposites, she could not have done better. Richard Webster, newly raised from curate to vicar, sat with his back to the engine. He had a good-natured face, not handsome but pleasing with its soft brown eyes and dark hair. It was a face which could be relied upon to give a welcome reception to a worried parishioner, to show sincere joy at a baptism and sincere grief at a funeral, to laugh at a joke against itself and frown more readily at its own failings than at those of others. He was soberly dressed in grey with a cassock vest and clerical collar. He had never yet been able to decide whether a train—being out of doors—required the wearing of a hat or —being an enclosed compartment—required the taking off of a hat, and compromised by alternate head-dress on alternate journeys. Today his broad-brimmed hat lay on the seat beside him. He wore Oxonian shoes with buttons.

It would have given some comfort to the Reverend Webster to know that had a young lady opened the carriage door her glance would have lingered not upon himself but upon the fair-haired passenger opposite him—for Samuel Delaford had an irresistible attraction for women. His father's income, his mother's approbation and his own mirror combined to give him a confidence of bearing not normally fostered by a curacy. Younger by two years than Richard, Samuel had, at twenty-five, all the advantages of the first-born son of a gentleman farmer. He had a sure and respected place in his community, the comfort of a well-established home, an interest in and talent for the running of an estate and no responsibilities. He had, moreover, an alpaca morning coat and trousers of impeccable cut and, since he was on his way to the country, a countryman's peaked cap which he had no hesitation in wearing. After the heroics of the Light Brigade he had taken to a moustache, and this, now luxuriant, he had a distressing habit of stroking whilst smiling wryly. He wore elastic-sided half-boots.

His peculiarly appraising eyes, which had raised more than one blush in the past fortnight and caused more than one mamma to ask her hostess whether Mr. Delaford had a wife in Dorset, were moving mechanically over the newsprint before him, but if he had bought his paper from a wish to ingest current affairs and not from habit then his fourpence was wasted. His mind was not upon what Palmerston had been overheard to say to Gladstone in the House but was moving idly over matters of a more social and domestic nature. He considered his fortnight's visit to London to have been a success and there had been one sweet Mary whose exceedingly small waist and exceedingly large eyes might have caused him to extend his stay had this month not been that of the hay harvest. There was no particular need for him to join his father in this activity since he was only the lieutenant and not the general upon the farm, but his interest in the land was so strong as to outweigh the attractions of the town—and the eyes which had so held his fancy would have clouded could they have seen how easily they were defeated by a field of grass.

In Samuel's thoughts there was an abundance of fine pairs of eyes but each harvest was the one and only harvest, the fruition of the labour of generations of Delafords. This attitude towards the source of his family's affluence had brought him some ridicule seven years before when he had first gone up to Oxford—where money was to be spent and not earned—but his talents and elegance, his ability to move with the fast set while still being able to satisfy the most academic of his tutors had soon lost him his nickname "Father Sam", and he quickly became more celebrated for his skill in turning Latin verse into lines which could melt a barmaid's heart. He had put this skill to good use and now, as he sat gazing out of the smeared window with his paper crumpled upon his knee, he was congratulating himself upon having continued his mastery of the second sex and his eagerness to be home was not only for reasons of agriculture.

He had noticed vaguely that the other occupant of the carriage did not seem to be attending to his paper either but, although the pages were not turned, the wall of print was held up between them for a considerable time and Samuel did not have the opportunity to amuse himself by engaging this silent clergyman in conversation.

At last the train drew to a halt at Salisbury and the paper was lowered. With an air of anxiety Richard listened to the cry of "Salisbury—Salisbury—all out for Salisbury!" and opened the door. He beckoned the porter.

"Am I in the right carriage for Sherborne?"

"Yes, sir, first five for Sherborne and Exeter."

There was a slamming of doors, a whistle and the train lurched on its way. Richard took a handkerchief from his pocket and wiped the soot from his hands, wondering why progress was so often accompanied by the need for a thorough wash.

Samuel raised his cap and broke in on this reflection.

"Perhaps I could be of help. I'm travelling to Sherborne myself."

Richard looked up, reached for his hat and found himself bare-headed. "I'd be obliged if you would let me know when we are nearing the station," he said; "I've never travelled this branch before."

"Nor I—or at least the complete journey only once, when I went up to town."

"You're a stranger to Dorset, too?"

"No, my family farms in Sherborne. The line is new." Samuel leant over and held out his hand. "Delaford—Samuel Delaford."

Richard reached forward, his fingers square and unassuming in Samuel's grasp. "Richard Webster," he said.

"The Reverend?"

"A green recruit. I'm to be vicar of St. Mary's, Bradford Abbas."

"Then you must walk over and call on us." The carriage jolted over the points and both men clutched their seats. "Or rather we upon you. Will Mrs. Webster be joining you? My sisters will be glad of the society."

"I have no wife and my sister will be remaining with my aunt in Aylesbury. I can offer no female temptation."

Samuel laughed. "Well, I can offer you temptation: I have one brother but four sisters and all of them unwed and all of them pretty—though Laura is so sweet on Sanderson her conversation is not all it could be."

To his surprise the parson seemed undaunted and it occurred to Samuel that he might have a friend in Richard—and so they met and, at the station, parted, two men of equal fortune and opposite mind; and Samuel, who could not read a character, had promised he would call.

Chapter Two

As he had told his family only that he was to be expected on the 19th or 20th, there was no one to meet Samuel at the station. Tipping the porter he had left his trunk to be collected later and had strolled over the level crossing and up the hill away from the Abbey. He was in no hurry: he was conscious of being at peace with himself and wished to enjoy his mood to the full. He had passed a very agreeable fortnight at the town house of his old school-friend—going to afternoon entertainments, going to evening entertainments, dancing, flirting, cheering at music halls, eating too many oysters—and now felt more than equal to the rigours of country life.

He stopped at the turning on to New Road and dallied to look down at the view. From his vantage point he could see the young cleric who had shared his carriage being driven up the street in Keating's trap. He imagined Richard would be showing an interest in the Abbey—yes, there was the servant pointing it out with his whip. Well, good fortune to him, thought Samuel. People must be christened and married and buried and there has to be someone to do it, but I can't see the attraction of a religious life. To be always in sick-rooms, always on your knees—no doubt Webster was a younger son who had had to choose between the Church and the Army and what choice was that? Thank God I was first-born.

By now he was beyond the town. Behind him the Terrace rose steeply and a breeze was soughing down through the beeches on the slope to where he stood. It was so light as to hardly stir the leaves, but it brought with it the dry smell of the barley field above and he raised his face to relish it. Idly, hands in pockets, he continued his walk. That was good land up on Dancing Hill and convenient for Limekiln, but it was part of Home Farm and belonged to Bernard Page; it was not likely that he would ever sell, not with so many children to support. How many was it? Married seven years and three sons and a daughter—and another on the way or so Laura had said before he left. That was the devil of marriage: you took someone pert and pretty and before you knew where you were your family was into double figures and your bride was a worn-out matron. It was not a prospect that held much appeal.

He was hot in the afternoon sun, so he took off his jacket and carried it over his shoulder—that was something he could not have done amongst his formal London acquaintance and it gave him pleasure. Town was all very well for a fortnight but this was where he was truly at home. His friend's sisters had laughed in amazement when he had told them he could not lengthen his stay because there was hay to be harvested—"Don't you have men to do that?" one had asked at this eccentricity—and now he laughed at them in his turn. From where did they think the flour for their exquisite teas came? And where did their father and their friends' fathers get the money to provide those teas and the silks they wore to eat them? From the land: that was where the life was. He could understand an uneasiness about Trade but that was different, there was no tradition there.

He gazed down over the sloping meadows to the vivid green of the grass and reeds beside the river. When he came to take a wife she wouldn't be one to be prudish about his work; in the spring he could put his hand to the soil and tell when the summer's yield would be from the heat in the earth and there was nothing but pride in the thought. He would expect his wife to recognise his skill. Naturally she would be a lady and there would be no farm labour for her, but she would be such another as Mamma, from good country gentry not a simpering town miss—however entertaining they were in their way. He remembered a saying he had heard once—don't marry for . . . what was it now? Don't marry for money but go where money is. Very well, he would go where land is. But why think of marriage? He would see this evening whether he had need of a wife.

He had come to the end of New Road and turned up the hill towards the farm, bearing diagonally across the track to the lane to Thornford; almost home.

The farmhouse of Limekiln was set in a triangle made up of

three roads with the narrowest point towards Samuel and Sherborne. Often when they were younger he and Laura had sat high on the wall above this point as if it were the prow of a ship and the valley the sea. Over the years the roads had sunk beneath the level of the enclosure and now the dry-stone wall which ran around it stood on the summit of a steep bank. This bank was higher than Samuel's head as he strolled up the lane to the gate and it was covered with rough grass, long stems turned dry and pale in the June sun. Valerian was sprouting from the wall and the tight, ordered buds of the foxglove were waiting amongst the hazels. Sheltered as it was, this was always a corner for early primroses and in March his mother and sisters would make round, butter-bright bunches to give to their callers.

He opened the gate to the house and climbed the steps to the garden. He and Jonathan had laid these flagstones ten years ago when they could hardly carry one between them, and had made Naomi and Beatrice go up and down them for an hour before they were satisfied they were safe enough for Mamma. He noticed how the old Georgian roses had flourished since he went away.

The path led him up to what was now the front of the house. When it was built the main entrance was at the far side opening directly into the farmyard which, together with a small orchard, formed the shortest edge of the triangle; but with the new century had come refinements and the ladies of the house were no longer expected to approach it through the mud of the yard, nor to have their comings and goings overlooked by the two tithe cottages which stood opposite the working entrance. Not that the occupants of these cottages could have spared much time for looking out of their windows. The Coopers lived in one—father, son and daughter—and all worked long hours for the Delafords in the fields and dairy, Rachel, the daughter, being always the first on the farm to rise and the last to bed. In the other were Luke and Anne Hartley and their three small children whom Anne cared for as best she could, between the pieces of plain sewing she took in to add to her husband's wages. Samuel would have raised their wages if he could but his father was content to pay his labourers what his neighbours paid theirs; his men had always had working wives and he thought it the natural way of things—but he had had pumps put into the cottage gardens, a course his own father would have thought unnecessary.

The sound of the piano was coming from the opened drawing-room windows and by the occasional wrong notes Samuel guessed that the player was Lucy. All the Delaford women were musical, but Lucy did not have the long, elegant fingers of her sisters and as yet she did not always find the note for which she reached. Samuel entered the doorway and went straight to the drawing-room. At his appearance Lucy stopped playing and ran over to him. Mrs. Delaford and Laura looked up from their needlework.

"Samuel! Samuel!" cried Lucy, attaching herself to his arm. "Did you have a good time? What did you bring me from London?"

He pulled her hair gently. "What kind of greeting is that?"

"Oh, what did you bring? Tell me."

"Did I say I would buy you anything, minx?"

"You always bring us something when you go away."

"Sit down, Lucy," their mother commanded. "Try to remember you are not a hoyden. Samuel, dear, we didn't expect you so early."

She held out her arms and Samuel went to her chair and kissed her.

"I couldn't stay away, Mamma," he said. "I'm quite exhausted with enjoyment."

Laura smiled her cool smile. "You look it," she said. "I never saw anyone so tried."

He snatched her scissors and made to snip her hair; she laughed and clasped them back.

"We've been quite peaceful this past fortnight," said Mrs. Delaford. "How warm you look, Samuel. Shall I ring for tea or will you change first? Don't sit on the arm of the chair, dear."

"I'll have cider, Mamma. I've a thirst after that journey."

She pulled the bell-rope on the wall next to her.

"What have you brought me?" Lucy whispered.

"Wait and see. It's in my trunk."

A solid, middle-aged maid entered and her mistress gave orders for cider and tea and whatever cakes there were to be brought. As she left Samuel sank deep into an armchair and enjoyed the feminine scene. He liked women and he luxuriated in their company as a male cat will lap cream after a morning's hunting. He liked everything about them in all grades and conditions of life: he liked the rustle of silk petticoats and the glimpse of cheap lace beneath a serving-girl's gown; he liked the immaculate coils and plaits of a lady's coiffure, with its delicate wisps of hair about the nape of the neck, and the tresses which fell down around a woman's shoulders as she worked; he liked smooth white skin which flushed pink and the tan of the harvest-girls; he liked the vulnerability of his own class and the self-reliance of working women; he liked the tenderness of them all and the softness which came into their eyes when they looked at him.

And because this enjoyment was aesthetic as well as sensual he could take pleasure in his own family, as he was doing now. The three women reminded him of a cluster of flowers as they sat grouped together in the coolness of the room. His mother, who abhorred the harsh aniline dyes of the year, was wearing a gown of pale green and grey complementing her auburn hair and hand-some face; despite the fashion she had never worn a crinoline frame and her skirts fell naturally and gracefully around her. Laura took more heed of the fashion-plates, but she adapted every change to suit her already attractive appearance and her cages were never ridiculous. Today she was becomingly dressed in white silk with blue ribbon at the waist, and Samuel thought he could have taken her tambour from her hands and led her just as she was into any London drawing-room without embarrassment.

Though his mother and all his sisters—even the school-girl Lucy—were well favoured, when he returned from a visit away he was always struck anew by how lovely Laura was. He would even call her fascinating. Another man would have wondered why with all this charm, she was unmarried at twenty but Samuel under-stood his sister too well. He was amused to know that she was as exactly aware of her attractions as he was of his. A girl did not have the same licence in using them as had a man, but the excitement and romance of a dozen flirtations were as acceptable to her as they were to him. Recently she had begun to hint to him that she thought the law a most agreeable profession and, as his friend the local solicitor had long admired her, Samuel thought it would not be long until he was greeting her as Mrs. James Sanderson. He hoped that marriage would play her a generous hand.

Lucy, who had not yet put up her hair, completed the picture by sitting on the floor at her mother's feet, idly twisting shanks of coloured silks. Scents of lavender and clean linen drifted to him from all three and mingled with that of baking as the maid re-entered the room.

There was the homely chink of china and spoon as the women poured and stirred their tea and Samuel filled his tankard from the earthenware jug of cider. Each year they made their own in the great cider-press built by Mr. Delaford's grandfather. Last season their trees had not produced their usual crop and they had bought in apples from Cerne Abbas which had made the drink sweeter than it would normally be.

When he had broken his thirst he told his mother he would go to his room to clear himself of the journey and went upstairs to the bedroom he shared with Jonathan. It was at the back of the house and the afternoon sun was slanting in through the open window, throwing its soft light across the floor on to the coverlet of his brother's bed.

He stripped off his shirt and tie and poured water from a china jug into the basin on the wash-stand. The water was cold after the heat of the train and the walk from the station, and it was pleasant to wash the grime of the day from his skin. He had towelled himself dry and taken a clean shirt from the chest of drawers when there was a knock on the door and he heard Laura ask if she might come in.

"A moment," he called, fastening buttons and fixing embroidered braces into place.

Laura entered and sat on his bed.

"Let me guess," said Samuel. "What are they wearing in London?" He turned up his collar and slipped his tie around.

She pouted. "Mayn't I visit you out of pure sisterliness? What did you buy Lucy?"

He adjusted the knot. "A musical box—and talking of which I have brought you such a piece of frippery," he held out an imaginary hat at arm's length and fluffed the lace and ribbon with his other hand, "as will make you the envy of Sherborne."

"Oh, Samuel." She smiled delightedly. "Did you choose it yourself?"

He took a pair of brushes and began drawing them through his hair. "Well, I couldn't face a milliner's on my own so I took Henry's sisters, but the choice was mine." He put down the brushes and sat on the other bed. "I'm sure you'll like it," he continued, "and it wouldn't surprise me if someone else did too."

She pointed her toes and studied the tips of the kid slippers she was wearing. She glanced up at her brother through her lashes and said nothing.

"No news awaiting me?" he asked.

"Oh, only the usual," she said. "Everyone's still talking about Mrs. Hirst's new carriage. We had a picnic luncheon in the Park last week . . ." She paused and the face that was usually so clear and still was slightly puzzled.

"Well?" he said softly. "What of the picnic?"

"Grace was there."

"Grace Palmer?"

"Yes. I don't understand—she always has a crowd of men around her."

"But not as many as you; not such attention."

"Of course not—but even so. And I don't see why. Her eyes are striking but she's not pretty, and when her father died he left hardly a penny—she can't have a dowry; she can't afford to dress well."

"So?"

"Then why do they all like her so much? She says things and they laugh but I don't see where the humour is."

"Laura, if you understood Grace Mamma would lock you in your room."

She raised her eyebrows. "Oh? Is it so bad?"

"It isn't what she says; it's her manner of saying it—a question of style. You keep your own: it seems to work well where it's needed. And what of James? I suppose he was there—was he around Grace?"

"Only enough to be polite; then he came to me." She patted the coverlet where her weight was creasing it; again her expression was uncertain and he waited for her to go on. In a moment she said, "We walked together. He wasn't like himself at first. He was quiet—dreamy. We walked almost to the lake without saying anything, and then he told me that we had been friends for a long time and he wanted to talk to me because he felt I would understand. We stopped and he turned to me and said, 'Laura, love is so . . .'"

"Yes?"

"And then we were interrupted and couldn't be alone again. Oh, Samuel . . ." She raised her face to him and he moved across to sit beside her and put his arm around her shoulders. She leant her head against him and he pulled her ringlet gently. She was such a naive coquette; he would not, for the world, have her hurt.

"Well?" he asked. "Have you seen him since?"

"Not by ourselves—Mr. and Miss Sanderson and James took tea on Monday. Emma said she would lend me her new novel—I forget what it was called."

"To be delivered by James?"

"Perhaps."

"You'd better be in the garden wearing that hat."

They sat apart and laughed.

"I can't be in the garden all the time," she said, "and anyway they're to dine next Thursday. The Pages are coming too."

"Ah," Samuel left his seat and went languidly to the chest of drawers. He lifted his pipe and peered into the bowl.

"If you're going to smoke I'll leave," his sister rose and shook out her skirts. "The smell clings to me for hours." She rustled from the room and the door was closed.

Thinking of nothing but the pleasures of home Samuel took a pipe cleaner and began threading it into the stem. The chest of drawers was to one side of the window and from where he stood he could see into the farmyard below. As he watched a dark-haired girl of about eighteen dressed in a plain cotton gown came through the gate with a rush-basket of eggs resting on her hip. She could not be called a beauty, but she walked with a lyrical grace and, though small, was so perfect in her slenderness that she gave the impression of height. Quiet, with a self-contained modesty, she was a rural English girl, Oriental in her restraint, whose every practised task showed reticence, whose eyes spoke repose.

Samuel moved closer to the window to be clearly in her view and reaching out of the open casement he tapped his pipe against the stone as if to clear it. Hearing the sound the girl looked up—then, giving no sign of having seen him, she continued to walk across the yard.

Dinner that evening was an affable, talkative affair. Mrs. Delaford took a pride in keeping a good table and her domestic arrangements were always well in hand. Her cook was capable and well trained, her maids deft and cleanly, her floors and furniture swept and dusted, her silver and china shining. She devised the menus and unlocked the store-cupboards once a week as her mother had done before her, but had substituted a grant of tea for the servants' beer allowance of her girlhood. She did not forbid kitchen callers but discouraged them; she allowed her maids as much butter as they wished. She personally supervised the brewing of wines and ales and the making of preserves and marmalades; when a friend was in poor health she made port jelly with her own hands. Had she not always looked and sounded so much the gentlewoman her daughters might have complained that she took too much upon herself.

Tonight she looked with satisfaction across the white cloth to her husband who sat at the head of the table. Her family was complete once more, with one son and two daughters to each side, and the conversation—fired by the desire to know every detail of Samuel's excursion—was easy and rapid. As she ate she wondered how much longer she would have them all together. Each of her children was reaching marriageable age and no doubt would soon be leaving her.

"Mamma," said Samuel, catching her eye. "You know Dr. Knapton at Bradford Abbas?"

"I thought he had died, dear."

"I met his replacement in the train. A Richard Webster. I told him I'd call."

"A young man?" She cut her meat.

"About my age, I think, or a little older. This is his first living. He seemed pleasant enough; I thought we might have him to dinner."

"Certainly, if you wish it."

"What about next Thursday? If there are people coming he may as well meet them: he doesn't know anyone here."

"Do you think he would be free to dine so soon?"

"I daresay. There can't be much ministering expected on a Thursday evening."

Mrs. Delaford considered her guests. "Does he bring a wife?" she asked.

"No, he's not married. Shall I invite him? I could ride over tomorrow."

"Very well. I'll write a note for you to take and I'll ask Margaret Rouse to make up the numbers."

The meal continued. Samuel's attention was taken by his father and talk of the harvest. Both thought the hay would do well: the grass was dry and sweet and rain was not threatened. It reminded Mr. Delaford of the year they had dredged by Darkhole and Laura had slipped from the bridge bringing the boys their ale. "Hardly more than a child and never a tear from her."

"It was Rachel." His wife passed him the fruit dish.

"Rachel. Ah, it would have been her," he nodded to his son. "She used to follow you about like a mooncalf, Samuel. Still would, I daresay, given the chance."

Jonathan said that, talking of calves, young Garvey from Oborne had told him that they expected to sell theirs for fifty guineas if the breed held true. Lucy asked her mother why she couldn't go to London if Samuel could and Mrs. Delaford said that they would see when she was older. A maid brought in the cheese.

When they had eaten Mr. Delaford withdrew to the estate-room —in theory to attend to business but in practice to smoke in peace—and the family collected in the drawing-room. Samuel spent a quieter and more domestic evening than he had done for a fortnight. He turned the pages of Naomi's music as she sat at the piano, he played a hand of cards with Jonathan and he read the local paper. At a quarter to ten, when the lamps had been lit and his younger sisters gone to bed, he folded the *Flying Post* with a yawn and told his mother he would take a stroll before going up himself.

Bidding her good-night he left the house by the back door and picked his way around the edge of the farmyard to the gateway, the light from the quarter moon being too faint for him to risk a direct route after the evening's milking. He passed the tithe cottages where candles glowed behind curtains and struck away from the town towards Thornford. There was Delaford land on either side of him now and he could taste the green plant-smells of the country—so different from the city, redolent of hot brick and cab-horse. He walked carefully for it was hard to see his way and the deep, dried ruts which changed after every rain were a danger to the unwary. In places his feet sank into the thick dust by the verge where it had not been stirred by a cart that day, and he thought he could make out the impressions of smaller feet as if someone had walked there not long before.

Coming to the edge of Honeycombe Wood he left the road and climbed the stile into the trees. It was very dark under the leaves but he knew this path well at night and, with his arm outstretched before him to shield his face from the over-hanging hazels, he made his way surely uphill.

Deep into the wood he paused, seeming to see a darker form in the dusk.

"Rachel," he said gently.

There was a light, dancing step, a rustling of bracken underfoot and the girl he had seen in the farmyard came from the bushes and clasped him from behind. Her fingers crept beneath his waistcoat and he put his hands on hers, holding them flat upon him, as he turned his head to kiss her. She leant against his back, standing on tiptoe for her chin to reach his shoulder, breathless with laughter at having caught him. He rested his cheek by hers and whispered, "Oh, Rachel, Rachel, how I missed you."

She laughed again, deliciously, quietly, as if it were something she rarely did and it was a pleasure to her. She had a quality of joy he had found in no one else; nor did he want to find it. His flirtations were of no importance to him beyond the gratifying of his vanity, his senses were a surface interest, and, as innocent in his way as his sister, he had come into the wood to seek a devotion too deep for him to understand. He did not question why he came to seek it. He was young and thought himself a roué; if he loved he did not know it. He held her tenderly beneath the trees and it seemed to him that this was his home-coming.

After a moment she stirred and he turned to face her.

"I have a present for you," he said. "Hold out your hands."

"Samuel, you know I can take nothing home," she was softly reproachful, but she made a cup of her hands and he put into them something which gleamed palely in the lessening light.

"The finest quality town-mouse," he said. "I saw a nest of them in a shop-window and I thought—Rachel is a sugar-mouse; she should have company."

She held the mouse in the air, rocking it so that its crystals glittered, and her smile was all happiness and welcome.

"I wanted you," she said. "I wanted you back."

He drew her to him and her body against his was as warm and strong as the love she bore him—then, slowly, gently, with anticipation, he began to draw the pins from her hair.

At Limekiln Laura was lying in bed with her hair tightly braided to give it fullness in the morning. These past months she had had a particular reason for looking her best. It had been good to have Samuel among them again; when she had a household of her own she would be sure to make him welcome there. She would have liked to have joined him for his evening walk, but he preferred to go without company and she realised that men must have time alone. She wondered if James would do the same when they were . . . then stopped herself with a smile; after all what was James to her? She must give up these assumptions; she must give up thinking of him as James; he was Mr. Sanderson and she must remember that.

She twisted the end of her plait and tried not to laugh. Surely she would not have to wait long now. She knew that he liked her, that he named her the most beautiful girl in the county. She had thought he would declare himself at the picnic but they had been interrupted; she could not see why Mrs. Palmer should think they had the mustard, anyone could see they were not eating. No matter, what were a few more days? And being courted was so delicious. She would remind Emma of the book tomorrow. She turned on her side and dreamed.

At the moment Samuel was meeting Rachel, Richard, having entered into the rich tapestry of domesticity and been dined and suppered to the point of grossness, was unpacking his case of books and placing *The Angel in the House* in convenient reach of his chair. A letter to his sister lay sealed on the desk.

My dear Maud,
    Please convey my love and duty to Aunt Sophia; to her I will write separately.

To you I say there was no need for your anxiety: my dinner was well cooked, my sheets are aired; you find me in spirits. Tired but exultant I tell you that I have feared this day for months and yet here I sit at its latter end. There are greater trials to come: there is my congregation to meet, my first sermon to make, my every word and deed to be passed and discussed by all the parish; but that is tomorrow and tonight "sufficient unto the day is the evil thereof."

You will wish to know who cares for me. I was introduced to my staff by Mr. Adam Keating who has already proved so generous in his welcome and whose letters I showed to you. I have a very pretty maid-of-all-work with a look of subdued longing in her remarkable brown eyes. Unless this longing is for something unusual in a maid I foresee a kitchen full of followers, tears, pleadings and a hurried reading of the banns. It would be cruel and worthless to forbid courting and who am I to dissuade young women from matrimony, a holy and sacramental state? Keating says that she is a sober, discreet girl but Mrs. Houghton, my voluble housekeeper, tells me that Keating himself suffers from the conviction that he has killed his wife—a lady whose death in childbed caused him to buy Abbotsbury House and there cloister himself amongst his papers—and, while not seeking their company, is noted for his courtesy towards women. Certainly he seems of a most composed and studious disposition, older than his middle years, and inclined to a reverent view of the sex. He said, with some bashfulness, that he has taken the liberty of lending books to this maid, who expressed a desire to widen her learning—and here, perhaps, my first impression has misjudged her.

I see that at my suggestion none of my staff are in mourning for the late doctor. How I dislike to see black worn for any but the nearest, dearest relative or friend; let us take what rejoicing we may from this life.

Oh, Maud! The beauty of this place and the hopes and longings I have for it. If I can but order my parish as the first sight of Sherborne was to my eyes. I had left the station—so new, so oiled and painted, so bestrung with geraniums—and taken my seat in the trap K. sent for me. Henley, his man, gave clicking of teeth and tongue, we moved off along the road that curves away from the line and there, screened by old yews, moated by lawn, was the Abbey—the Abbey!—rising from its ground splendid and comforting, square and decorative in the glow of its West Country stone. It was power and tradition yet a grocer was wiping his hands on his apron and setting his watch by its clock, women were harrying children past its porch. It was the one picture to please me—town and church in harmony.

I was then of a mind to be pleased by all I saw. Here they do not build with the red brick that we know; the twisting streets are lined with stone soft and warm as sunlight in September and when you leave them the country is lush and sweet as the scent of lilacs. It is a green land, the rich green of fields of sheep and cattle, the pale silver-green of unripe corn, the deep smoke-green of woods and distant hills.

I was told that "there is a living to be made here if you're a farmer" and that that living is made by the Delafords. I had shared a railway carriage with one of this tribe ("farming men; oh, great farming men, sir") and I think now that harvest fever had made him free with his words. Indeed he had cause to be joyous for the land that we travelled was heavy with his crops. His father owns four farms—and such names, Maud! Limekiln (their residence), Darkhole, Lenthay Dairy and Silverlake—and I was driven several miles through the two last. He has promised to call and threatened me with sisters; I am like to have company. There is much to be said for a female companion. I could not help wishing as we wheeled down the lanes, lifting white dust like fog in still air, that you, my dear sister, were beside me to be mistress of my home. When all the care of a parish is to fall to me, when dilemmas are put before me concerning which I cannot turn to my superior for help, it is hard to have no trusted confidante at my fireside. Before I left my vicar told me that had I realised how often in the past years our congregation had evaded the parson to reach the curate, the knowledge would have done much for my self-confidence but little for my humility; I cannot believe it.

It was strange to me to be journeying to a place I had never seen, to a house I would not recognise, with the intention of remaining there all my life. Mr. Keating had described the church and parishioners at length but had written only briefly of the Vicarage and I had no notion of what I would find. Too soon, before I was composed, we turned into the village and the mare, eager for her stable, quickened her pace. Henley said, "Parsonage orchards to your left, sir." I looked to the left to glimpse trees, then to the right to see my church standing on a high bank, and we were there.

I sat for a moment with the cob tearing grass from the foot of the wall. I had had no particular expectations, but if I had I would not have been disappointed. My home is a plain, unornamented building more than large enough for a single man. The design is symmetrical with two sash-windows to each side of the front door, five on the first floor and three dormers in the tiled room. The whole has been washed with a deep pink, a little green in places from damp and age. There is a lawn before divided by a straight path from the door to a wrought-iron gate hugged between two cypress trees trimmed to solid, reassuring, blunt ends.

I cannot tell much of what has happened since; it comes back to me in short waves of remembrance. I was greeted by Mr. Keating at the gate, met my staff, was taken into a hall that opens country-fashion on to the garden behind and given tea and converse in the drawing-room. (The furniture is old, the carpet shabby, but all is clean and cared for—and the light from north and east, the gaiety of the muslin curtains stirring at the opened windows would make your heart sing.) I ate and drank, we talked of this, we talked of that—each, I think, finding the other cordial and willing to judge by first impressions—and K. took me to my church. I will write more fully tomorrow, now suffice it to say that there are stone steps to the churchyard and that it is as you thought—there is a tower and not a steeple. We entered by the south porch and stood in the nave facing the north aisle. It was quite empty and deep in the silence of late afternoon. At the far end of the nave before the rood screen I saw an oaken pulpit . . . .

I awoke to hear K. saying ". . . mostly fifteenth century. You see the barber's pole effect on the beams and the red and white roses on the roof. Must have been most attractive in their day." I said, "Yes." He mourned the two year loss of the box pews. "Yes," I said. He, though it was none of my intending, knew we were a crowd—he smiled and left me, poor fool, to my glory.

Your loving brother,
Richard

At eleven the last volume was in place, the crate empty, but their owner was so unsure of sleep that he saw no use in retiring. He could not rest and, at length, took a walking-stick from the hallstand and went out into the darkness. The moon was in its last quarter and he could see little, but he had no desire to learn his way. Tonight he was conscious only of an unknown village lane and it was enough. He wandered to its head then, on impulse, turned left, right, right again up a steep incline and found himself on the high road to Sherborne. The hill made him feel his body's exhaustion but his mind was too wakeful to let him go back. He was almost at the fork where he and Henley had turned off for the Vicarage before he paused to take his breath. There was a small bank beyond the ditch at the edge of the track; he climbed it and sat canopied beneath an oak.

From his seat on the grass he was aware of all the silence and stillness of the land. He sat motionless, a quiet figure radiant with innocent humanity, looking out at the grey-black countryside, at the early stars in the grey-black sky. He felt the presence of the hills and gratitude and anticipation rose in him.

"Oh, ye Stars of Heaven," he whispered, "bless ye the Lord, praise him and magnify him forever.

"For the Lord is a great God, and a great king above all Gods. In his hand are all the corners of the earth: and the strength of the hills is his also."

He was content.

Chapter Three

In the evening of the following Thursday Laura was in her room preparing for her parents' dinner party. She had renounced that afternoon's meeting of the Literary Society in order to give all her attention to her appearance and she did not doubt that Patience and Emma had done the same. Naomi, who shared the bedroom and who was also to be present, had generously collected all her own belongings and gone to dress with their younger sisters so that they could each have a mirror to themselves. Beatrice and Lucy were neither of them thought old enough to dine at a party and had already eaten a cold meal from a folding-table upstairs. Fortified by a promise of having two glasses of wine sent up to them later they were now kneeling on the carpet with a mouthful of pins fastening knots of ribbon and sprays of artificial lilies of the valley to Naomi's breadth of skirts. They would gladly have helped Laura; she, however, preferred to perfect herself alone unless her hair was to be particularly intricate.

It was still light enough to see without lamps, but Laura had drawn her curtains and lit candles to reproduce the background of the evening. After dinner there would be oil lamps in the drawing-room, but her mother thought the softness of candles more gracious and always lit their dining this way. "Never choose women or linen by candle-light," Mr. Delaford would comment as he looked around the table at his wife and daughters in the flattering glow of the flames.

She had begun her preparations after tea by having the hip-bath taken to her room and filled by a procession of steaming buckets being carried up the stairs. She had swirled a little honey and a handful of lavender into the water and sat in it for longer than she needed, dreaming of a certain young lawyer she would see that night. Every movement she had made since she came up to dress had been a thread in a net she was weaving for James. She hoped that her mother would place her next to him at the table. She had told her feelings to no one except Samuel, who had always been her closest friend, and she thought that she had been discreet enough not to have aroused gossip—but surely a mother must notice that her daughter loves. She was glad that the Sandersons were such an acceptable family; there would be no difficulty after James had spoken; no one would think it anything but a suitable match.

She dried herself on a large white towel and unwrapped the cloth she had wound around her hair to protect it from the steam. Next she dragged the bath into the corner of the room and waited for the water to stop slopping from side to side before draping the towel over it to prevent any more moisture rising into the air and so spoiling her evening gown. She clothed herself carefully in a lawn shift, drawers and camisole—all three miracles of ribbon and embroidery—silk stockings with frivolous lace garters and white satin slippers. She sprinkled herself with lavender water and let it dry whilst brushing out her hair that hung loosely down her back. Biting her lips to make them red she took a puff of swansdown from a box in the drawer of the dressing-table and gave her face, arms and neck a light, almost imperceptible dusting of pearl powder. She clipped herself into her satin corset and laced it less tightly than was fashionable to avoid looking stiff. She stepped into a small watch-spring crinoline frame, passed the tapes around her waist and tied them in a secure bow in front. With her hands on her hips she appraised herself in the mirror.

Now she was ready to dress.

All over Sherborne guests were preparing for the evening; servants were shining boots and curling hair. At Home Farm Bernard Page was lying on the bed with his collar unbuttoned and a brandy and soda in his hand recovering from a day in the fields. Through the open door he was carrying on a conversation with his wife, who was in the nursery in her dressing-gown bending over the cot and telling her youngest to "be good for Mamma". There had been a sudden rush for fairy stories and comfort when it was learnt that Mother and Father were to be out for the night, and Patience had left herself little time to attend to her appearance. She had spent part of the afternoon letting out the seams of her moiré gown and Bernard, who liked her too much to worry about her waist, had said that really you could hardly see her condition and what would it matter if you could?

At the Sandersons' Emma was sitting on a stool heating a pair of curling-tongs over a small spirit lamp. She had already dressed but had stepped backwards on to the hem of her skirt and her maid was crouched upon the floor biting off the thread she had used to repair it. James and his father had been in evening-dress and carpet-slippers for ten minutes, and were in the drawing-room discussing the conveyance of a house in Acreman Street as they waited for their boots to be brought.

Margaret Rouse was lying motionless on the chaise-longue in the parlour of Lenthay Dairy House with her elbows in two scooped out halves of a lemon and her hands coated with salve inside a pair of wash-leather gloves. Her hands and arms were a great trial to her. She had been brought up in a household whose women had done no work beyond arranging the flowers and providing music, and her skin had been as white and unblemished as she could wish. She had married for love a man considered by her family to be beneath her and had proved her advisers wrong by living very happily with her husband, a tenant farmer.

Rouse was a self-educated man who had worked himself hard to reach his position and he had aspired to the luxury of an idle wife—a wife who was unmistakably a lady. While he lived Margaret had gained a theoretical knowledge of farming from listening to him talk, but she had done nothing more practical than scattering corn for the poultry. When Rouse died leaving her with two young sons Mr. Delaford, who was their landlord, had expected that the widow would give up the farm and return to her father's house in Devon; but on visiting her to discuss business arrangements he had found himself sitting at the table reading the accounts with a changed woman, a woman of pride and independence.

"No," she had said, looking at him through swollen eyes with her hands clasped in her lap, "I will not go back and tell my family that my husband has left me with nothing. I will not be spoken of as 'poor Margaret—she married badly, you know.' And my sons will not be dependent on their grandfather's alms. If you will give me leave I'll farm this land myself until they are old enough to take my place."

The desire to pass on land—even rented land—from father to son was something Delaford could readily understand. He had no knowledge of whether Mrs. Rouse had any private income and, of course, could not ask, but he assumed that she must or she would not attempt such a venture. He expected that she would hire a good foreman and live much as before. It was soon plain this was not what she intended. She dismissed all but two of her workers —one man for the heavy labour and a girl to combine the roles of dairy- and nursemaid. She made herself stout overalls of calico and went out into the fields herself to hoe and scythe and milk. Life would have been easier for her if she had lived either as a widowed daughter with her family or completely as one of the peasantry, but she was determined that she and her sons would not lose their gentility. At seven in the morning she might be scouring the pig-buckets in ankle-length skirts and gaiters but at seven in the evening she would be dressed for dinner. She was so careful to observe the proprieties away from the farm that the ladies who did not know her well enough to pay unexpected calls would not believe the rumour that she worked in the fields.

When he saw what she was doing Delaford sent Margaret a letter by his wife who was her close friend. The letter told her that as a show of respect to her late husband he would waive the rent for that year. He could afford to carry a loss and would have waived it for longer, but he knew that even this would hurt her—however badly it was needed—and make her believe she was receiving charity. He never discovered how much it had been needed —neither ever mentioned the gesture again—but it had meant her survival. The difference in return between a well-staffed farm run by an experienced man and a depleted farm run by his inexperienced wife was naturally great, but the money retained from the rent sent her sons to school and within five years there was once again a profit. She took on more labour but not enough to exclude her from all manual work, and the one thing her efforts could not disguise was the soiled hands of the working woman. She could conceal them with kid during day calls but with evening wear her skin would show through the lace and it was not the skin of a gentlewoman. She did not complain of her position to anyone —not even to Mrs. Delaford—but it was matters such as these that made her weep when she knew herself alone.

"*. . . elephanto beluarum nulla prudentior,*" finished Percy who was sitting at a table near her reading aloud his preparation for the morning. "There, you see, Mamma?" He shut his book loudly. Mrs. Rouse sat up and removed the lemon skins.

"Very good, my dear. I think you're even better than David was at your age." She wiped her elbows with a handkerchief. "Go for your supper now; I must finish getting ready."

The summer twilight was giving St. Mary's House at Bradford Abbas the air of peacefulness its inhabitants were feeling. Since the master was dining out there was no meal to prepare, and Dinah and Mrs. Houghton were taking their ease on a bench outside the kitchen door watching the shadows lengthen across the lawn. The housekeeper was sitting placidly with her hands folded before her and the maid was indolently teasing the old cat with a long twisting piece of orange peel. From the kitchen-garden there drifted the rhythmic scrape of a hoe in the dry earth and out of a back bedroom window came the faint splashings of the parson getting out of his bath on to the india-rubber mat.

Richard was feeling satisfied with his new life. The spectre of the first sermon had been met and vanquished five days before and on Tuesday he had been asked to visit the sitting-room of the squire's mother, a woman known to all in the district as "Old Mrs. Thornhill". This name was usually followed by a comment upon her age. She had borne her only son in her thirty-eighth year and her son was now fifty. She had become frail in the past decade and had gradually stepped back from public life until now, when she hardly stirred from her room. She had given instructions that if Webster seemed acceptable he should be brought to her for a quarter of an hour that she might see him for herself; if he were unsuitable he was not to be brought.

Since her retirement she had been engaged in improving her soul and had had her bible and prayer-book constantly by her side; but she had been brought up in the old ways and looked on the clergy as the figureheads of the Established Church and not men in whom to confide and find guidance. In her day they had hunted and sworn and swilled good wine, and it had never occurred to her that they should do otherwise—just as it had never occurred to her that the villagers were anything but inferior to herself or that she was not personally responsible for their welfare. She had no patience with those who taught labouring men to read nor with those who let cottage roofs fall in upon these same men. When her husband had died she had done as her mother had done before her: she had had her wedding ring enamelled black and a skeleton engraved upon it. She was not afraid to become a skeleton herself.

Now she sat in her winged armchair, in her black gown, as straight-backed and composed as she had been at thirty-three when the serving-man had run in to tell her of the victory at Trafalgar, and regarded this earnest young man with the strange collar who had asked after her health. He had a queer, mixed look about him, a blending of humility and self-confidence. She thought there would be many who would see only the first and find to their cost that he would do as he chose. He had an air of having been treated better than he deserved and of not knowing why —not like the parsons when she was a girl. Well, well, the world changes. He reminded her of the brother who had died when she was so young—how long ago? Sixty—seventy years? She had drifted a little and recovered herself to hear him talking of his idea to introduce allotments. Perhaps he was a practical man.

"Pigs," she had said authoritatively. "Let every poor man have his pig and there will be thrift in his household."

Wrapping his gown around him Richard went across the landing to his bedroom and dressed himself in evening clothes, with a white silk waistcoat and a conventional stand-up collar instead of his daytime wear of the cassock vest. Since he was to drive himself to the farm he stowed his white doeskins in his coat pocket and put on his old buff gloves. With his hair scented and the late sunlight gleaming on his gold watch-chain no one who did not know him would have guessed that he was a clergyman.

The Delafords' barton was crowded when he arrived. Already a carriage and a loaded hay-wagon harnessed to two shires were in the yard, and a dogcart pulled by a solid chestnut was being backed out of the entrance by a middle-aged labourer with a patriarchal moustacheless beard. Richard just caught a glimpse of blue skirts vanishing through the door of the farmhouse as he drew up to let the dogcart pass into the field opposite.

"Ah, parson," said a voice.

He looked round to see Samuel approach, and, gathering whip and reins into one hand, he offered his host the other. Neither man had dressed with particular care and both wore the same uniform of black and white, but Samuel had an air of elegance which Richard could never rival and Richard gave an impression of integrity which Samuel would never show; his every button breathed reliability.

"Here, Cooper!" called Samuel as Richard straightened up. The labourer paused in fastening a sacking-nosebag on to the head of the chestnut. "Put this one in there as well, will you?"

The man nodded.

"There's no more room in the yard," Samuel explained. "You might get out now. She won't stray, will she? Cooper won't be a moment."

Richard changed his gloves and jumped down. They walked towards the house.

"How's the parish?" Samuel asked.

"I'm alive to tell the tale."

"Not been crunched up and swallowed by the Thornhills? Watch that mud."

"No—Mrs. Thornhill's father and my grandfather were at Oxford together."

"What more could you ask? Come in."

They scuffed their feet conscientiously on the doormat and went into the passage where Mrs. Delaford, regal in burgundy satin and black lace mittens, was waiting to greet him.

"How do you do, Mr. Webster? I'm so glad you could come."

Richard surprised his companion by bowing urbanely and kissing his mother's hand. The lady found this quite delightful from a priest and the priest wondered whatever had come over him.

"Everyone is here except the Pages," Mrs. Delaford said, "and, of course, my eldest daughter."

She led him to the drawing-room and there was a burst of polite introductory remarks as he was presented to each guest. Mr. Delaford was there, his daughter Naomi, James and Emma Sanderson and their father, Margaret Rouse and, only a moment after Richard's own arrival, the Pages.

"Guess who's late," Samuel said. "Oh, no. Here she is." He pointed to the door and Richard, who had been standing with his back to it, turned around.

There was a girl poised in the doorway. She was dressed in lavender silk with a deep lace-berthe that framed the cross which fell from a white ribbon about her neck; her fair hair was arranged in long ringlets over one shoulder and she carried a crystal phial of scent and a fan of lace and ivory. She hesitated on the brink of the room with the diffidence of a fawn.

"Wonderful!" cried James. "*Quelle toilette!*" He kissed his fingers into the air.

The girl laughed and covered her face with her fan, her eyes showing that her entrance had been calculated to the last degree. If Richard had not loved her on sight he would have loved her for that laugh. He stood still as the women moved forward to greet her. He was filled with a sense of great comfort; he had been walking alone in the night and now he had come home, he had taken his seat in warmth and serenity. He was touched by her innocent vanity; he loved her for her acknowledgement of it. She had thrown her net and caught the wrong man.

"You haven't met my sister," said Samuel. "Laura, come over here."

The angel, the enchantress came towards them. He stood dazed and dazzled as the girl reached him, bringing the essence of lavender with her, a perfume which would always recall for him this first meeting. Brother and sister glanced at each other aware of their attraction, then Laura turned her eyes to those of her lover. She said something to him, some word of welcome, and he replied. As he finished speaking he could not remember what he had said. He gave himself up to her but she did not see it. She saw only what she had seen in a dozen other faces—the look of a man who admired her beauty and would take pleasure in a harmless, formal flirtation. She had no wish to hurt; her life lay at the other side of the room with the man who was guiltlessly dallying with Mrs. Rouse even as she was dallying with Richard.

Under their hostess's guidance the diners were forming themselves into couples to go to table. Richard found himself given Emma, who was to sit beside him, and Laura was passed to another. As in a minuet they trod in pairs into the dining-room and were assigned their places, Bernard Page being ushered to the end of the table opposite Mr. Delaford so that each person might be flanked by two of the other sex. Richard had Emma to his right and Mrs. Delaford to his left, the elder Mr. Sanderson sat directly across from him with Laura between him and Mr. Page.

The evening had darkened and the brilliance of the candles in their branching silver sticks made a sanctuary of light in the encroaching shadows. Richard watched Laura as she was seated; a candelabrum was set between them and the brightness of its burning made her colouring chaste and cool. Her eyes were luminous with the reflected glow, and he thought of the altar candles making the wine in the chalice glisten on winter mornings when his breath curled from his words and the coldness of the cup chilled his lips.

There was sherry soup at his elbow and he filled his plate. He ate and drank and conversed with all the appearance of normality but his heart and mind were with the girl who sat talking with other men. The soup was removed and replaced with cod in a shrimp sauce; it was rich and flavoured but he could taste nothing. The table-talk gained strength and speed, knives and forks clinked, wine glasses were lifted. The cod was replaced by a fricassee of chicken and mutton pasties; again for him it was as air. A great joint of beef was brought in and Delaford carved with the assurance of one who has reared his own meat and knows it to be good. All the men had second helpings while the women fanned their flushes and gathered themselves for the next assault. Warm masculine smells rose from the men—oil of bergamot, bay rum, eau-de-Cologne and sandalwood drifted and mingled with the flower scents of their partners. A window was opened and the candles flickered and rightened.

"I'm glad that tea is going up," Mrs. Delaford was saying. "The wives of the labouring men spend too much of their time and money on it as it is. You cannot go into their homes but you see the kettle boiling. It's a weakening drink and shouldn't be taken more than once a day by women who need to be lusty. If they want to keep their vigour they should drink herb beer . . . Oh! You're not teetotal, are you Mr. Webster?"

"No indeed, ma'am."

"Tea and sugar up, wine and brandy down," said Page, "and quite right too."

At the other end the hay harvest was being thrashed out. James was asking if it had all been cut and tied. Very nearly, he was told, it would be over by luncheon tomorrow.

"Better make an early start," said Delaford, "I smell rain."

"Will you be visiting the market, Mr. Webster?" Emma asked.

"Is there a market?"

"On Thursdays."

"I daresay I shall. May I have the salt, Miss Sanderson?"

"When you do come," said Mrs. Delaford, "call on us afterwards. We shall be pleased to see you."

Richard's eyes went to her daughter. "Thank you. I will." He put down his knife and fork and drained his glass. The maids cleared the plates and a dish of roast ducks was borne in. Mrs. Page dabbed her forehead with her handkerchief.

"Of course, that's only the workaday market," Emma went on. "*The* market is on Pack Monday in October. That's when the fair comes and the servants for hire. Or am I telling you what you already know?"

"No. I'm innocent of all knowledge of Dorset. I've been reading the Reverend Barnes's poems but I can't understand the dialect. I must practise."

Conversation ebbed and flowed around the table. What words can I use to describe her, thought Richard: radiant—yes; sublime —yes; graceful—oh, yes.

". . . superphosphates," said Mrs. Rouse. "You see, gentlemen, I wasn't a farmer's wife for nothing." Laughter rose and drifted.

"Let's see you ring a bull," said Samuel.

"Make an appointment."

Delaford stood and uncorked more claret. A large Eve's pudding was placed on the cloth and surrounded by lemon jellies and gooseberry fools marvellously decorated with cream and angelica. Knives were abandoned for spoons. Richard stretched his legs beneath the table then drew them back, fearing to touch Laura.

"Now they've made picketing legal," said Delaford. "Damned nonsense."

"That's Palmerston for you," James said. "I'll have a little more of that fool if I may."

36

"This is what comes of educating the working men—it makes them no happier in the long run: they only want what they can't have. That's what those Christian Socialist fellows don't understand. There's old whatshisname over at Durweston—parson chappie . . ."

"Osbourne," Samuel prompted.

"Osbourne . . ." went on his father; "now I've forgotten what I was going to say. Everyone finished? Where's the cheese?"

A large and crusted Vinny was put before him. He prepared to portion it.

"I don't agree," said Samuel. "If you educate your workers you teach them to think for themselves, to reason—then they're not taken in by every Tom, Dick and Harry who gets up on a barrel."

"We all know you're a democrat."

"I wouldn't go that far—but listen," he leant forward, tapping his forefinger on the table-cloth to make his point, "take the labourers who don't know how to read and write—how do they amuse themselves? By drinking themselves stupid. Result—unpunctuality, poor work and their families in want. Now take the Coopers—hard-working, well-behaved, decent livers and pence put away every week. And why?"

"Because they're Dissenters," James put in.

Samuel waved this aside. "It doesn't matter, it all adds up to their having learned prudence from the little schooling they had. You can't deny it."

". . . burn moxa," said Mrs. Delaford, "then pick the slugs off by hand."

"My aunt lures them to their deaths with beer and jam," said Richard.

"Lure me with beer," laughed Page, "don't know about the jam. What do you say, Miss Delaford?"

"Lure me with jam," said Laura, "don't know about the beer."

Richard's heart swelled within him; he left his cheese unfinished. There was a pause as the table was cleared and a vast cut-glass basin of fruit carried to its centre. Nuts and dried fruits were handed round in baskets. Patience protested no, really, she could eat no more—well, perhaps a few strawberries. James showed Samuel how to crack a walnut with one hand. Nut shells showered the cloth.

At last the ladies rose and were led from the room. The men resumed their chairs, their feet on fallen napkins and the port was passed. When they were young men Sanderson and Delaford had both been used to seeing their fathers come out from these interludes staggering, and Sanderson had twice come down to breakfast to find his respectable grandfather sleeping stoically under the table—but habits had changed. Nothing was said that could not have been heard by wives and sisters and the bottle went round only twice before the drawing-room saw their return.

The women were already recovered when their escorts re-appeared. They had adjourned to the bedrooms to make use of hair-brushes, mirrors and cold water to the temples and now looked almost as fresh as when they had arrived. Each was seated next to an empty chair. A small and unnecessary fire of fir-cones was burning in the grate for the sake of its cheerful appearance, lamps shone softly throwing shadows into the corners of the room and two white candles lit the music-stand on the piano. The second movement of the evening had begun.

Richard was invited to sit beside his hostess. It was only as he saw James go to Laura that he remembered what Samuel had said on the train—"she's so sweet on Sanderson."

He tried to determine their relations to each other from observing them surreptitiously, but he could not hear what they were saying and their attitude displayed no positive evidence one way or the other. They could be lovers—or they could be familiar friends. He felt hot and slightly ill; he determined not to sing.

The musical entertainment began with Naomi who was conveyed to the piano amidst protestations of not having practised, compliments, assurances and general pretty speeches. She ran her fingers up and down the keys to indicate a beginning and all attention was upon her.

> "Will you hear a Spanish lady," she sang,
> How she woo'd an Englishman?
> Garments gay and rich as may be,
> Decked with jewels had she on . . ."

She was followed by Mrs. Rouse, with her black hair and blue gown, who played Mendelssohn with the enjoyment of a performer who rarely has time to show her skill. Patience and Mrs. Delaford sat out their turns on the grounds of matronliness but James, who had been sitting with his face close to Laura's so that they might whisper together beneath the music, stood with his hands behind his back and gave "Oh, I feel like beef without mustard" to a bouncing accompaniment from his sister. He lingered at the piano to turn the pages for Laura.

Laura was doubtful of her right to be last. She thought that her face allowed her the privilege of a dramatic entrance but she believed—mistakenly—that Naomi and Margaret were the better musicians, so it was with a shy tremor in her voice that she took off her rings and began her song.

"I saw my lady weep,
And Sorrow proud to be exalted so
In those fair eyes where all perfection keep . . ."

The candles lit up her hair as she leant over the keyboard in concentration and Richard looked at the aureole about her face and tenderness hurt within him.

"Enchanting," he murmured. "Enchanting."

"Yes," said her mother, "we think her quite an artist."

The girl finished and turned to her audience for applause; once again the robust, hearty evening took Richard in its toils.

The door was opened from outside and two maids rattled in carrying a precariously laden tea-table between them. Samuel slipped out as they set it down and singers and listeners prepared to refresh themselves. Richard was handing a cup and an iced bun to Mrs. Page when Samuel re-entered with his arms full of lemonade and soda.

"Come on," he said, flourishing a bottle. "Support local industry. Away with your champagne; bring on the Seymours! Everyone sign the pledge."

He shook the bottle violently and the soda fizzed out over the stopper. Naomi, who was standing close by, screamed and jumped from his side, her belled skirts swaying.

"Oh, 'ill tak zum o' that in a moog," said James and emptied his cup into the slop-basin.

39

Samuel took tumblers from all his pockets and filled everything he could see.

"Toast," he said, "toast, toast. Your turn, Webster."

Richard stood up. He cleared his throat.

> "Here's a health to all those that we love,
> Here's a health to all those that love us,
> Here's a health to all those that love them that love those
> That love them that love those that love us."

"Bravo, Mr. Webster," said Laura and everyone drank.

Under cover of discussion of the drinks Richard retired to the shelter of a window. He drew back the heavy damask of the curtain and looked out into the night. Laura, he thought, Laura, Laura, Laura. Down in the valley lights were pricking the darkness—pale candle-light, yellow gaslight. All around was stillness. Laura, Laura, Laura. Far away, subdued by distance, a dog began to bark and every sound beat with the rhythm of her name. He turned and went back into the warmth of the room.

Chapter Four

The next day the weather broke.

The night had been hot—too hot for comfort—but for all that it was noticed in the main bedroom of the Vicarage it might have been the lightest, brightest spring morning. Richard had floated home intoxicated with love and Laura. He was too adoring to undress and had lain on his bed fully clothed, dreaming and romanticising through the night as the girl in lavender silk passed and repassed his bedside, smiling and turning her eyes to his.

He fell asleep at last and woke a few hours later to find himself still in evening-dress with his collar adrift and his mouth dry and thick. He raised himself heavily from the crumpled eiderdown and undid his tie, rubbing the red indentation on his skin where a stud had pressed into his neck. A cool breeze was blowing through the window he had not thought to shut the night before and he went across to pull the curtains, revealing a morning that was grey and overcast with a suspicion of rain. The blooms on the lilacs that had been so late this year had finally turned to brown and were bobbing and swaying in the wind. It was a sad change from the night before; a man in love should have the sun to cosset him.

He told himself that he had letters to answer and a sermon to write, but somehow when he got to his study it was not these that he began. He took out the journal that his sister had given him at Christmas and searched for words to describe his evening. Finding that there were none he fitted a new nib to his pen, wrote "Thursday, 29th June. Miss Laura Delaford", ruled a line and blotted it carefully. Then he took out his personal account books. He hardly dared admit to himself why he was examining them but the reason was there unasked—he must know whether he could afford a wife. He had thought when he came here that his expenditure would be directed towards local charities, but all at

41

once there was a new dimension in his life and, however unromantic it seemed to calculate for it, it was an expensive luxury which would have to be paid for. It would be nothing short of cruelty to take a gently-reared girl from her home without being able to keep her and her children in comfort. But there was no need to fear—with the income left to him by his father and his stipend he would have almost eight hundred pounds a year; more than enough for his purpose.

He leant his head on his hand and doodled idly on the blotting-paper. He had cleared this hurdle easily but he did not know how to continue. He had met her only once and they had hardly spoken; what would she say if she knew that he was sitting at his desk deciding whether he could provide for her family? Would she be flattered by his interest or angry at his presumption? How could he meet her again and would she be satisfied with a dull, dark, plodding parson when she wanted a lively, polished lawyer? Of course she might not want Sanderson at all; brothers did not always read their sisters aright. From what he had seen of James the night before he was inclined to think his rival heart-whole and therefore no active rival at all, but he could not be sure; it could be that his own feelings were blinding him.

The object of his thoughts had spent a more restful night than he. She had gone to bed aglow with the pleasure of her amicable conversation with James. It had been a disappointment to her not to be placed next to him at table but, of course, that had meant he could sit beside her in the drawing-room; she expected that that had been the thought in her mother's mind for, naturally, unless a couple were betrothed they could not pair at both. He had also chosen to turn her music for her when it would have been quite in order for him to withdraw after his song and leave this privilege to another. And then, as the good-natured Naomi had pointed out to her as they lay cuddled together on their feather mattress, Mr. Webster's eyes had been drawn to her again and again, although so discreetly that only the percipience of a girl who was herself husband-high could have noted it. At this they had both smothered their giggles in their pillows.

If there is one thing above another that will make a young woman sleep well it is the knowledge possessed by Laura: she knew without doubting that she was more than pretty, more than pleasing, she was beautiful. She had never entered a room of strangers but all attention had turned to her. In form she was a queen among girls. This was neither conceit nor egotism; she had no haughty airs, no presentions. Like a bird of paradise she had been born with fine feathers and she saw no reason to hide them. That she added to the recipe a dash of frivolity and a dash of folly did her no harm in an age when women were not admired for being bluestockings.

She had awoken as happily as she had gone to sleep and had hardly known what to do with herself all morning. The men of the family had risen at dawn and run to the hay fields to gather the last of the crop before it could be spoiled by rain, but obviously she could not spend her energy in helping them. She was too buoyant to settle to needlework or reading or even to daydreaming of the delights of being a wife, and had been glad when luncheon had arrived to divert her. During this all-female meal—for the men were too busy for more than a snatched bread-and-cold-bacon at their work—Beatrice said that for goodness sake, if she couldn't sit still and stop wandering about getting in everyone's way, why didn't she go out for a ride? Since the weather was cool enough for exertion but had not brought the threatened rain, Laura accepted the idea as good and had changed into her riding-habit: an outfit flattering in its severity with its white linen shirt, closely-fitting black jacket, a skirt held out by only a single quilted petticoat of black satin and a hat with veil and peacock feather.

As all the farm servants were occupied she saddled the mare herself, mounted from the block and guided her out of the yard on to the lane. Since she was so full of the ardour of life she decided to hack to Lenthay Common, where she could dispel the emotion that fermented inside her with some zealous galloping. This meant taking the road down to Sherborne and along Ottery Lane before turning to the left for the half-mile to the Common. She had learnt early—and this was why she so enjoyed flirtation—that most of the pleasure of an act comes not from its consummation but from the anticipation, so she kept Tansy to a sedate walk as they progressed through the town, luxuriating in the general benevolence of a life which seemed to go out of its way to pour treasures at her feet. She had never needed to be told to count her blessings for she revelled in every one.

The weather was growing cooler, and the breeze fluttered the trailing muslin of her veil and brought a flush of pink to her cheeks as she rode. She sat her gentle mare well, moving easily in the saddle in time with the strides, and the consciousness of the appealing picture she must be making had almost lulled her into a more placid mood when her notice was taken by two figures coming towards her in the distance. As the lane neared the common it narrowed until it was hardly wider than a bridle-path and the bushy profusion of the hedges obscured her view. At first she could make out only that they were a girl in walking costume and a man leading a horse. They were moving close together as if deep in conversation, but whether this was from choice or necessity Laura could not tell. The man held aside a hawthorn branch for the girl to pass and she judged it was from necessity; they glimpsed herself, edged a little apart and she judged it was from choice. Still she was not near enough to make out their faces—though she thought she knew the gown. Then—yes. There was no mistaking it. James—her James—was accompanying Grace Palmer. How could this be? Why should it be? Did he make love to herself in the evening and to another the next day? And to one who was so fast that she would walk openly and alone with a man in such an unfrequented place—for unless she had been suddenly struck blind there was no chaperone to be seen.

She was about to kick her mare on and shoulder past them, combining dashing canter with social cut, when she took herself in hand. Every wicked thing she was thinking was nonsense. She was being rash—was not her mother always warning her of this trait in her character? Of course, there would be a good and perfectly innocent reason for their being discovered here.

The three drew close.

"Good morning, Miss Delaford," said James. He took her gloved hand from the rein and kissed it. Laura withdrew it and returned Grace's nod.

"It's the afternoon, Mr. Sanderson," she reproved him.

"So it is. This is what comes of 'Mr. Weston's good wine'—a certain oversleeping, a certain confusion of mind, a certain need for air and exercise. . . ."

"A certain disgraceful headache." Grace turned her dark, almond eyes upon him.

James leant his forehead against his gelding's neck.

"I wouldn't count on making your fortune on the stage," said Laura.

"And why should I need to?" he said. "I shall make away with this concert pianist here and live iniquitously upon a woman's earnings."

"Don't be foolish," said Grace. "I've just been up to Lenthay Dairy to borrow some music Mrs. Rouse promised me," she explained to Laura, "and I met Mr. Sanderson as I came back. He's been trying to clear his head on the Common and has done nothing but abuse me all the way."

"And how have I abused you?"

"For one thing you've said I need to work for my living."

"Have you no shame, Miss Palmer, to turn a sick man's jokes upon him?"

"You don't look very ill to me." Laura pulled Tansy's head up from the verge.

"And you, madam," said James, "look more ravishing every time I see you. Tell me how you do it and I shall make a potion of it to sell profusely to ladies of a certain age."

"You're very commercially minded today."

"Ah, I've done no work since yesterday and the poorhouse doors gape open."

"I hope you don't expect Grace to escort you all the way to Dorchester," Laura said a little coldly.

"Oh, no. In fact I think I shall abandon her here—I don't want my reputation ruined." He twisted his stirrup-leather and mounted. For one joyous moment Laura expected him to turn his horse and go with her to the public seclusion of the Common—the very place, the very opportunity for a short and longed-for question, but instead he raised his hat, bid the ladies good-day and started forward. The narrowness of the path and the position of the talkers made a short boiling and jostling of movement inevitable, and the result was the break-up of the triangle: James riding onwards to the town, Grace following at a stroll and Laura moving away from them both.

She continued at a walking pace, this time not from a wish to tantalise her senses but from weight of thought. Her warning to herself on recognising them had been right—there had been good reason for them being found together—and yet . . . It seemed to her the meeting had not been quite—she didn't know how to describe it—quite comfortable, she supposed. James had not seemed to greet her with the preference that he should have shown—but then that would hardly have been courteous of him in front of Grace and he was a courteous man. And then if he had drunk too well the previous night he would not be feeling particularly gallant—though she had not noticed him drink himself into his altitude. He could have continued at home, perhaps; she knew he had a fondness for Cognac. Grace had seemed to have a possessive air about her—but she had known James as long as had Laura and it was Laura who had interrupted their tête-à-tête, not the other way around. She was being excessively foolish. What had she to fear?

She twisted in the saddle to look back at them. She was some distance apart from them now but it appeared to her that James was riding slowly and Grace walking fast. Foreshortened as her view of them must be, it seemed the gap between the two was narrowing. She swung herself back and heeled her mare violently, sending her bouncing into the hedge. Jealousy, suspicion and hurt surged within her, welded together with guilt at feeling thus for no reason. She imagined herself to be proudly indignant but it was truer to say that she was piqued. She had a second cousin in India who was addicted to opium: the taking of it gave him pleasure but the more he took the more he needed, and so it was with Laura and admiration. She had been given a generous dosage the evening before and she wanted it continued. Very well, then, she would have it. She would not gallop on the Common, she would go on to Bradford Abbas where there was now a most acceptable parson. Naturally she would not call on him but if she hacked through the village she might just chance upon him.

With the handle of her whip she hooked open the gate on to the Common, where, it being summer, the cows from the Dairy were grazing, crossed its shortest breadth and trotted in a businesslike manner past the farmhouse on to the Bradford road. She continued to trot through her father's land for some time until she had descended the long slope from Silverlake and let her mare take the steeper rise at a walk. The air was still cooling and a few drops of rain began to fall as she took the fork to Bradford Abbas, but she was in a mood to ignore them until she was within a few hundred yards of the village when—as her mother would have described it—the heavens opened. The sky grew suddenly and frighteningly black and water poured down as if the earth were being sluiced. In a moment Laura was chilled and drenched. There was nothing for it but to take shelter: home was too far away. She had no particular friend to go to and so—her mind being already on Richard—she decided to turn to him. No one could possibly question the propriety of being aided by a clergyman on dining terms with her family.

She took the village at a slipping, slithering canter, the mud flying up behind her, pulled Tansy up sharply at the Vicarage, tied her to the gate-post and ran for the front door. Dinah answered the knock almost at once and had only time to say, "Dear life, Miss . . ." before the bedraggled figure was inside the hall and dripping copiously on to the floor. Dinah recognised her, noticed her dress and realised the predicament. She ushered the unfortunate into the drawing-room, where a fire had just been lit to combat an English summer, and went to tell her master of his guest.

Richard was in his study in the throes of long division as he reckoned up the accounts of the parish and did not particularly want to be disturbed.

"Yes, Dinah?" he said as she entered, ". . . and thirty-five is . . ."

"Miss Delaford is here, sir. She was caught in the rain."

He put down his pen.

"Have you shown her to the drawing-room?"

"Yes, sir."

He got up from his chair. "And is the fire lit?"

"Yes, sir."

He adjusted his jacket. "You'd better make tea."

Laura was standing in the greyness of the room. She was holding her hat in one hand and looking disconsolately at its fall from glory. Wet as she was, she was a slim and elegant sight in her black and her hair was almost perfect. To her the one saving grace of her plight—without which she would not have called—was that her hair had been dressed high and been protected by the brim of her hat. Only one stray, damp tendril had escaped and clung to her neck.

If there was one outfit Richard liked above another it was the simplicity of a riding habit. It put him in mind of demure Puritans and in it Laura seemed less of a porcelain figure; less girlish and more womanly. It tore at his heart that she, who must have so many friends, should have turned to him in her need. Under his nervousness ran a strain of thought that no one could help her or cherish her more than he.

"What must you think of me, Mr. Webster?" she said, indicating the circle of water that was soaking into the carpet around her skirts.

He came further into the room. "'A sweet disorder in the dress . . .'"

"'Kindles in clothes a wantonness'?" She plucked out her ruined feather and threw it on to the fire; it sizzled, curled and disintegrated.

"Oh, no. Not wantonness, Miss Delaford."

Laura looked at him kindly; he had spoken in a tone she recognised. "I wish you would ask me to sit down and take tea. I'm cold, forlorn and completely at your mercy."

He explained that tea was on its way, pulled an armchair for her as close to the fire as was possible, arranged her hat on the hearth, took the tray from Dinah, gave her Miss Delaford's jacket to dry in the kitchen, ordered Barratt to stable her horse, poured, finally sat down himself and there began an afternoon of serendipity for both of them.

The rain continued to beat down outside. Richard offered to light the lamps but Laura prevented him because of her dishevelled appearance, and they sat together in the darkness of the weather and the glow of the fire. The cups in their hands steamed, Laura's skirts steamed, her hat steamed; they joked of living in a laundry. She put her feet on the fender for a moment and the tips of her chamois leather trousers protruding over her boots lent a pleasing frisson to the atmosphere. From the way Richard glanced at her but could not look her in the eyes for long Laura became more sure that he admired her, and the more sure she felt, the more she recovered her self-confidence and the more encouraging she became. And the more Richard was encouraged the more encouraged he felt. And the more encouraged he felt the more he showed he admired her and could not look her in the eyes. Around and around they went.

He wanted to give her roses. Dr. Knapton had had no interest in gardening, but the Thornhills were keen horticulturalists and had always presented him with the latest species of rose; Richard wondered if they would survive the downpour and if so could he give a bunch to Laura? But how could she carry them home on horseback?

From time to time one of them wandered to the window but there was no release from the rain. At half-past four they had cake and more tea. At six Laura was worried about getting back to the farm. As the storm seemed to have settled in for the night Richard invited her to stay for dinner and then use the spare room—it would surely have stopped by the morning. It was impossible to say which blushed the deeper as the realisation of this indiscretion struck them. Hurriedly Richard offered to leave her in Mrs. Houghton's care at the Vicarage and go to sleep at Keating's, but this also she refused. Prepared to go to any lengths of presumptuousness for her sake he then said he would borrow Keating's carriage and stableman and have her driven home in safety and shelter. Again she thanked him and said no. Not wanting to cause disturbance or be involved in long explanations she determined to ride home as she had come, and, with some anxiety, for the darkness was growing and she would not hear of his accompanying her, Richard was forced to watch her splash away alone.

The following morning he sent a messenger to Limekiln with a dozen *Gloire de Dijon* from his garden and a note hoping Miss Delaford had taken no harm from her wetting.

Chapter Five

As always Rachel was the first to wake at Limekiln. Her days were all begun early for cows will not wait a dairymaid's pleasure and neither will a father and brother with stern ideas of duty wait to be served their breakfast; but today her rising was even earlier than most, because this Monday marked the start of the corn harvest and there would be extra work for everyone.

Rachel had the gift of awakening within a few minutes of the time she had chosen the night before and it did not fail her on this morning. It was only a little after half-past three when she opened her eyes to the grey pre-dawn. She had no wish to get up: her bed offered her no comfort, the mattress was hard and lumpy and her head ached from sleeping on her back with her pillows too high, but she felt safer there than outside. She was tired and lethargic and would have liked nothing better than to have turned over and ignored the world, but work was work and had to be done. She pushed back the single sheet she used as cover on these hot nights and wearily sat up, head in hands, with her feet on the rag rug she had made from old gowns and aprons.

One elbow slipped off her knee and the jolt and the swinging of her hair made her realise that she had started to doze again. This would not do, she told herself, and stood upright heavily. In her nightgown she went across to the window—not a great journey in this tiny bedroom—and drew aside the curtain to look out at the mid-August morning. The fine weather of the previous month had continued and already there was a promise in the air of heat to come, although she could see dew enough to give the fields a blessing and white mist lying in the river-valley down by Darkhole Farm.

The window was too small and the hour too early for anyone to see her movements, so she left the curtain pulled back while she poured water from a large china jug into its matching basin. It was a handsome toilet set; it had belonged to Miss Delaford who had been going to consign it to the lumber-room in favour of a more modern design until Samuel had suggested that she give it to Rachel, and washing in this disguised present—for neither dared risk an open gift—lifted the girl's spirits enough to give her strength for her first tasks.

She was not long in dressing; there was no frivolity of clothes for her, no frothing petticoats, no delicate stockings. Her father would have beaten her if he had found her tight-lacing, but it caused her no distress. She did have a secret, guilty yearning for a silken gown for Sundays, but her tastes were simple and the plain, sprigged cotton she wore suited her calm, Quakerly carriage.

Tying a large and functional apron around her neck and waist, she left her room and banged on the wood of the next door until a voice, thick with sleep, told her the men were awake, then went down the stairs to the chamber which served as kitchen, dining- and living-room.

The night before she had laid a small fire of kindling and newspaper of the exact size to boil a kettle without further waste of fuel and she lit this easily, grateful for having been born into an age which had the use of matches. Like an automaton she switched herself into her daily routine. The obscurity of the room perceptibly lightened with the growing dawn and the flaring flames as she passed to and fro from the scullery to what the family called the "parlour" and back again. She spread the cloth and set two places with plate, knife, mug and spoon. She cut three portions of bread and cold boiled bacon, putting her own share into her apron pocket, measured tea into the pot—a mixture of the cheap leaves she bought herself and the Assam slipped to her by Samuel, who at least had never offered her money—and poured milk into the pewter jug that had been her mother's.

Then, with the sound of footsteps from above and the water timed by long practice to boil as the men reached the table, she slipped out into the birdsong of sunrise. She had always loved the break of day in summer with its quietness and sense of solitude and the moisture being drawn from the ground into a knee-deep cloud as the heat rose. She often walked the meadows with bare legs just to feel the cool dew on her skin, but this morning she was too preoccupied to give much notice to such familiar pleasure and she went to gather her herd as if in a trance.

Had anyone seen her they would have said that she was not yet fully awake. Samuel, with his quick perception of such things, had recognised the latent streak of sensuousness held in restraint by this demure, religious girl and had released it for his own exploitation. Occasionally he thought he should have disliked himself for it, especially as he had to admit that her innocence and her bursts of resistance, which inevitably gave way to his persuasions, lent an added fillip to his enjoyment of her. Surely he was excused by his fondness for her. She had always loved him; they had always been friends. He thought no harm would come to her and somehow life did not incline him to be hard upon himself. He was turning over in his sleep when she opened the field gate, and if his heart had been as heavy as hers he would have started from his pillow in a sweat.

On an ordinary morning the herd would have been lined up in an orderly string headed by the little Jersey cow kept for the Delafords' private use—and called Belladonna for her dark, lustrous eyes—to follow Rachel in a slow, udder-swaying procession to the yard. Today she was three-quarters of an hour early and so she circled around them crying "Cush! Cush!" as they raised themselves in their ungainly fashion, hindlegs first, leaving dry patches of grass where they had lain amidst the dew.

Disliking the break of their routine the red and white milchers were not to be hurried and Rachel was forced to walk behind them, driving on stragglers with slaps on the rump until they reached the barton. When they arrived both Luke and Anne Hartley were waiting to help her with the milking. Anne was due for another child in six weeks and was not of a size to cut corn, but she had agreed to take over what she could of her neighbour's dairying —skimming, churning and seeing to the cheese presses—to leave Rachel free for the reaping. The three settled on their stools, foreheads resting on the warm hides of their animals, and the milk began ringing rhythmically through their fingers into the pails. Cow followed cow and, as they were nearing the end and Luke was carrying two brimming buckets into the dairy, Samuel emerged into the now clear sunshine in a workmanlike outfit of corduroy breeches, linen shirt and neckerchief, cheerful at the prospect of harvest—the highest point of his year.

He went over to Rachel's crouching figure—the lover in him admiring the charm of her rural appearance, the farmer her expertise—and, in a voice too low for Anne to hear, reminded her that his mother would like cream set aside to be soured for the making of curd cheese. He tried to infuse this unromantic message with deep fondness and succeeded. Her hands constantly moving, Rachel replied that she had not forgotten and, encouraged by his tone, without lifting her head from her work she asked softly if she might meet him that night. Agreeing, he moved on and Rachel called over to Anne the request of the mistress.

The day wore on in the fields and Rachel became a figure in the annual formal dance of harvest. Mr. Delaford would rather have waited another week before cutting but, hearing how rain was devastating the crop in Suffolk and mindful of the downpour which had driven his daughter to shelter with Webster, he had consulted his sons and determined to move it forward.

Every labourer on the farm together with his family had been put to the reaping, and every wanderer who inquired at the farm for casual work was quizzed on his skills and hired at once if he showed experience. Mrs. Delaford had been calmly efficient in the vast preparation of refreshment for the workers; each was entitled to a gallon of cider a day, on top of an extra shilling a week during harvest, which had to be measured and drawn from the barrels; ginger beer and barley waters had to be brewed for those who preferred them; quantities of materials for the Harvest Supper had to be assessed, ordered and begun. Young girls to guard the children and present babies to be fed while the women worked also had to be found and organised.

The only people on the farm who did not participate actively beyond attending the Supper were the Delaford sisters. Prevented by their modern gentility from doing anything more robust, they continued their ordinary lives whilst watching their mother's stately arrangements and being teased by Samuel, who was a practised hand with a scythe, for not reaping. Had they taken up his challenge he would have felt demeaned, for this was no longer something acceptable for a gentlewoman to do unless forced to as Mrs. Rouse had been, but he would have appreciated a more regular appearance with the baskets at midday. This was, after all, their living that was being earned.

This, however, was only a slight irritation, and Samuel barely thought of it after shrugging his shoulders and deciding that if they had any sense—and he believed they had—they would see, when they had establishments of their own, that it was perfectly proper to copy their mother and combine gentility with production. His mind was concerned with other things. More than Jonathan, more even than his father, Samuel was in harmony with the cultivation of nature. There was no part of the harvesting that he could not do better than his fellows, whether it was binding a sheaf or driving the swaying, top-heavy waggons that brought the grain to the barn to be threshed.

It was a joy to Mr. Delaford to watch him wielding the scythe with strong browned arms. He had seen his friends' sons finish their schooldays full of new notions of what was beneath them: they would hunt and shoot but not plough; oversee their men from the back of a blood mare but not go to market; their pride prevented them from doing any kind of manual labour but not from living on the labour of others. Now this was one thing in a woman—he was glad that his daughters kept to the house for this was a reflection of the success of the males in the family—but it was foppishness in a man. When Samuel had proved himself so quick academically Mr. Delaford had been afraid that he was lost to the farm, but he had returned from Oxford laughing at the distaste among his contemporaries for "honest work", forgotten his easily won baccalaureate and thrown himself into the life he had spent all his terms missing. He revelled in every aspect of farming and there was no question of a purely administrative involvement.

The problem now was what to do with Jonathan, who had steadfastly declined to go on to university now that he had left school, and showed no particular interest in anything except agriculture and the engineering papers he was always reading. The brothers agreed well enough now, but what was he to do with the younger when both wished to marry and have children of their own?

The heat pressed down on the corn and the workers' thoughts flowed on as their bodies automatically bent and cut. They had come to the field as the dairy herd had wended its way back to its grazing. The dew had not had time to dry and their clothes had become lightly damp as they waded thigh deep through the rustling, sighing barley to their positions. The field had spread out before them—a dusky blanket of pale gold dropped on the hillside, stippled scarlet with poppies, blue with cornflowers and cranesbill, white with chamomile. Delaford had cut the first stroke, then the company had swum forward breaking like a wave on the corn, swinging their blades to the beat of old songs that set their rhythm for later, when they would be too tired and too far from the end of the day to sing. The men and some of the women used scythes whose wood was worn smooth from years of use, but most of the women stood closer together and used sickles—some gathering each bundle together with a crooked stick before cutting. In the time of Delaford's grandfather the female harvesters had not been allowed to wear gowns and had been forced to work in their shifts, but that rule had been relaxed and now they wore prints or wrappers of brown holland and bonnets with long cotton flaps to protect their necks from the sun.

Behind the reapers came the binders, the stubble pricking their arms raw above their strong gloves. Bending low they scooped armfuls of the fallen barley from the ground and bound them together with stalks drawn from the previous sheaf; then, in groups of ten, they stood each sheaf upright and leant it against those of their companions to form a shock. Hook and cut; hook and cut. Bend and stoop; bend and stoop. The hours went by marked only by the changing shadows. The sun rose to its zenith, and the scent of the honeysuckle in the hedgerows and that of the clover wafting from the meadows grew almost unbearable in the heat.

Steadily they progressed up the field. Delaford's mind was already on the threshing; Jonathan dreamed idly of a machine which could do this ten times more quickly than a man with ten times fewer labourers; Samuel reaped with a long, fluid stroke, happy to feel the handle in his hardened palms, happy to feel his wet shirt stick to his back and pull against the sweat with every movement; far to his left Rachel worked with a dryness in her mouth and sick anticipation in her stomach. Now and then she broke the regular swishing of her sickle to wipe her forehead with the back of her hand and listen to the ring of hones against metal as blades were sharpened in the distance.

At midday Mrs. Delaford came, walking beside a cart filled with the rattle of stoneware as it jolted up the track, and they dropped their tools to eat and drink, not realising their exhaustion until they sat down. Mothers with babies sat together in a patch of shade and suckled their infants as they drank the oatmeal-water the mistress prepared to keep up their strength. There was little talking—just the request for more cider and the slow chewing of bread and cheese, and then it was back to their labour. There was no singing now and, to eyes veiled by the hours of toil ahead, what they had felled seemed no more than a nibble at the edge of what they had still to do. Keeping their eyes down they shunned the sight of the other yellow acres spreading across Delaford's land, and even Samuel was conscious of muscles which had been resting since the hay-mow. This was what Delaford called "the noon-tide low" and had to be endured, but gradually, as the sun lost strength and their clothes ceased to burn against their skin, the prospect of evening and the end of the first, worst day put new energy into them and the work regained the morning's pace.

They broke again at five. Rachel drank but did not eat, and when the others went back to the reaping she left the corn and returned to the dairy. The herd had been collected by Anne Hartley and was standing in the yard, but she could not milk alone: some of the beasts were particular and would let down only for familiar hands. Rachel sat heavily on her stool and brushed the dripping udder clean of flies. She wished that she was less skilled at this for then it would need some thought. As it was her fingers caressed and coaxed and squeezed by themselves and her mind was left free to wander; but what else did she expect after all this time? For six years she had come here night and morning and for three of them she had been placed in charge. It was an acknowledgement of her craft, a position of trust—for how much longer could she hold it? No use to think this way, no use.

She was meant to go back to the fields when she had finished at the dairy but she could not bear it. Instead she collected the potatoes and bacon she had left with Anne to boil for her return with the men, and took them home to cook herself. They were ready by the time her father and brother came in at half-past eight and the three took their seats at the table. She could not eat; she had no appetite and to prevent waste—a fearsome word in their household—she scooped her food on to the other two plates. Her father looked up.

"Are you ailing?" he asked, and the concern in his voice almost made her cry. "You didn't come back."

"It was the sun," she said. "It's made my head ache; that's why I came straight here—but it's so close indoors."

"You should sit outside in the cool air. Or go down and get some butter-milk—the mistress won't grudge you in harvest."

"Yes, I think I will."

"Only don't forget you've got to be up early."

"No, Father." How could I? When have I ever risen late?

She waited for him to say the concluding grace before she could clear the table.

Samuel was waiting in the dusk. He was pleased with his day: the crop was good, the labourers were good, the feel of steel biting through barley as if it were butter was good, the idea of finishing such a day with a soft, loving girl was heaven. At present, with the skin on his arms and face still glowing from the heat, his body aching with satisfaction from his work and his mind teasing him with the thought of Rachel making her way to him, he could not imagine any way to make his life better.

Like his sister he never needed to be told to count his blessings: he knew and appreciated them without that. Only this morning he had received a letter from a friend who had taken to schoolmastering and the contrast between their two professions had sharpened his appetite for his own; not that Edward was unhappy as a teacher but Samuel knew that he would be if he found himself in such a position. But, he thought, I never shall: I am the eldest son of a gentleman-farmer; I eat breakfast of milk and eggs and bread and ham from my own land, step out into the sunshine and see what? A most delectable dairymaid who asks if she can meet me that night. I am one of the elect.

He sat down on the bank where they had met so often and amused himself trying to roll a cigarette in the darkness under the trees. This was a new occupation, not thought of before last week when he had seen the papers on the tobacconist's counter, and he was not altogether successful in it yet. The lesson he had been given in the shop had faded, but he persevered and was deep in the attempt when Rachel slipped through the wood and sat beside him.

He brushed the tobacco from his breeches and leant to kiss her. Her lips were still sweet from the cider she had drunk and her cheeks were warm. In low voices they talked desultorily of the harvest, then fell silent. To Samuel she had seemed different lately—at once more distant and more desirous of reassurance than before—but their affair had lasted for over a year now and he was used to her bouts of guilt: they meant nothing.

She sat with her legs bent up before her and the backs of her hands resting on her knees as she nervously peeled the seeds from a grass. He would not let her down, he could not; she was safe, quite safe. She felt his arm come round and stroke her waist. He tried to lower her to the ground but she did not yield; instead she took his face into her hands. "You do love me, don't you, Samuel?" she asked.

He was in a mood to pamper her: he answered that he did.

"Truly love me?"

"Truly love you."

And so she told him and silence fell again—but this time it was harder, colder.

"Are you sure?" he said at last, knowing from her voice that she was and yet hoping he was mistaken.

"Yes, I've missed twice; I feel ill in the mornings."

The motion of his taking his arm from her waist made her want to scream. It's all been make-believe, she thought incredulously, all of it; if he cared for me he would have held me tighter. She was surprised how aloof her mind was from the hysteria that bubbled within her. She thought of her years of devotion and did not want to see that its object had been worthless.

"You told me you wouldn't let me down," she said. "You wouldn't desert me."

"Nor will I."

Oh, thank God, she thought, thank God. Why was I ever afraid? She almost laughed with relief. "If we marry quickly," she went on, "we can pass the child as premature."

"Marry?"

"Yes," she was puzzled. "You said . . ."

"I said nothing of marriage."

"But . . ."

He interrupted her. "You must know we can't marry. Look at our positions. How can I give my mother a farm girl as a daughter-in-law? It's unthinkable. You must have known that."

His words were so composed, so assured, that she knew he did not see the horror that was before her. Yet this was the same man who only a few moments before had kissed her and said that he loved her. The same man whose child she was carrying. She clutched again at his promise.

"You said you wouldn't let me down."

"Nor will I. I won't deny paternity; I'll make you an allowance; I'll see that . . ."

"No," she said fiercely, not understanding that she had lost. "That's not enough. You must marry me—my father will turn me out. Samuel, please!" She reached for his hand in the dark but could not find it.

"You'll be found somewhere to live. You wouldn't be in want."

"You always meant this." Still she was unbelieving. "You must have known what would happen in the end. You knew I'd think you'd marry me because you loved me."

"Rachel," Samuel was so angry with himself that he could have struck her. He, of all men, should have realised that if you sow a seed you reap a harvest. But no—what is trouble later compared with pleasure now? He ignored the words that were battering against him and concentrated on putting his tobacco into his pouch and the pouch into his pocket. He could have been alone in the wood. He stood up and was almost surprised to find a desperate girl clinging to him, begging him to marry her. Calmly he took her wrists and pushed her from him.

"I cannot have you as my wife," he said, as undisturbed and sedate as if talking to a child. "I am a gentleman and you are a serving-woman. You have worked for my family all your life. Come to me again when you're more reasonable and I'll take care of you."

He dropped her hands and left her to her grief; she would see things more clearly in the morning.

Chapter Six

The sound of iron scraping the cobbles told Keating that his horses had been harnessed and the carriage was being brought round to the front door. He took his watch from his waistcoat pocket and smiled. Two minutes to eight. He had told Henley he wanted to start for Sherborne House at eight and eight it would be. A smooth-running household. He replaced the watch, adjusted his necktie in the mirror above the fireplace, collected hat and gloves from the parlour-maid and stepped outside as the hall clock chimed the hour.

"Perhaps I'll take my great-coat for the journey home, May," he said, turning at the door.

"It's already in the carriage, sir. I thought it might turn cold."

"Ah."

He climbed into the brougham, its body leaning a little under his weight, and took off and replaced his left glove. The diamond he wore on his middle finger had caught against the leather and twisted the ring awkwardly. I'm getting old, he thought. I must have everything about me comfortable; I must cling to old habits. It's September so I have a fire lit although I'm not cold and I'm going out—and then the evening air seems chilly. Old fool. Well, at least I won't have to drive home alone. Young company is what I need in autumn.

The brougham wheeled out of the drive and turned left into the village. There was a hint of moisture in the dusk, a cool water-bringing breeze, but the rain had not yet fallen and the greys' hooves thudded dully on the summer-hardened roads; the branches of the trees barely stirred in the wind. It was a good night for a ball, Keating thought; there was that air of anticipation the coming of winter brings. The young would be persuaded that they were in love with all or any of their partners, and the old would be glad of the lights and music and laughter to protect them from the fear of cold and darkness. Or was he the only one who had this fear?

They rolled past the corner of the churchyard and stopped outside the Vicarage. Henley jumped down from his high seat and went to knock at the front door. Through the carriage window Keating could see that there were lights burning upstairs, which meant the parson was either still dressing or had been in too much of a hurry to turn out the lamps behind him. He wished that he could still feel the enthusiasm for life that would make him late for engagements.

As he waited the door opened and Richard could be seen holding a cloak over his arm and talking to a servant in the recesses of the passage. He gave a last instruction, said a few words to Henley and followed the coachman into the lane.

The carriage rocked as both men stepped up at the same moment. Keating clutched at the hanging strap while his guest arranged himself on the seat with the audible relief of one who has almost missed the train.

"Dear oh dear," said Richard looking round for somewhere to put his hat and deciding upon his knees. "I didn't think I would be in time. I . . ."

They both lurched as the horses moved forward with unexpected zeal.

"Let me take my coat," said Keating when they had gained a more orthodox pace; "you've no room to breathe." He lifted the great-coat from between them and laid it at his feet; Richard did the same with his cloak.

"I thought I'd better bring it," he explained. "There's a feel of the season about."

"Yes," said his host, "another summer gone."

"Apples," the young man went on complacently, "harvest-festival, bonfires, Christmas," and his friend felt a little warmer.

"Of course," he said, "this must be your busiest time."

"It's hard to say which is busier; there's a lull in mid-summer certainly. I suppose November to March is the worst but it depends on the weather. That's why I was almost late: I've been over at Ryme Intrinseca all day talking about tickets for blankets and coal and so on with Mr. Croxley—his parish is quite well organised. I only went to lunch and I didn't get back until half an hour ago."

"And what did your respected cook have to say about that?"

Richard pulled down his cuffs and smoothed his trousers. "Fortunately for me she'd gone to visit a friend and left my maid in charge of the dinner; then it seems some sort of crisis developed in the pantry while we were both out so she was glad I didn't arrive. We've entered into a conspiracy not to tell tales on each other."

"Disaster avoided?"

"I think so. I couldn't make head nor tail of it. I got as far as the bread not rising and from there I'm lost. I'll let it sort itself out—the master of the house is superfluous in these matters."

It was dark when they entered the town and joined the line of carriages converging on Sherborne House. As they drew slowly up the steep slope of Green Hill the house lights spilled across the pavements and down into the submerged road, giving the figures which leant over the railings to watch them pass an abnormal emphasis. Richard sat quietly staring at his spectators through the window until they turned off towards Newlands. He felt surprisingly calm and confident as the prospective meeting with Laura approached. It was the confidence of one who has been too occupied to think of what he is about to do: he had jumped from fantasy to reality without suffering the period of anxious anticipation which can cripple an encounter.

"Worn out by today's good works?" Keating asked.

Richard came to suddenly. "Intended benevolence is not very tiring," he said; "it's carrying it out that calls for the brandy."

Keating gave a short, gruff bark as if he was unused to laughing and recommended port for sustained philanthropy. On the journey he and Richard had imperceptibly changed moods: Richard had become less ebullient and more pensive—he did not know how the evening would develop but he was determined to take any opportunity that offered itself; his companion felt happier than when he had left his home, more comforted and less solitary—he would cultivate his friendship with Webster he was sure.

The carriage rumbled, they felt the horses strain as the wheels crunched on gravel and they followed the battered landau in front of them into the lantern-lit drive of Sherborne House. The mingled scent of the shrubbery, stables and cooking crept around the edges of the doors and expectancy invaded the brougham as Henley reined in before the flood of light from the library windows. Richard moved to get out but Keating put a hand on his arm.

"Not yet," he said. "We're just waiting for our turn at the front door."

"Oh," Richard sat back, "is this not it?" He pointed to the pillared entrance beyond them.

"You'd think it would be but it's round the corner. It's a pity you won't get a good view of the house tonight—you need to see it from a distance for the true impression. It's worth seeing if you like early Georgian."

"I do." Richard was engrossed in searching the crowd within for a sign that the Delafords had arrived before them, but could find no one he recognised. Already most of the guests had shown themselves unashamed to be early, and the sound of a congregation determined to be glad rose beyond the subdued courtesy of the greetings. Friend had met friend and had gathered into knots of sociability. Immaculate footmen and highly-starched maids with trays of steaming silver cups brought cheer and comfort with a deep red punch. From the curtained room above the muffled squeaks and indecisive pizzicato of a small orchestra preparing itself promised large appetites and torn skirts far into the night.

Hardly had Richard begun to feel a most unclerical enthusiasm for such sport when the landau rattled out of the drive and the brougham pulled forward to take its place. The carriage door was opened from outside, both men got out, put on their hats and almost immediately took them off again as they entered the hall.

"Is Mr. Macready not here?" asked Keating who was unable to see his host.

"He's been called away for a moment, sir," said the butler, a monster of accomplishments who had beckoned a tray-bearer and passed on two top-hats to a man-servant without noticeably moving a finger. "I believe Mr. Sanderson had something of importance to discuss with him."

Cups in hand they went stoically into the press. The party had not yet spilt upstairs but this was to Richard's advantage and he joined the other first-time visitors in congesting the hall, heads bent back, examining the murals with the interest of a company of surveyors. Keating, who was fanning his punch with his invitation, had told Richard that the house had mythological paintings by Thornhill, but he had expected merely a border, a frieze to decorate the panels, and here were bold, flamboyant scenes reaching to the ceiling and across, glowing with deep reds, blues and greens. Classical heroes leant on their spears; lavish goddesses welcomed them with Grecian eyes.

A surge of newcomers forced Richard to look to his wine and he edged to the library door. From this vantage place he could see pockets of the room which had been hidden to him in the carriage. The royal blue of a gown caught his notice and he saw Mrs. Rouse standing at some distance from him. They bowed to each other through the throng and Richard felt irrationally encouraged, as if because one member of the Delafords' dinner party were there then all must be expected.

A glimpse of lavender passed the corner of his sight—he turned, ardent for Laura, and saw dull, brown hair. The pain of loss was as sharp and sudden as the rise of hope, and now he was sure she would not come. He told himself not to look for the same colour, she would not be wearing the same gown, but he had first seen her in lavender and he waited for lavender.

The women had come in silks, brocades and velvets, satins, muslins and lace, in virginal pastels and matronly primaries. They were pretty, plain and passable but to Richard they might as well not have been there: there was no young beauty amongst them —no cool fair girl who laughed at her own devices. Only one held his interest even for a moment—a vivid, animated girl with an unusual, dark attraction. Her lips were as rich as rose-leaves and she had a knowing air about her foreign to Laura. She was half-facing him, talking to a companion he thought he remembered as Miss Sanderson although he could not be certain from behind. There was no sign of the male Sandersons nor of his host.

The doors of the room above were opened and the first bars of a quadrille were heard above the voices, repeating themselves twice to call the attention of the dancers. Excitement shivered and rustled through the skirts like the wind in the beeches, and a movement towards the stairs swept round the room.

Keating tapped Richard on the arm. "Shall we move on before we're trampled?"

Richard assented as he felt the pressure mount at the library entrance and they were borne forward whether they would or not. Jostled in the flood of polite amusement Richard was being carried up towards the half-landing when the front door, which had been at rest for some time, was held back once again and Mr. and Mrs. Delaford came into the hall followed by their two black-clad sons and three white-dressed daughters. They made a striking picture standing on the black and white stone slabs like chessmen and Richard smiled to think he had expected Laura to enter the stage with the common players. She was standing beneath him, so near he fancied he could smell her lavender scent, but she was speaking to Beatrice and did not look up. He tried to turn on the stair to reach her before another could claim her, but the press was too strong and, surrounded by revellers, he was swept away.

"Now," said Laura, "to beckon you must hold the fan just *so*."

Beatrice watched the demonstration with a worried face. "I shall never remember," she said, "never."

"Nonsense! We must all begin somewhere. You managed very well at home."

"But that was at home. I wish I hadn't come."

Laura patted her sister's hand; it was Beatrice's first ball and Laura could remember the alarm she had felt at her own.

"It will seem better when the dancing has begun."

"Perhaps no one will ask me."

"Of course someone will ask you; see how pretty you are in that silk. Come, we're being left behind—there's Mamma on the stairs." They glided across the floor to their family and each took one of Samuel's arms.

"Hold your skirts up next to me," he instructed, "or I shall tread on them: there isn't room for three in these extravagant times." Fearful for days of sewing they did so and followed Jonathan and Naomi towards the music.

"Wasn't that Webster leading the rout?" Samuel asked. "Most unbecoming to the cloth; I shall tell him so."

"I didn't see . . . Oh, there's Grace Palmer," Laura inclined her head to her friend who was engaged in the quadrille. "Not looking her best I see."

"Charity, sister, charity. How could anyone look their best compared with us. Mark, Beatrice! We are arrived."

They composed their expressions for a serene entry and joined their parents at the edge of the dancers.

The Delafords had not intended to be last, but had it been

planned they could not have been better pleased. Mr. Delaford was experiencing the relief known to any man with a wife and daughters that he had arrived at all; Mrs. Delaford was relishing the effect of her handsome family upon the onlookers—the stirring, the turning of eyes, the whisper of their name; Naomi and Beatrice were confident that once Laura was safely married the first regard would be accorded them—and Laura? As always the Red Sea parted before her and she was satisfied: she felt herself glow as the wave of admiration washed over her.

Of them all, as Beatrice shed her anxiety, only Samuel was less than complacent. Since Rachel had told him of her pregnancy a shutter had slid down over his mind, cutting out the capacity to feel either anguish or pleasure. He had no interest in what occurred around him—he thought of nothing but his work; he knew himself to be drifting but had no compulsion to alter his attitude to the girl. The one certainty to which he clung was the senselessness of a marriage between them.

On the farm he could not avoid her entirely and when he passed her by he could see clearly that she was ailing: there were lines beneath her eyes and for all her condition she seemed to him to be growing thinner. He had arranged to meet her alone the week before to give her the chance to change her mind and accept his offer of an allowance, but she would have none of it and, for an evening, had roused him from stupor to resentful anger. He had planned to remove her from Sherborne, perhaps from Dorset altogether, to take her somewhere where she was not known. There she could wait her time, have the child put out to nurse and return home, saying that she had gone to be in service but it did not suit her. If she was foolish enough to wish to stay with her baby then he would provide a small income—the interest on the money left to him by his godmother would be more than enough.

The future was simple, neat; he had all but bought the tickets —there need be no fuss, no scandal. But Rachel had refused and held to her idea that he must marry her. He could not believe that a working girl could hold herself so dear, but he could not move her. Now he could do nothing except wait until her fear got the better of her pride and she yielded—for the time being he must suffer this lethargy.

After the quadrille there was a waltz, then a cotillion, another quadrille, the lancers. The room with its many candles grew heated: the young people talked rashly of opening windows and were overruled by their guardians. Richard could not tell if he were hot or cold and did not care. Through five dances he had been unable to reach Laura: always he had been snared into taking a nearer partner or had seen Laura led on to the floor before he could find her. The sight of her so tantalisingly close to him and yet not his fed his need for her until he barely had patience to be civil to his neighbours. She was cool and tranquil amongst the flushed, laughing dancers—a magnolia, a lily amidst violets and rosebuds —and to his eyes there was no one to compare with her. He saw the vivid girl of the library whirl by with Jonathan and wondered why he had thought her pretty.

Before the second waltz he could contain himself no longer. He made his way across the room to her, ignoring the looks which asked him for his company, bowed past his acquaintance, past Samuel who was talking to a farmer—"We put in Chevallier; the yield was better"—and forced a passage through her suitors. He had taken her hand before he spoke and her followers fell back in the face of his self-assurance. Amused and flattered, Laura made no complaint: she knew the action must have cost him more courage than she would have seen in anyone less diffident in his relations to her. Letting the invitation seem long-standing, she floated to the centre with him and he took her in his arms as the gentle lilt of the measure was sounded.

Down and around, touching, swirling, dipping: the dancers span and wove romance in the candle-light. Beneath the music were the swish of skirts and the rhythmic tread of soft shoes. This was Laura's natural sphere and Richard danced in her enchantment. She was more than human to him this night: she was ideal, angelic. The flickering light played on the curves of her face, lit her white shoulders and filled her eyes with imagined love. The sweet scent of rose-water drifted from her warm skin, enveloping him, and he forgot his dreams of lavender. His heart beat so hard he was afraid she could feel the blood pulsing in his hands. He could not wait beyond tonight; he must have her for his own.

And Laura was surprised by his lightness and grace of movement. She found him strangely altered for the better each time they met; perhaps, she thought, because it became more obvious how he valued her with every meeting. If only James would make himself so clear. She wondered why James had not asked her to dance —but he had asked no one; he had not yet come up to the dancing at all and she had only to wait. Until he came she would let herself be idolised by other men. Richard looked down at her too deep in love to smile; the night seemed arranged to fascinate her and she it.

The music stopped and she broke away. "No," she laughed. "No. How could I? Two dances! I've promised the next to Captain Ewart. See, he comes for me," and somehow Richard had Mrs. Rouse's hand in his and she too was laughing.

"Mr. Webster," she said, "this is the Tempete; don't try to waltz."

"I beg your pardon. I wasn't attending."

"So I can see. Would you prefer to sit it out?"

"I think I'd better. May I find you another partner?"

She tapped him with her fan. "Am I such an old married woman that I can't be talked to?"

"I think," he said, leading her from the floor, "that from the way you're reading me I don't need to speak." He found two empty chairs against the wall.

"Oh, you must speak—but not to me. How this gown gets in the way; I wonder I ever sit down. There. That's better. Do you see the dark-haired girl in the lace in the lower set? Yes, the very one—a friend of mine. Her name is Grace and she has grace in a way. And yet she is not such a one as Miss Delaford."

"You're very deep this evening. What of her?"

She put her closed fan to her lips. "Not one word more. You must discover for yourself. Now, let us talk of the weather and crops and be altogether sober and respectable."

They watched the dance to its conclusion. As it ended and the couples dispersed Mrs. Rouse laid a finger on Richard's sleeve. "Macready," she whispered and looked towards the door. Richard followed her gaze and saw the London Theatre enter the room and make a slow progression through his guests—shaking hands, bowing, exchanging compliments—towards the platform where the orchestra played. He stepped up and faced his audience. Richard could almost see the shine of the footlights—he tried not to applaud.

"Ladies and gentlemen," Macready began, his thumbs in the

satin pockets of his waistcoat, his voice carrying effortlessly to the far side of the room, "dear friends and welcome. Forgive me for this interruption. A host should know his place and at my age it's not on the dance-floor, but I come to give you most happy news. Some of you may have wondered why I was not at the door to greet you, and in answer I may say that I had abandoned you for a bride. Not my own, sorry though I am to tell it, but that of Mr. James Sanderson, lawyer and son of our esteemed . . ." he paused to let the ripple of exclamation die out, "of Mr. Phillip Sanderson, known to us all as—but you grow impatient and you have reason. Ladies and gentlemen, I am most honoured to announce that Miss Grace Palmer will . . ."

His last words were as nothing; the name said, a crest of concealed astonishment and open congratulation rose, crashed and drowned the speech.

"My dear! I never was so surprised."

"The Sandersons and Palmers—such a suitable match."

"They say she has almost no money of her own."

"Dearest Grace."

"Of course I could have told you months ago but . . ."

"Dear James."

"So pleased."

"Here's a commotion," Mrs. Rouse innocently relished the moment, her dark eyes gleaming. "I declare a fox in a chicken coop is nothing to it."

"You knew," said Richard absently.

"I guessed last week and taxed her with it. I've been at my wit's end to keep silent. Such excitement!"

He did not look at her; he was staring hard at the Delafords who were standing together near the platform. Fear made him blatant in his attention but only his partner noticed. In that moment he had been more afraid and more relieved than he had ever been before. Hearing Sanderson's name he had waited horrified for Laura to be brought forward and given to a man who could never care for her as he did—but it was not she; it was the girl he had seen downstairs, who had been pointed out to him by Mrs. Rouse, who was in the cluster of friends receiving good wishes. He had turned immediately to Laura, to find how she took the news but she, so poised, so used to praise, made no movement in shock or sorrow. She was standing turned half-way from him and he could see only the side of her face, but it seemed to him her expression said nothing: she neither flushed nor grew pale. He saw Samuel glance at her with concern, but her family gave no other sign of expecting her to be distressed. There was a dry, sudden note on a violin and the orchestra began a bouncing, crackling polka; her partner claimed her, she smiled and went to tread as brightly as the rest.

Richard took no part in the dance. Now he had no intention but to take his opportunity; he wanted only to find Laura alone. He remained where he sat, half-listening to Mrs. Rouse's chatter while she was there, opening no new conversation when she was taken from him. There could have been nothing between them, he thought: her brother was mistaken. Mrs. Rouse knows her well and encouraged me to speak for her; she knew Laura would not be disappointed. Samuel was mistaken: there was nothing between them. Were they never to be alone?

He saw her finger a loose piece of hair that had fallen to her neck, excuse herself and make her way towards the stairs as if she were withdrawing to the maid's room to have it put up. He followed her, telling himself he would look in on Keating at the card-tables, that there was a promise of supper and he would not be missed. When he reached the stairs she was gone. He idled in the hall waiting for her return but she did not come. From the door of the resting-room he heard voices he could not place and saw only strangers pass in and out. He pretended an interest in the murals. Then, bringing a gust of cold air, a couple came in from the garden, shivering and bantering at the change in temperature, glad to be again in the warmth. He thought how much she had been dancing, how welcome would be the cool of the night, and he took the door the young man held back for him and went out into the garden to search for her.

Darkness had fallen while they were inside and with it had come a frost. The Plough glittered in the clear, cold sky and the leaves and grass were beginning to stiffen. Laura's thin soles crushed the fragile ice to powder as she paced back and forth in the shrubbery behind the house. She could not be comfortable: if she walked she wanted to be still; if she took a seat on one of the benches she wanted to walk. She dropped her flowers and hugged her arms to her in her distress. There was a dull pain in her temples, she was suffocating with tears that would not flow and the bursts of young laughter from the ball only made her seem more solitary.

She was suffering from a hurt she had never thought she would feel. She could not understand James's engagement; she herself was undoubtedly the most beautiful woman at the gathering, and for her this was the first intimation that a man wishes to marry more than a face and that love does not fall where you choose. Her beauty, which she had relied upon to bring her all that she desired in life, had proved to be no protection and she felt alone and naked in a world with no security.

When she had heard the announcement she had been stunned by the shock of rejection. She had had no idea that such a thing could happen. It was true she had had the occasional pang of jealousy when James had shown interest in Grace, but she had thought it a passing fancy; not this. Not this. She could not understand why he had chosen Grace instead of her. She had felt sick and dizzy; she had been frightened she would faint and give herself away, but the turmoil hid her from comment and in an instant her pride had come to her help and held her as straight as a sapling in its cage. Her partner had come to her and she had danced automatically, her mind far away. As she swept down the floor she had glimpsed James and Grace standing together, as they would now always stand together, receiving the congratulations that should have been for her, and everything within her screamed as she smiled at her partner's remarks.

At last she could not be sure she could keep back her tears and, using her hair as an excuse, she escaped from the house, hoping to recover enough to go back. But outside, with no one to support her, the knowledge seemed all the worse and she tortured herself with the thought that she must now be a laughing-stock, a woman who had tried for a man and lost. She had been deliberately led on to hide a different courtship and she was now abandoned when her use was over.

Had she known it there had been no deception, no intended cruelty. James had never meant to hurt her nor to keep the secret of his addresses from her more than from anyone else. He had not realised she loved him and had failed to see his sudden blossoming of love for Grace.

What had happened to him was no more than had happened to a thousand men before him: he had gone to collect his sister from the home of a friend—and found he loved the friend. He had gone liking the girl; he had come away loving the woman.

He had kept silent from discretion—and from surprise. He had not prepared Laura because he had not realised how he had touched her. She, too, had been discreet: she had never crossed the boundary between the familiarity of an old acquaintance and the display of her heart; confident in her attraction, she had waited for him to move.

The fault could have been hers, it could have been that of a world that bridled girls' tongues, it could have been that of a young man who did not have eyes to see, but she did not think this—she thought only that she had been deceived and humiliated. She imagined James and Grace ridiculing her. To her mind she had been publicly shamed.

The sound of a man's footsteps came towards her through the stillness, pausing as if to pick something from the ground. She patted her cheeks and hair and turned with as normal an expression as she could muster, trusting to the night to disguise her. Richard approached with her discarded flowers in his hand. He hesitated when he saw her, unable to think how to begin, then came closer.

"Miss Delaford, I saw you dropped your corsage." He made no attempt to give them back.

"You're very kind," she hoped he could not see her clearly, "but they'll be spoilt now."

"I saw them given to you in the cotillion."

"Did you?" All the flowers had been the same; he could not have known they were hers unless he had followed her.

"I thought you might have wanted them."

"Thank you but they're spoiled now."

"Yes," he looked down at their crumpled petals and laid them aside.

"Yes, I know. I didn't come out here to give you these."

"No?"

For a moment he halted, then went on. "I—came to ask if you would marry me."

Laura stood silently, her breath clouding in the night air, misting the laurel that hung inches from her lips. She had not thought she had affected him so far. She tried to speak, to warn him not to go on, but before the words would come the chance was lost.

"I know you'll say that we have hardly met, but from the very first time I saw you, when you came into the room at your home, I was sure I loved you. You must have seen it—I can't hide my feelings and I wouldn't want to. I'm clumsy in my words, Miss Delaford, I don't know how to tell you what I feel—but if you'd come to me there isn't a man here I wouldn't be doing a wrong. . . . I'd hurt everyone for they'd never find a wife to match mine." He stopped, uncertain how she was listening to him.

Again she said nothing. Surely he had not guessed? No, he would not ask her if he had.

He reached out as if to take her hands but stopped before they touched.

"Oh, Laura, all my fresh springs shall be in thee."

Being in such pain she could not hurt him; she could not do to him what had been done to her that evening. There was adoration in his voice and she had need of being adored.

"I—I don't . . ."

He waited, but she could not continue.

"Marry me," he said. "Please marry me."

She was almost crying. She wanted to say she did not love him and could not be his wife—but she wanted to be a wife: the wife of a man who could love her more and raise her higher than James could ever do. She was twenty and unmarried—but she did not love him.

"Would you give me a week?" she asked.

"As long as you wish." So she had not refused him outright; he felt light-headed with release.

She took a step away, considering. "If I say next Friday? Not at home—the Abbey, St. Katherine's Chapel at three o'clock, I'll answer you then."

"Yes, anywhere," he paused. "The air is very cold; may I take you in?" He was afraid for her now—afraid she would come to some harm without him.

"No," she said, drawing further from him, aware of his concern. "No, please leave me. Don't press me. I'll stay by myself a little longer."

73

Chapter Seven

"Another?"

Richard's hand came out of the depths of the armchair and presented a glass, empty except for a hint of port at its rim. Keating leant from his seat with the decanter.

The atmosphere in the small room was mellow, ripe for confidences. They were sitting in Keating's study in two high-backed winged chairs drawn up close to the fire against the chill. Thick velvet curtains shut out the night and they were lit only by the low flames and an oil lamp behind them. A spaniel, its nose brown and dry with age, lay in the red glow on the hearth-rug, meat juices on its ears. They were cocooned from the world.

To have the second chair in use was unusual; it was rare for visitors to be entertained in such a private place. Keating had bought the two as a set and, once bought, could not bring himself to admit his loneliness by breaking the pair; he had filled its emptiness with piles of books and papers or spread a cloth over its cushion on which the dog could rest. The spaniel would lie with its muzzle on the arm, watching him with its great dark eyes and its master would wonder bitterly if this was the best he could do for company after forty-eight years. But tonight there was no sadness in the room; it had a younger, fresher climate.

An arch of burnt-out coals crumpled and fell sizzling into the heart of the grate, making the spaniel start. Richard stretched out his leg and scratched its belly with the toe of his boot; the old dog lifted a paw lethargically and settled to sleep.

This was the nearest Richard had come to calm since the night of the ball. It had been five days since he had asked Laura to be his wife and every one had seemed unendurable in its length. The weather had turned to the bad and sharp easterlies had alternated with drenching rain. Much of the time he had been unable to get relief out of doors and had been confined to the house where the pungent smell of wet mackintosh crept into every corner. He could not concentrate during the day nor sleep at night. Every knock at the door had been a message from Laura; every letter a refusal.

This evening, unable to be alone in his agitation about tomorrow, he had put on his damp coat and riding boots and splashed up to Abbotsbury House in the hope of solace. He had been there two hours and they were both a little bedazzled by the wine.

The wind blew a scatter of rain against the window. Keating watched his friend from behind his pipe. It was obvious that something was preying on the young man and Keating could guess what it was. During the drive home from the soirée he had begun to suspect that Richard had met a lady entirely to his satisfaction —nothing else would have made him so quiet—but he himself had spent the evening at whist and had not been able to find who she could be. All that week he had noticed Richard going about his business with that mixture of muted elation and melancholy that at once points to love. Only that morning, meeting Mrs. Vaughan in the street, she had remarked how vague the vicar had been about next Sunday's hymns. There was only one explanation that could fit such behaviour.

"So Sanderson is to marry Grace Palmer," he prompted.

Richard moved his attention to the spaniel's chest. "Yes. It seemed to take everyone by surprise."

"Every marriage is a surprise."

Richard looked up. "Oh? Are you not in favour of it?"

"Oh, yes. I meant that considering the courage it takes to propose, the difficulty of seeing the lady alone, the chances of her not returning your feelings and so on, it's a wonder anyone gets to the church at all."

"I know exactly what you mean," he rested his foot—the dog lifted its head and thumped its tail ingratiatingly; Richard obliged.

"Of course," he said, "you've been through all this yourself."

Keating did not remark on the assumption that he knew more than he had been told. "Perhaps not as badly," he said. "I was rather full of myself at your age; it never occurred to me that Anne would say no. I was a complete fool; I could have married her years before I did but—no—I wanted to 'enjoy' myself first so I let her wait for me. I don't know why she did. And then we were hardly married before she died." He went on before Richard could speak. "Don't start telling me it was God's will and don't start saying you're sorry; I don't deserve any sympathy."

"You're very harsh on yourself."

"I was harsher on her—and she so kind, so gentle . . ."

"You've never wanted to marry again? Forgive me if I . . ."

Keating raised his hand. "Yes and no. There could never be anyone to take her place, of course, but I've missed the companionship of a wife; I would have liked to have taken a second."

"But you never found her?"

"Oh yes. At different times there were one or two I could have been fond of—as a second, you understand—but—I'm sorry if I'm too free—you know Anne died in childbirth?"

Richard nodded.

"I couldn't risk doing that to another woman; I've felt so guilty. I did consider a platonic marriage but how many women want to be childless? It would be too selfish. And then, the temptation of a wife. I wouldn't say I was an overwhelmingly carnal man—but the temptation . . ."

Richard watched his wine swirl around his glass, embarrassed and flattered his friend had been carried so far, to confide his own apprehensions.

"Certainly," he said, "the carnal matters are a problem: it's so hard to reconcile them with spiritual love. How can your wife believe you love her? It all seems so—so undignified."

"Indelicate?"

"Yes."

Keating bent to the fire to light another taper for his pipe. He hoped he had not given fears where none had been before; his own life had been poisoned with guilt; he had no wish to infect others. "Do you have a particular lady in mind?" he asked lightly.

"Did you see anything different in me last Saturday?"

"On the way home? I noticed something."

"I'd asked Miss Delaford to marry me."

"The eldest girl?" He drew on the stem, smoke straggling upwards.

"Yes."

"Then you've made a fine choice: she's very lovely—and impulsive, I'd imagine."

"Oh, no," her lover defended her. "Serene and demure. You don't know her as I do."

"You haven't told me her answer." Don't let him be hurt, he thought, don't let such innocence be hurt.

Richard looked uncomfortable, his face showing his sleepless nights. "She didn't give one," he said, turning his head at the sound of the rain on the window. "She asked for a week to decide; I'm to go in tomorrow to see her. Thank God it's Thursday, that's all I can say; this week's gone on for ever."

It went through Laura's mind to pretend she was ill. She had woken that morning to realise that it was Friday and she was still undecided; the week had gone by too quickly for her to clear her thoughts. For a few moments she had lain in the comfort of her bed, listening to Naomi's quiet breathing, and illness had seemed the only way to rid herself of her responsibility—but, she thought, turning restlessly on to her side, it would bring too many complications. She could not let Richard wait in the Abbey forever; she would have to send him a note and then, no doubt, he would be on the doorstep full of concern for her and the secret would be out. Even if her letter explained that there was no cause for worry, there was nothing seriously wrong with her, she only needed more time to decide, someone would have to be called to her room and entrusted with the message. No, he must have an answer and it must be today.

She slid out of the bed and went stealthily across to her clothes. Naomi stirred at the movement, nestling into the hollow where her sister had lain, but did not wake and Laura slipped quietly out of the room so as not to disturb her more. She would dress in the boxroom, then go down to the kitchen to beg for early tea. The downstairs fires would be lit by now and in the peace of the early morning her answer would come.

But the answer did not come; the morning was as the week that preceded it, she could not focus her thoughts, trivia crowded her mind. It was of concern to her that the store-cupboards should be checked, that there was no hint of dust in any room, that Lucy should seam exactly straight, that letters should be written at once. The chiming of the clock felled the hours but she was no nearer her future.

Luncheon passed and she realised at last that she could not

evade her duty. Declining company she put on bonnet and pelisse and left the house for Dancing Hill. Her skirts bunched in her gloved hands, she climbed the mound opposite the farm with a tread that was firm and steady from long practice. Here the rise was almost vertical, so steep it defeated strangers, leaving the breath rasping in their throats, their heads dizzy, but from a child she had scrambled up and rolled down—it was no challenge to her. At the top she turned and looked down at her home, the wind fluttering the ribbons at her chin. Would this always be her home? Would she live on there, sinking into old-maidism because she had lost the man she loved? Would it be only her nephews and nieces that would climb with her—until she was too frail to do more than watch? There were tears in her eyes and she could not tell if the wind was too cold or her hurt too wounding.

She clasped her hands in her muff and walked on across the Pages' land towards the Park. The stubble was standing in the heavy, wet earth and here at the field's edge the beech leaves oozed beneath her boots, the water soaking upwards beyond her hem.

Half-way between the farms she sat down on an old stump and gazed unseeingly through the sighing, waving trees that clothed the terraced slopes, out across the town to the Abbey. She wondered if Richard was already there and one of the tears that might have been the wind ran to her cheek.

If the weather had only been better she could have thought more clearly. If it had been spring with its optimism, its promise for the future, or if it had been the drowsy heat of summer lulling her into confidence in new and ideal lovers, her way would have seemed more open—but autumn with its dampness and decay depressed her and underlined her loss. There seemed nothing but winter and spinsterhood before her. Oh, a week had never been so short, there had been no time to decide—but, she thought bitterly, could a hare with its head in a trap decide whether it would go free? Could a fox outrun the hounds?

There were Fungi growing from the stump; everything about her seemed in ruins. James, James, why Grace and not me? It was no use, she could not marry this man that she called by his Christian name only because he had proposed to her. How can you give yourself to one you think of as "Mr. Webster" when there is another who is constantly, tenderly in your dreams as "James"?

But he was now only a dream; the door to her life with him was shut and bolted. It was of no importance that she ached for him, that she cried in the nights, she could not have him—however much she loved him, she could not have him—and if she were not to wither into an old maid she must marry someone. She might never have a better offer than the one she had had last week.

She was twenty now; it was not a great age to be unwed but her sisters were growing: they had only to begin marrying and she would be labelled a failure, useless. Only a few more years and the whispers would be heard: "It's a pity Miss Delaford never married, she used to be so promising . . . Do you think she was ever asked?" "My dear, she was disappointed. Sanderson, you know."

And then her pride rose in her, strengthening her will, making her choice. She would not wear the willow for James, she would snap her fingers in his face. If he was gone from her then one man was as good as another. Richard Webster loved her, James did not. Very well then, she would take Richard. There would be no deceit in marrying him: she had never said she cared for him; he could not say she promised more than she gave—and she could give a great deal: she had her beauty—when she walked into a crowded room on Richard's arm it would be he who would be envied not Sanderson—what was it he had said? "There isn't a man I wouldn't be doing a wrong; they'd never find a wife to match mine,"—she knew how to run a house, she was accomplished; he would never have cause to complain of her favour. He was pleasant, obliging, adoring; he would be easily handled, easily moulded into what she wished. She would marry Richard—and she would marry before Grace.

She stood up and shook out her skirts, turning for home with a purpose. She walked the grass border with comfort and safety awaiting her. She had only to go down to the chapel and security and love would be hers, but as she neared the farm the flush of decision ebbed and died; she felt the chill of the wind. She would not change her mind but she could not speak to him this afternoon; she could not bear to see his joy.

She approached the house from the orchard, sodden windfalls beneath her feet, and as she followed the wall of the dairy she thought of Rachel. Unlatching the door Laura went into the cream-house to find her.

The girl was standing at a churn leaning with both hands against the marble counter beside her, her head bent as if she were faint. She looked up as Laura entered and smoothed her apron uncomfortably.

"Aren't you well, Rachel?"

"Yes, ma'am, only I've been churning and churning . . .." She stopped and pumped the handle wearily; there was a liquid slushing.

Laura went over to her. "Won't the butter come?"

"No, miss," Rachel pushed her hair out of her eyes with the back of her hand. "I'm fit to weep with trying."

"Then leave it for a while; take a letter down to the Abbey for me instead. Tell Mr. Delaford I sent you if he asks."

Rachel abandoned the churn, the milk reeling inside the barrel. "I'd be glad of the air," she said, rolling down her sleeves. "When shall I go?"

Laura fumbled at her coat buttons and looked at the watch pinned to her gown. It was half-past two. "In a quarter of an hour."

"Very well, miss. Shall I come to the house?"

"Yes. . . . No, no. I'll bring it to you here."

She covered her watch and slipped out of the dairy into the house, patting her coat front nervously. She did not want to be seen. She heard voices from the drawing-room, but no one noticed her enter the hall and she almost ran up the stairs to her bedroom. If she could only give the note to Rachel without having to answer her family's questions she could live her ordinary life for another two days. She wondered what had been wrong with the girl: it was unlike her not to be in command of her work; they could always trust Rachel to be diligent. However, it was useful to herself to have such a messenger.

She tugged off her outdoor clothes, throwing them on to the bed, and sat down at the writing-desk. As she reached for a pen she saw that her hand was shaking; she cradled her right in her left and felt they were clammy. She could barely breathe. Her whole life was to be written in this letter. She couldn't write it, she couldn't, she didn't know what to say. She sat motionless in the quiet room, her head bowed, holding her own hands until a sound from the farmyard roused her. She looked again at her watch. Ten minutes had passed, she had only five left. So little time. She took a sheet of paper and dipped her nib in the ink.

Still she could not find words, she could not tell this stranger she loved him and yet did not want to be cold. She held the pen a fraction above the paper. Was he at the Abbey yet? Did he believe she returned his feelings? She saw her poetry books piled on the window-ledge. Yes. She hesitated for a moment then bent to the desk. "My true love hath my heart," she wrote. She wished she could go on, "and I have his," but she could not. The first was true but not the second and she would not lie.

She took a second sheet of paper and wrote that her papa worked at home in the estate-room on Monday mornings and Richard could find him there between ten and twelve. She signed herself "Laura". She would fold the sheets together with the quotation in the middle so that he would read that first. He would understand. She placed the papers side by side in front of her and read what she had written, then she took the half-moon blotter by its handle and rocked it over the wet ink.

Richard had once been ignorant enough to believe that waiting for the bishop to grant his ordination had been the most harrowing point of his life, but crossing the yard to be interviewed by Mr. Delaford at five past ten the following Monday he realised that he had been wrong. He had met Laura's father twice and it was quite likely that if they were to meet in an unfamiliar town they would pass each other in the street without remembering they were acquainted. Yet here he was, coming to the man's house like a pirate to steal away his eldest daughter with hardly an introduction to recommend him.

He felt inside his jacket for the letter Laura had sent and rang the doorbell. This morning, at least, could not be worse than the previous Friday afternoon. He had arrived at the Abbey half an hour early and had wandered aimlessly and sightlessly around the church, reading and rereading inscriptions, fingering his hat and gloves, constantly drawing his watch from his waistcoat pocket until a quarter to the hour. He had stood for twenty minutes that stretched like twenty years with the stained glass of St. Katherine's Chapel weakly patterning his back, unable to bring himself to take one of the chairs that faced him squarely at the tomb within. It was not the reminder of death that troubled him; it was the effigies of John and Joan Leweston lying side by side beneath the canopy, silent and content, resting placidly together through the centuries for everyone to see when he had another six, seven, eight agonising minutes to endure before he would know whether he too was to have a wife. For if Laura refused him there would be no one else.

He had come prepared to persuade her. He expected shyness at the last, a hesitation, an inability to make up her mind. He didn't pretend to himself that she loved him as ardently as he loved her, but she must care for him a little or she wouldn't have considered his offer. She hadn't seemed eager to accept him but, then, brought up as she was, how could she? It was one thing to dream of marriage, another to see the man standing beside you—and it was undeniable that there were aspects of the union from which a gently bred lady would recoil. He acknowledged he had not been a gallant suitor, he was no Tennysonian knight. He loved her truly and could offer her all his heart, but he was racked by the worry that this might not be enough.

He was interrupted in his anxiety by the entrance of a pale, pretty girl dressed as a servant. She enquired his name, handed him the letter she held beneath her mantle and withdrew. She's refused me, he had thought looking down at the delicate script on the envelope; she hasn't dared to tell me herself. It had hardly seemed worthwhile unfolding the pages—he didn't want to read her reasons—but he had read them and they had brought him here to steal her from her father.

"I'm afraid the mistress and the ladies have gone to Yeovil, sir," the maid told him at the door.

"It was Mr. Delaford I wanted to see," said Richard. "Could you give him my card? My business is important. Shall I wait in the hall?" He entered without invitation; his intention was to carry his purpose. "Are none of the ladies at home?" he asked, passing the card and taking off his gloves.

"Miss Laura is here, sir, but she asked not to be disturbed. I won't keep you a moment."

The girl left him long enough to consider elopement, returned and presented him to the estate-room.

Mr. Delaford had not wanted to accept the visitor. He had been spreading field maps and day books on his table when Edith tentatively informed him of the arrival and his mind had been full of crop rotations. Has the man no work to do? he thought irritably; I daresay not on a Monday.

"I don't think he will go away, sir," Edith ventured.

Her master laughed. "You anticipate me. Go and fetch him then if he doesn't mind seeing me here. I expect it's some charity or other."

The two men had greeted each other civilly and critically, neither wishing the interruption to take longer than it must. Richard saw a family resemblance he had not noticed before; Laura's face and composure might be her mother's but her eyes were those of her father. Delaford saw a young man with an air of calm determination that seemed out of proportion to the occasion. He wondered what good works could call for such resolution.

In an hour all was said; the father bound and tied, the bridegroom victorious. Delaford was not a timid man, but Richard had pinned him with a pulpit stare and delivered an address so concise, so measured, so outwardly confident that there was no weakness left to be attacked, no argument to be made. His daughter's surrender was laid before him, her suitor's love, respect and devotion displayed, his financial position, properties and prospects explained. The power of the Church was exerted; its unfortunate opponent could do nothing but submit. The lady's settlement was offered, waived, pressed and accepted at half the original sum. The maid was summoned and appealed to to bring Miss Delaford and a bottle of Madeira.

"So this is why she didn't go shopping," Delaford said indulgently as they waited. "I thought it wasn't like her. You'll need a long purse, Webster; she'll be a damned expensive wife."

"I'd anticipated that."

"More fool you for not taking all her dowry."

"I'd rather not take any."

"Well, you'll learn," he shuffled his papers on his desk. He knew he could have no objection to Richard beyond his very existence. He knew that this was a suitable marriage, a match in birth and rank and expectations. He knew Richard could provide an income that would shelter Laura from the troubles of the world. It was obvious that Richard loved her. He knew all this. There was no disappointment that she should choose such a man, no embarrassment. Even so, it was hard to give away your daughter, to appoint someone else as guardian to the tumbling child that had fallen over its petticoats to run to you, that had once let out all the lambing ewes in one afternoon. And she was only the first: in the next few years he would be overborne by three more young strangers who came to take away his youth; mortality felt a good deal nearer.

It was strange so much could have happened so quickly without him being aware of it. He had had no hint Laura felt this way. There could have been no more than friendship for the lawyer after all. It seemed to him she had barely met Richard. How could she be sure of her choice so soon? But he had been sure of Elizabeth from the day he had met her and there could be no more successful marriage than theirs. There was a light step and a lighter rustling in the doorway and Laura came in. She was wearing a dark woollen gown that made her face seem paler than it was, but when she saw Richard she coloured. Her hands were clasped in front of her and her fingers locked tightly. She stood aside to let Edith pass and set down her tray.

Nothing was said as Delaford poured the wine, spilling it in heavy drops on the silver. He had thought to toast his daughter's happiness but could think of nothing joyous to say. To both men she looked very young, standing so uncertainly with the blush spreading down to meet her collar. She had come from her room a free woman and found herself promised to a man she did not love and hardly knew; only now did she realise what her pride had done. It was not too late to change her mind; at any time until the wedding she could say no. Dare she go on? Yes, her pride would not let her fail; no one would say she went back on her word—nor that she had been afraid.

She interrupted the stilted good wishes that eddied around her. Her father had mentioned June brides; she could not trust herself to wait so long.

"Not June, Papa," she said, gripping her glass. "I had thought of a month's time—if Mr. Webster would agree." She gazed at her lover beseechingly.

He was surprised. "It would please me more than anything," he said. "Can you be ready so soon?"

She smiled, nodding passively, and lowered her eyes to her wine.

Chapter Eight

The calm of the night was deep and satisfying after the turmoil of the farm. It was Pack Monday and the chaos and commotion of the town were being enacted in the house where the family's first bride was preparing for her wedding the following Saturday, but here on the hill that led down to Westbury the Delaford brothers were alone in the peace between tumults.

Jonathan, his hair a shade darker than Samuel's, his build a shade lighter, was peering closely at a catalogue of farm machinery, straining his eyes into the darkness. Samuel was prowling beside him with his hands in the pockets of his cutaway. He was experiencing a reawakening of feeling as the revelation of his fatherhood faded, and its resurgence made him restless and eager for excitement. Rachel's docile silence had gradually persuaded him that her position was of no importance—one more love-child born to a serving-girl was nothing—but it had been the news of his sister's betrothal that had shaken him back to the awareness of emotion. He had been her only confidant in her longing for James; her apparent unconcern in the week after the announcement of the Sanderson-Palmer alliance had upheld his disinterest in what was happening around him, but when he heard that she had accepted an offer from a man he had brought to their home only three months before—three months she had filled with allusions to James's perfection—fear for her unhappiness had crept through his armour. He had taken her aside the evening he had learnt of it and taxed her on her reasons for accepting.

"Reasons?" she had said archly. "Do you ask an old spinster for reasons?" and he had seen all the workings of her mind. It had been of no use to argue with her, she was set on her course. He had tried to make her wait for a man who touched her as James had done—she said she had been mistaken in her feelings, his engagement mattered so little to her that she realised she had not loved him after all; Richard, she said, would do very well. When he insisted that what she was doing was wrong to herself she had grown angry. Where, she had asked, was she to find a more suitable husband? Was she not capable of discovering a good man without *his* help? Was she still in leading-strings? No? Then perhaps he would keep any poor opinions of Mr. Webster to himself.

He admitted to her that he had no poor opinions. He acknowledged that if she had brought Richard forward as her first love he would have thought him a perfect match; it was only the rashness of a cold marriage that worried him. Three weeks later it still worried him. She was showing no joy, no gaiety, no anxiety over her coming change of state; she moved towards her wedding with a grave formality that her parents put down to good sense but he knew was a mask for folly.

"What about this one?" said Jonathan. "Listen: 'A New Improved Horse Gear with Intermediate Motion for Driving a Small Chaff Engine.'"

"What firm is it?"

Jonathan turned the brochure to the front. "Ransome, Sims and Jeffries."

"We'd need a new shed."

"Not necessarily. If we moved the corn bins out of the old pigsty and lifted the roof a couple of feet that would do. Do you think the governor would buy one? He'll be digging deep for this wedding."

"Ask your new brother-in-law to pay; he can afford it."

"Yes," Jonathan gave up trying to read in the darkness and thrust the rolled-up catalogue into his pocket. "Yes, I hadn't thought he'd be so warm. Still—if she goes on the way she's started he'll have his work cut out paying for her."

They looked back on the last weeks with masculine gloom. Preparations for the wedding had begun with a vengeance on the Tuesday when Laura had proved adamant in refusing to put back the date. There had been an expedition to Dorchester for materials suitably splendid and dazzling for bride and bridesmaids, and a glass case to petrify the bouquet. Two dressmakers had been summoned to help with the trousseau and the Delaford women had hardly had needles out of their hands. There were ribbons here, laces there, embroideries here, tissue-papers there; there were bonnets in need of trimming on the tables, half-packed boxes on the chairs; the house was overflowing with finery. Mr. Delaford had not been niggardly in his allowance, and his wife had channelled all her natural excitement and concern for her first loss into the managing of the arrangements.

Both parents wanted their eldest daughter to display their standing, to compliment their family, and she had not denied them their wish. She had chosen her dress with care as the outward celebration of her position; not as an Afghan bride decorates herself with gold to show the world her husband's wealth, but to show one man that she was a prize he had been foolish to miss, one woman that her beauty could not be rivalled and herself that if she could not truly be joyful she could at least appear to be so. Her body could rejoice if her spirits could not.

Samuel had accused her jokingly of marrying simply to upstage Grace Palmer. "Oh, Samuel," she'd said, "you've found me out!"—and he had not been quite convinced that her words were said in play. Certainly all the attention of the town had been diverted to her. The talk was all of Laura. The announcements in *The Times* and *Flying Post* and the issuing of banns in the Abbey had brought a flood of letters and visitors to the farm, all anxious to give congratulations and devoid of any suspicion that she had wanted James. Indeed, the names Sanderson and Palmer were as if they had never been and James was privately suffering under the eclipse of his lady by Laura.

Samuel had briefly considered telling Richard of his doubts regarding Laura's feelings but he could not be so disloyal. Marriage was the goal of a woman's life. If Richard were to reject her because of a connection with another man, the humiliation would ruin her however innocent her attachment had been. No one else would take her; his interference would have been as disastrous as if she had sold the land from under him.

They jostled up Cheap Street through the crowd. The road had been closed to traffic but was densely filled with pot-valiant spectators celebrating the ending of the day and the beginning of the night. This was the 16th October, the first Monday after Michaelmas, the day when labourers were engaged for the agricultural year and the fair brought the normal habits of the town to a halt. The Delafords had spent the day rehiring their workers; officially they had had no workforce for the past week—every autumn Delaford declared he'd be damned if anyone would prosecute him for breach of contract, dismissed his men and maids and took them up again on Pack Monday for a period of fifty-one weeks, thus being obliged to make no contracts and avoiding the Master and Servant Law. That he paid them a shilling over double the week before dismissal and that they provided a week's work in exchange was incidental and convenient. It was not a policy Samuel relished but his father was not to be moved.

Now the streets were full of labourers and their girls with the signs of their trade pinned to their jackets, bent on squeezing every drop of enjoyment from the fair. Cheap Street had been lined with the travelling shops and the cheap-jacks had done most of their business with the housewives during the day; the heart of the night-fair, the throbbing, blaring centre of flamboyance, was to the north of the town between the Coombe and Bristol roads and it was here that the flow of humanity led them.

Inside the fair-ground all was clamour and noise and bright, flaring lights. There were wooden stalls on the trampled grass where men in golden earrings and dark, unwashed women sold beer, cider and gin, meat pies, hot sausages, brandy-snaps and greasy pastries. There were drinking tents, coconut shies, shove-ha' penny, darts, Aunt Sallies and roundabouts. There were freak shows: the fattest woman in the world, calves with two heads, chickens with three legs, performing dogs, educated pigs. There was shin-kicking and grinning through a horse-collar, boxing booths and Cornish wrestling. There were fortune-tellers, acro-bats and girls in tights walking on the high wire. There were jugglers and conjurors, and couples dancing in a roped square to a band playing above the shrieks and laughter of the night. An artificial excitement held its audience in thrall.

The brothers wandered through the side-shows paying out their coins to lose their money. They shot and shied and bowled as they had done since they were boys and together they battered a coconut from its cup, but to Samuel the brightest attraction was dressed in her Sunday clothes passing a baked potato from one hand to the other as she waited for it to cool. He lost sight of her as he turned to see Jonathan duck under the barrier with their prize, but he found her again as his brother brushed the milk from his coat and suggested they return to the farm.

"You go on," he said, looking past his companion's shoulder. "Tell Mamma I've met friends."

Jonathan followed his eyes to the girl standing alone in the crowd, tapping her fingers against her skirt to the music of the band, and raised his eyebrows.

"That's Webster's maid."

"I know."

Jonathan shrugged. "Well," he said, "it's your funeral. I'll wish you good hunting."

Samuel approached his quarry from behind. He was tall enough to have to bend to whisper, "Will you dance, Dinah?" and rich enough not to wait for change as he took her into the square. He thought throwing away a half-crown would impress her but she was not so easily taken in. She danced because she wished to dance not because she was a fool. He held her to him, gazing down with heavy eyes, and she smiled at him, amused that he could be so sure when he was so wrong. She was tempted by his closeness as a young girl will be tempted, but she was too worldly-wise to give up her dreams for the luxury of one night. She had spent three weeks in preparing a home for his sister so that Laura might marry a man who would never accost a servant at a fair, and it had strengthened her yearning for a better, higher life; a life where you did not slave as an undermaid until your children came—only to give up your daughters to slave as undermaids. Samuel thought she was such another as Rachel but he was mistaken; he was holding ambition in his arms.

She let him treat her to beer that he thought would ease his way, to a one-act melodrama in a steaming, overheated tent and to the Amazing Spectacle of the Fire-eater, but when he suggested he walk her back to the village she laughed and pushed him away with the flat of her hand.

"It's not walking alone in the dark that's dangerous," she said.

Samuel took her hand from his chest and clasped his own around it. "There's no danger in me."

She tried to free her fingers. "Why didn't you call me Miss Hillyard?" she asked.

"Miss Hillyard?" He was taken aback; it hadn't occurred to him not to use her Christian name.

"Why didn't you?"

"You're too pretty, my love."

"Too pretty. Dinah, the too pretty housemaid."

He did not understand the expression in her eyes; this was not how Rachel had looked at him. There was no adoration masking her intelligence and he had no experience to make him cunning. He could think of nothing to reply and she took what might have been pity on him. She did not yet know what she wanted of life but was realistic enough to see that her choices were few. She did not despise Samuel for finding her attractive and it was the world's disrespect that chafed her, not his own. If she encouraged him enough could this end in more than a hedgerow? Could she raise herself this way? Her hand was still in his and she did not withdraw it. She smiled and he noticed how softly her hair curled amongst the violets of her bonnet and felt safety return.

"But, sir," she straightened his clasping fingers one by one and looked into his waiting eyes, "on Saturday Miss Delaford will be my mistress—if you chanced to visit her . . ."

Laura woke early on her wedding-day. It was one of many wakings that had disturbed her night. She stepped out of bed in her nightgown and went softly across to the window, the coldness of the polished floor biting into her bare soles. She could hear her sister's gentle breathing as she had heard it on the morning of her decision. "Oh, Naomi," she whispered, "you're happier than I today." She parted the curtains and looked down on Sherborne, grey in the morning twilight. There in the town James and Grace were sleeping with their newest clothes set out so that they might celebrate her wedding. Knowing that she must and would, she wondered if she could carry it through.

She turned to look at her clothes. They had been lain over a chair and covered with a muslin sheet to protect them from dust and all she could see were the backs of her white kid boots. She could not connect them with herself.

Her gaze went back to the window. I may never see the dawn break over this view again, she thought; when I come back from Weymouth I'll look out over the fields of Bradford Abbas. How strange I should be moving there—preparing to spend my whole life there—when I've never seen the view from my new bedroom window, nor seen any room in the house except the drawing-room. Would this have happened if I hadn't been caught in the rain? How strange I should be going to this man, willingly putting myself in his hands, to live with him, care for him, have his children. . . . She leant her forehead against the cold glass until she could no longer see out for mist on the pane. Aimlessly she drew a "J" in her condensed breath, then brushed it out with the back of her hands. She picked up the framed photograph of Richard's sister that had been set on the window-ledge. Maud's face was like her brother's, pleasant, intelligent but not immediately memorable; only her grandmother's Egyptian earrings hanging beneath her dark hair gave her appearance a touch of the exotic—it was the second glance that told you she was handsome.

Well, there was no more time to worry—by noon she would be Mrs. Webster and must call this girl sister. The chill in her feet creeping upwards, Laura slid back into bed and sat propped against her pillow, watching the room get lighter.

Had her sight reached as far as Bradford Abbas she would have seen Richard, dressed for an ordinary day, close his front gate and cross the obscurity of the lane to the church. He, too, was unable to sleep and had decided not to waste his morning tossing uncomfortably in his new bed with its elaborate, shining brass, but to spend his time more profitably in prayer. It was not likely that he would forget his faith on this day when the care of the one he loved most was to be entrusted to him, but the enormity of that charge made him fear his own inadequacy. He would cherish Laura to the very end of his life and beyond, but there was nothing he could give that would equal the favour of her love.

"Lord," he began, kneeling in the chancel with the dim eastern light before him, "thou knowest how busy I shall be this day; if I forget thee do not thou forget me." Repeatedly he touched the thin gold wedding ring that hung round his neck on a silk ribbon, unable to convince himself it was there.

The silence and sombreness of the empty building lulled him into that suspended state that comes before an anticipated event when there is no consciousness of the passing of time, and some hours had gone by when Dinah surprised him with her whisper of "breakfast". He got up stiffly, rubbing the numbness from his knees, and followed her back to the house. He drained the pot of its tea but could not eat and at half past nine, to be ready for the wedding at eleven, he went up to his room to dress.

He had everything new from boots to a black frock coat still wrapped in its tissue-paper and a top-hat with the dark, rich sheen of polished jet. His collar and cravat were an obstacle race for nervous hands but the finished effect was of sober, unconcerned affluence; he might have been preparing for the wedding of a second cousin. He looked at himself curiously in the mirror; where was the self-conscious student that he usually saw behind the mask? Perhaps ability rose to meet responsibility.

He brushed and rebrushed his hair. It still wanted twenty minutes to when Keating, his groomsman, was to collect him. He sat down on the bed and smoothed the nap of his hat with his cuff. It came to him that when he returned he would have Laura beside him as his wife—even now, at this late moment, it seemed a strange, impossible thought. He stared around the room. He had done all that he could think of for her comfort: he had had every inch of the house painted and every room papered—the smell of the paste still hung in the air; he had bought a round work-table she had admired in Yeovil and this soft-mattressed bedstead to replace the vast and hideous edifice that had been the doctor's, but no other furniture thinking that its choice would occupy her mind when she was homesick. There were new curtains of Nottingham lace and frothy Irish bed-linen embroidered with Laura's initials. The background had been provided and she could paint it as she wished.

He idly straightened the counterpane and wondered whether she wore her hair plaited or loose at night—he hoped loose. He had never seen it unbound; he thought it must reach to her waist. He shut his eyes at the memory of its wheatsheaf colour. His sister wore hers untied but then she dressed it more plainly. If only Maud could be here to see him married; his aunt must be ailing if she could not spare her niece. He must remember to send them flowers from Laura's bouquet.

Keating had gathered him up, taken the ring and ushered him through a side-door into his place in the Abbey before he realised what was happening. Time was playing tricks on him, coming in rushes and gaps he could not explain. He had seemed to be preparing in the shelter of his room for hours yet he could not account for his arrival in town. Surely it had been a moment ago he was at home.

A whisper that the bride had come ran up and down the pews, there was the rustle and shuffling of a congregation rising to its feet and finding its place in its hymn-book and Richard was standing in the aisle beside Keating. The calmness and confidence of one who has achieved his desire, reached a goal that had seemed as distant as a mountain-top, descended upon him. He turned to see his wife approach and for one dizzy, faint moment imagined that she could not be for him; he was here as parson to marry this exquisite figure to another—she could not be for him.

She looked as delicate as porcelain as she drifted towards him. She was wearing a white satin gown, a little creased on one side where her father had crushed against it on the journey from the farm, a berthe dipped low between her breasts and left her shoulders bare in imitation of the Princess Royal. Her veil had been her grandmother's and was of Limerick lace washed in milk; it flowed from a headpiece of artificial orange blossom and lilies-of-the-valley. She carried a circular posy of white chrysanthemums and she was followed by her sisters in white muslin and ribboned bonnets. She was altogether glorious; she was the perfect effigy of the 'sixties bride and she knew that in this she had defeated her rival, but there was bitterness in every step that took her to Richard. Here at last it was too late to go back and she did not know whom to blame.

She kept her eyes to the ground through the service until Richard took her hand for the ring, then she looked up at him with a wide, startled glance as if she did not know why she was there. He thought how painful this must be for a girl who had never left her family—and how cold her touch.

They were swept back to the farmhouse in a shiningly new Victoria lent by the Armstrongs of Oborne with white rosettes on the horses' browbands and white bows on the driver's whip. Afterwards neither of them could have described the wedding-breakfast as anything but a confusion of voices and speeches and a blatant display of food and wines. They had been joined until death, made one flesh, and yet there seemed nothing linking them. The binding threads of flirtation had been discarded, the anticipations and uncertainties were gone and their relations were flat and dull without them. They were players in a drama with no emotion. To Richard this was no surprise: he had seen this stranded bewilderment in every couple he had married and he knew it to be artificial; but since she was a child Laura had regarded this day as the purpose of her life and its hollowness frightened her. Only once did she see Richard as the lover who had courted her. As they cut the cake his hand folded strongly around hers, giving all the force for the stroke, sparing her even this small effort, and she knew he would always try to protect her from what she had brought on herself.

And presently she went upstairs to change and came down to be taken from her home. Her whole demeanour had altered with her dress: she was no longer the magnificent puppet acting out a part but a shy, scared girl who had found herself to be a wife and was covering her timidity with a veneer of smartness. She was wearing a grey and lilac silk gown with a tight grey sealskin jacket and muff, neat grey gloves and square-toed boots and a grey bonnet with lilac ribbons—all very sedate and suitable for an October honeymoon, but the handkerchief she clenched in her palm gave her away.

Richard was waiting for her in the hall at the foot of the stairs and she took his arm to be led out to the carriage. He preferred her in these clothes; he knew she had had to be decked as splendidly as she had been and he had thought her beautiful, but he was relieved to see her more natural, nearer her everyday self. He did not want "a bride", he wanted Laura; it was the woman herself he desired not simply the state of marriage.

The mood of the party had also changed as they moved outside and Laura kissed her family good-bye. Her mother was smiling but crying at the same time and when she clutched at her father she saw that there were tears in his eyes too. Richard guided her into her seat and wrapped a fur rug across her knees leaving none for himself as he took his place beside her. Naomi stood on tiptoe, balancing against the body of the carriage, and handed up the bouquet.

Her hands clumsy in her tight gloves Laura pulled out one

flower and threw it blindly into her audience. All the unmarried girls tried to catch it as it flew, but her aim had been so wild that it passed over the guests into the servants who had gathered to see her leave. Jostled in the laughter Rachel reached for it without thinking and all the applause went to her as the Websters wheeled out of the yard.

She could not help but glance at Samuel; he, however, was looking resolutely after the favourite sister who was being taken away from him by a man who could treat her as he pleased. She was Richard's property now, every sixpence in her purse, every ribbon in her costume belonged to him and if he abused his power neither brother nor father had the right to help her. He felt afraid for this delicate creature who had begun her marriage so foolishly and who could not fight ill-treatment as he could do. It was hard to see his sister made so defenceless.

It was a cool, brittle afternoon with sun as clear and light as Moselle and a bite in the air. The wheels of the victoria were half-hidden by mist in the hollows, and the hills before Cerne Abbas floated like wooded islands in the sea. They rode with one half of the hood open that they might watch the country pass and as they rolled through the landscape—unnaturally still in its autumnal greens and browns—Richard took his wife's hand and held it safely beneath her fur.

They paused two miles from home to remove the rosettes from the harness—Laura pleaded they drew too much attention—and a woman beating a carpet over a fence stopped with the back of her hand on her hip and thought nostalgically of her own wedding ride. Richard had been ready to travel anywhere to please her; he had suggested Scotland or the Lakes or indeed anywhere Laura wished to go, but she had been seized with an irrational alarm at being so far from her home and had asked for Weymouth—the nearest seaside town that had come to mind. It had seemed to Richard an unadventurous choice, but when she explained she was not used to leaving her mother he had been concerned enough to suggest she bring a sister. To his relief she had held out firmly against this, privately she had wondered why he should feel her in want of quite such a degree of support. He couldn't expect her to need consolation unless he had seen through her masquerade

—and yet he gave no sign of not believing she returned his love.

She adored the hotel he had chosen; it was rich, new, a hushed, sensual world of thick carpets and stiff draperies, alert with deference to herself as a married woman, a world which invited you to bask and wallow in its comforts. Their room was just as she wished; overlooking the sea, with dark brocade curtains to shut out the night and lace to shut out the day; there were tasselled plush cloths on the multitude of tables and ornaments on the multitude of cloths. It was all too heavy and reminiscent of the seraglio for Richard, but Laura looked at the glare of the fire on the brass and mahogany and thought how much nicer this was than the farm. If she could only have the Vicarage this way.

They dined together in the warm intimacy of the full dining-room and here Laura saw a new problem approach. How could she undress with this stranger in the room? Even behind a screen it was impossible, not even her own brothers had seen her in her shift—but as the time grew nearer Richard saw her shyness increase as she tried to linger over her ice and said he would come down for a brandy when he had escorted her upstairs. He longed for a cigar to steady his nerves as he waited to go up to her, but he thought it would do too much damage to his breath: no woman wanted to taste tobacco and tonight of all nights he must not revolt her.

When he entered she was lying in bed feeling the weight of the unfamiliar ring, twisting it round and round her laden finger, her hair—released from its coils—gleaming in the lamplight.

"Richard," she said, her voice almost lost in the lushness of the room, "don't you think this design is lovely?"

He laid his jacket over a chair. "It's very modern. I thought you'd like it."

"May I do this when we go home?"

He went over to her and sat beside her on the edge of the sheet. He looked at her with inexpressible tenderness as she rested against the pillows. She seemed very young, very fragile. He touched her hair softly. "You can have anything you want, my love."

He was leaning close to her and he gave off a slight, heady scent of sandalwood. She was struck again with the oddity of sharing her room with a man. He stroked the length of her hair and she found her heart to be quickening. One rim of her collar was turned under—he straightened it gently and the brushing of his knuckles against her neck sent an unknown shiver down her body. He was looking at her with love but there seemed something different in his expression, some peculiarity that for a moment reminded her of Samuel.

He lifted her left hand and put his lips to the palm, folding her fingers down to hold the kiss, and left her to undress. As he went behind the screen where her own clothes were laid neatly on her trunk she thought how well he had looked that day. Tall, distinguished; a suitable foil to her own beauty, and in the emptiness of her loss of James she felt a faint stirring of affection for her husband.

She could not watch him as he lay down beside her and in her bashfulness began to describe how she would make their home —the china and the silver, the flowers and colours—and he let her talk on until it did not seem strange that they should be together; then, the dark hair showing through the opening of his gown, he stretched to turn out the lamps and with gentleness and innocence he reached for her.

Chapter Nine

Rachel crumpled the petals of the chrysanthemum and dropped them like fouled snow into the river. There was a grey-black mud on the banks where the water lapped and over this a grey-green slime pocked with the holes of rats. Months before this had seemed a shining river, alive with voles and moorhens, but now she thought of the stench of the trapped, stagnant inlets and the animals were rats, vermin. Everywhere about her there was vileness and corruption. The willow beside her dripping dankly on to the grass had lost a branch and the wound it had left had erupted into a luminous orange mould. Her head ached so badly as she stood balanced at the water's edge that her sight was blurred.

She had kept the flower she had caught at Laura's wedding until it had turned brown and withered. Superstitiously she had seen it as a sign that she might still be married, but that hope had passed. There had been no reconciliation with Samuel and now that she was in her fifth month she could not hide her pregnancy much longer. She was surprised that she had not yet been discovered, but then she had kept healthy and tiredness was a thing easily explained away.

The revelation that Samuel cared nothing for her had sickened her. She would wake in the night and see two eyes above her: cold, blue eyes that could persuade her with a glance and yet had never really seen her at all. She had loved him with all the passion of her old saints, with all the respect and deference and obedience of the serving-girl to her master. He was Delaford's eldest son and she had been in awe of him; nothing that he could do could be wrong. And the joy of it! The flowing emotion and physical release of giving herself to him, the escape from the cage of work and damnation that was her life.

The nausea of fear was always with her. She had convinced

herself that he loved her; now she saw that she had been no more than an entertainment, a relaxation, no more than his hunters or tobacco. She knew that they had sinned and because she was the woman her sin had been the blacker; yet she felt that he had played her on his line.

Since she had told him of the child she had met Samuel alone only once and then, when she had humbled herself and begged him to marry her, he had refused, seeming insulted that she could think of such a thing—and, indeed, if there was no love between them it was foolish to expect him to bring himself so low. She saw that there was no escape for her—she would soon be found out and unless she accepted Samuel's offer of shelter she would have nowhere to go but the Poorhouse. Please God she hadn't dallied so long he had even changed his mind about that.

He had wanted her to give up the child, but she prayed that there would be no child to give up. There was no future for the illegitimate, a still-birth would be a mercy to them all, but if that couldn't be she hoped it would be a boy and so never suffer this way himself. Oh, God, to be Samuel's sister, loved and wedded, with a good man and a good home and nothing to fear. Dear Lord, sweet Jesus, have mercy on me. . . .

She heard the striking of midday from the Abbey clock come faintly up the valley and drew her cloak around her to go back to the farm. She had come down to the meadow by Mill Lane to look over the herd and had wandered along the river-bank on to Darkhole land. She climbed slowly back to the cottage through the fields and cleaned her boots on the scraper by the door. The fire was lit and the kettle singing when she entered, and she cut the cheese and peeled the onions as her father and brother came in from drilling the winter wheat, stamping their feet against the cold.

With his mouth full of bread Malachi told her she looked pinched, but she said she was only chilled through—it was no matter. When the meal was over Rachel gathered the plates and took them into the scullery to wash. She felt very tired and the food lay in an indigestible lump in her stomach. Without thinking she put one hand in the small of her aching back and arched it, resting the other hand on the baby. Since the cold weather she had laid aside her print dresses and gone back to her traditional smock and its voluminous folds, plaintively embroidered with blue hearts, had disguised her condition, but this afternoon she gave herself away. Automatically she had tied on the apron that lay by the sink and as she stretched the waistband rode up under her breasts, emphasising her swelling figure. No one who saw her could help but know that she was pregnant.

Eyes shut, she clasped her hands behind her neck and twisted her head from side to side to ease her tension. Something quiet and malevolent in the air awoke her and she opened her eyes. Her father was standing in the entrance to the scullery, holding the boiling kettle she was to use for his dishes and looking at her with horror and revulsion on his face.

For months she had dreaded this, but now that it had come she found that she wanted not to scream but to laugh. Joseph Cooper, patriarch, lay preacher, corner-stone of the Connection, was standing in a kitchen clutching a pan of hot water like an old wife, staring through his foolish rim of beard at the terrible sight that was his daughter. All she could think was that he and her prosing brother would have to do their own scrubbing now and a high, screeching laugh came up from her throat and surrounded her.

Cooper slapped down the kettle, steam rising from the slops, and took her by the shoulders, shaking her to and fro until the laughter stopped and the combs fell from her hair. He was shouting, cursing and reviling her, accusing her of whoring, and when she did not deny it but smiled at him with a hard smile and hard eyes he hit her face with the back of his knuckles until Malachi pulled him away.

In the panting calm after the storm she put up her fingers to her brow and cheeks. There was blood on her skin; a little, a very little, but enough. All her resilience left her; she cradled her numbed face in her palms and the weeping she had kept back for five months began. Her father was ordering her out of her home. She pleaded to stay, telling him she had nowhere to go, but he only taunted: "Ask the father. Ask him for shelter, Jezebel!"

"I can't," she said. "I can't—he won't have me."

"Won't have you? Is he wed already then?"

She had never heard his voice so harsh, never felt so divorced from his love. She turned towards Malachi and he backed a step away as if even her look was foul.

"No, Father," she said bitterly.

"Then he can marry you."

"No, no, he can't. He's . . ."

"Well?"

"He's too far above me." She touched her falling hair, but he grasped her wrist.

"No man," he said, his face close to hers, "who can sire a bastard can say he's above another."

"He won't, he won't," she cried, pulling away from him. "I've begged him but he won't."

"In God's name, we'll make him take you! Tell me who did it and I'll make him take you!"

Afraid of him and afraid of Samuel, Rachel kept silence.

"Damn you! Damn you! Tell me." In his anger Cooper tightened his grip; she drew breath sharply but did not speak. He turned to his son, "Who's looked on her with lust?"

"None that I know—except the young master."

The knowledge of what had occurred, the old story that they were powerless to remedy, came to both men as he spoke—and Rachel saw that now the father had been named the guilt would be all hers.

Seated in the drawing-room with her family about her, Mrs. Delaford allowed her married daughter to pour the tea and looked across to her husband with contentment. Laura's wedding had brought back memories of her own courtship and—perhaps it was only that she was older—she couldn't see that Jack was any less handsome now than then. He was a straight-backed, full-haired man with a greyness at the temples that was spreading and a carven, authoritative face. He held himself with the consciousness of being descended from generations of good county stock and, except for his calloused palms, his occupation could not be guessed from his appearance; he and his sons were instantly recognisable as gentlemen. Miss Haverly of Sturminster Newton had given herself nothing of which to complain when she had joined her hand and fortune to his.

"Well," said Samuel as Laura passed the last cup, "what's the opinion of the Church?"

"Richard says it's quite wrong to have slaves and if people can't see that for themselves they won't give them up for the asking. He says there's bound to be civil war. There, you thought you were the only person who supported the North, didn't you?" She received the sugar with equanimity; since their return from Weymouth she and Richard had dined at the farm as a couple, but this was her first visit without him and she was enjoying her position as one of the family, yet far superior to her sisters.

"Oh, there's something to be said on both sides," Mr. Delaford laid down his saucer and stood up. "I'd better be off, Elizabeth."

"Drink another cup before you go, Jack. It's so cold outside. Laura, pour another cup."

"No, no. I told Cooper to wait with the trap." He bent and chucked his daughter under the chin, "Richard says . . ." he teased and kissed her as she blushed. "Where's poor Papa now, then, eh?"

He went out into the yard at ease with life, but an irritation awaited him. The pony was harnessed to the trap but Cooper was not beside it and the stableman said he had not yet appeared. Delaford was put out; he had purposely lunched early in order to take his most experienced cowman over to Silverlake to look at their cattle and now he wasn't to be seen. It was the more annoying because it was unusual. If you could trust a damned Dissenter for anything it was hard work and punctuality. What would Richard say about that?

He crossed the lane to the cottages to fetch the recalcitrant and as he entered the Coopers' garden he heard angry voices coming from the house. This, too, was unlike them and he almost turned back, but as he hesitated before knocking he heard the cause. In the space of a moment three separate emotions held him in turn—annoyance at being kept waiting by a family squabble, aversion and distaste for the morals of labourers and a dark wrath that this should have been his son's doing. He wondered afterwards that he should have been so sure that Samuel had been involved, but he knew and trusted this quiet girl who had grown up on his farm and he had seen Samuel's eyes when he looked at women.

He went into the house and confronted them. Cooper dropped his daughter's arm as he saw his master and his face grew sulky. He could not hope to save his respectability by marrying Rachel into this man's family; she had lain with gentry and was lost—now all that was left was to disown her.

Delaford ignored him and spoke to the girl. "Is this true?"

She nodded, nursing her wrist.

"Joseph?"

"I haven't known her to lie."

He watched Rachel crying and his anger with his son and with the world deepened. It was true that he did not pay his workers well, it was true that he deprived them of rights over him by his terms of hiring, but he had always seen this as the natural position of master and servant. He had always striven to do what he had seen as fair and this was not fair—this weeping girl hunched against the wall was not just, Samuel had had no right to treat her thus; she was not—or had not been—a loose woman; she was a decent, modest girl whose life was irretrievably spoiled.

He turned to the men. "Go about your work. Rachel—stay here while I talk to Samuel."

Her father looked at her with scorn. "I'll not have her here," he said.

"Just for an hour, Joseph, until we see what is to be done."

"No. Why should I have the whore in my house?"

"*My* house."

"And your grandchild—but he won't have your name, will he? Will you have your son marry the slut?"

Furious that he should be answered back Delaford rounded on him. "God damn you, Cooper, remember who you are! I could turn you all off tomorrow."

Behind her hands Rachel listened to them argue without making a defence. There was no defence to make: she was no longer the loving, diligent girl they had known for eighteen years; she was a heifer who had taken the bull before she should; she was a black harlot not fit to be in company with the pious. One sin had wiped away her humanity and there was nothing more for her but to let someone else decide what was to be done; she had no strength left. If Samuel had only been standing by her as tender and protective as he had seemed—but there would be no more tenderness from Samuel.

Her father was adamant in his refusal to have her in his home and for the first time Delaford gave in. He felt himself at a disadvantage; these were his people and this was his house, but it was also his son's selfishness that had brought them to this pass and he knew the revulsion he himself would have felt if one of his own daughters—no, that was unthinkable.

With bad grace he ordered Rachel to wait in the dairy and strode back to the farmhouse, afire with rage that his humiliation should have been added to the mess.

He returned to the drawing-room. Everything was as before except that Samuel was standing with his back to the fireplace, cup and saucer in hand. A cosy, domestic scene. His family looked round as Delaford entered and the expression on his face hushed them.

"Well, sir," he said, regarding his son's easy stance. "Let me hear your explanations."

"Of what, Papa?" Samuel was surprised—he could think of nothing he had done that would merit being stared at so coldly.

"Of what? Do you have a choice of evils to explain? Rachel Cooper is with child; are you the father?"

"Jack!" Mrs. Delaford half rose, but her husband gestured for her to be still.

"Samuel, I will have an answer. I can tell by your look but I will be answered."

Samuel put his cup on the mantelpiece; he might have been accused of forgetting to wind the clock. "Certainly," he said: "I've never intended to deny it."

Laura gathered up the reins of the trap, flicked them and began to jolt out of the farmyard and along the Thornford road to Bradford Abbas. She was resentful and tired of revelations. She pulled the rug more closely around her waist and tightened her already tense hold on the whip. She was bitterly angry with Samuel for taking advantage of Rachel.

Her attitude to life had changed dramatically since her marriage. Before her wedding-night all sexual matters had been a mystery to her. She had known that for a child to come there must be a man and a woman, and from whispered hints scattered throughout her life she had known that "a something" occurred between husband and wife, that a man had desires unfelt by women, that there was something given by a woman that was considered a great gift, but she had thought of this as a spiritual not a physical joining. From seeing young children bathed she had learnt the shape of the unexcited male, but she had never been allowed to see a mating and she had had no idea that there could be such a thing.

She did not know that she was a victim of fashion. She and her mother were gentlewomen and neither could be mistaken for anything other, yet their upbringing had brought each a different education. A lady of Mrs. Delaford's generation had thought it no shame to have practical experience of all that contributed to her comfort. As a girl she had learnt to spin and weave and sew her linen, to brew and bake and tend medicinal herbs; she could milk and churn and press fine cheese; she could purge a sickly calf and assess her ewes for lambing—and none of this had coarsened her manners or lessened her delight in music.

When she had married she was shrewd enough to see that the world had changed and respect could not be won for her daughters by the old ways. The girls had been kept within doors; with a day governess and visiting tutors they had learnt to sketch and play and do close stitching; they learnt French and reckoning and the use of globes, but for once in her capable life Mrs. Delaford failed. She forgot that a girl in seclusion does not see the procreation that means the continuance of a farm nor have those acts explained to her with laughter and naturalness. She had given her daughter to a kindly man and never guessed at the ignorance she handed him.

Had Laura loved her husband, or had she been of a passionate temper, that ignorance would have been of small importance, the shock of her new knowledge would have faded in a night; instead, it festered within her and damaged her idea of men.

On that first evening she had been tired by the excitement of the day, shy at being alone with this young man whom she barely knew and nervous about the step she had taken, but her nervousness had been for the new life she was to lead—not for what awaited her.

She had been grateful when Richard had suggested she go up to their room before him, no man, not even her father, had seen her undress, nor she them, and she had been too diffident and self-conscious to watch her husband as he changed and took his place beside her. She expected him to kiss and caress her and though she longed to be dreaming, longed to wake and find herself with James, she did not begrudge him this. She had made a bargain and would keep it—but she had imagined her bargain to have been for this and nothing more. He had been so gentle, so loving, that even when he had removed her gown she could not have complained of his treatment of her. She thought her humiliation would be quickly past, and for a while as she lay in his arms she felt the warmth that would glow within her as she danced or saw that she had made a new conquest. But then, to her horror, she had been hurt. She was shocked and scared; she did not know what he was doing; she only knew that she was in a strange town with a strange man and was too afraid to cry out or push him away.

Afterwards she had lain thinking Richard asleep but he had turned to her and told her not to be brave, to cry if she needed. She had stiffened and drawn away from his touch, fearing that he would repeat what he had done, but he had said, "No. No, my love, we'll wait a few days. Don't think me cruel, Laura, it's only the first time; it won't be like that again," and then she had cried. This was her first hint that the experience which had seemed so terrible, so outrageous, was shared by every wife, and as he explained it to her through the night she had felt a malicious comfort in thinking that Grace would suffer the same disillusion with James.

She felt that life had cheated her; if someone had only warned her she would not have married a man she did not love, perhaps she would not have married even James—and this she supposed was why girls could not be told. The whole act disgusted her with its intimacy.

She was in a confusion of spirits when she thought of Richard. Here, as she drove his trap which he had needed for himself to the home where she was given everything she wished, eager to talk to him and sure of his concern for her distress, she was forced to admit to herself that if one thing were taken from her marriage she could not have done better. But why did he have to be so kind to her all the time? Why love her so much when she didn't love him? It was so hard to resent someone who gave you no cause. He was generous and attentive, considerate and undemanding, but relations with him were so—so distasteful. And to think Samuel had been out in the hedgerows—no, she would not even imagine it. She would tell Richard; he would understand—just as she understood why married women whispered, why newly-weds blushed, why there was so much stress on a wife's obedience to her husband. She thought, too, that she understood another thing: this madness was for men, for men's pleasure alone, they were the initiators, they were the benefactors, they took from women what they did not want to give—in short, she decided peevishly, it was all men's fault.

Today's events had seemed to confirm it. She had known Rachel since they were children; she had been born at the farmhouse, Rachel at the cottage. She knew her to be quiet and modest, not fast nor even flirtatious, as she had been herself—a soft-hearted girl. Samuel had admitted that she was in love with him and, as their father taxed him with taking advantage of her and the unmarried girls had been hustled from the room, he had protested that she'd been willing. Laura had not believed him, but the notion that Rachel had revelled in the affair had not seemed unlikely to Delaford, he merely disregarded it as an excuse.

"Don't you realise girls in love are weak and foolish and must be protected from themselves?" he'd asked savagely. "Don't you realise that now she'll never marry anyone else?"

"Jack," Mrs. Delaford broke in, "you surely don't mean Samuel should marry her?"

"Of course I don't, but he must still take some responsibility for our grandchild."

His wife looked away sharply.

"Well, madam, will you have her go on the parish?" He turned back to Samuel, "Yet you look so calm. For pity's sake, man, who's going to marry her now? Who's even going to employ her?"

"Can't she go on working for us?" The first inkling of what he had done seemed to come to Samuel; Laura was amazed that her loving brother could reveal himself so callous—but the world had been a different place since October and everything she knew was changed.

"Do you seriously expect your mother to have your bastard running around her dairy?"

"I thought she could give away the child."

"Then you know nothing of women, sir, for all your philandering. She may be a harlot but she won't abandon her child. No, Cooper won't have her in the house—you can't blame him.

You'd better pay her maintenance, but where the devil can she go?"

They had argued back and forth where to send her, but could decide nothing worthwhile. There were few landladies who would be prepared to accept an unmarried mother, she could hardly become a living-in servant before the baby came and a girl of her position suddenly appearing in a strange town with a private income, claiming to be a widow, would be too suspicious to be believed. Nevertheless, Delaford said, she must be taken far enough away—perhaps to Bournemouth—to prevent as much embarrassment to the family as possible and roomed at whatever expense until her confinement. Until this could be carried out she must sleep in the dairy.

As she rattled home with the dusk growing Laura could not feel satisfied with this arrangement. She entirely blamed Samuel for the affair and she thought it unjust that it should be Rachel who was vilified and hidden away from her family and friends. She knew herself the vulnerability and muddleheadedness of being in love, and for Rachel to lose everything that was her world because of her weakness made her helplessly angry.

It was almost dark when she reached the Vicarage and she could see lamps burning in the drawing-room. As she let herself into the hall she stood a moment, remembering the glory of the day when Richard had led her into her new home and her own staff had curtsied to her. The cook had put the housekeeper's keys into her hand and she loved to hear them clink as they swung on the silver châtelaine Richard had bought her in Weymouth. This was what she had looked forward to in her marriage—this and the calls and honours paid to a bride—and her new status and powers as her own mistress excited her. She began unfastening her gloves as Dinah came down the stairs. Laura looked at her in surprise.

"What's that you've got, Dinah?"

"It's a book, ma'am; the master lent it to me."

"Oh . . . Oh, well, take these, will you?" She handed her outdoor clothes to the maid and opened the door to the drawing-room. Her hands were chilled from the drive and she went over to the fire to warm them as she greeted her husband. Richard was sitting with his feet on the hearth and an unfinished letter on the floor beside him. He caught her as she passed and drew her companionably on to his lap, kissing her softly at the curve of her neck; she was so preoccupied with what she had to tell that she forgot to resist. She tapped him authoritatively on the shoulder to get his attention and put up the other hand to protect her earring.

"Richard, have you been giving Dinah novels?"

"Yes, I found her reading instead of dusting so I lent it to her. Why?"

"I don't know if you should."

He took her chin in his hand and lifted her face to his. "What's the matter with my Laura?" he asked gravely.

"It's so awful," she said and buried her face against him; he could feel her tears trickling uncomfortably into his collar, but she had never clung to him before and he held her to him as he coaxed the muffled story out. Gradually, as she saw he took her side, she recovered herself.

"Isn't Samuel going to marry her?" he asked.

"Of course he's not," Laura said from behind his handkerchief. "How could he? Don't be silly, Richard."

"It seems quite natural to me. Where's she to go, then?"

"That's just the point. Papa says she's got to be taken where no one knows her, but until then she's to stay in the dairy."

"The dairy?"

"Yes—and in this freezing weather. It's too bad. I nearly brought her home with me."

"You like her, then?"

"Certainly I do. I was brought up with her."

"Well, bring her here," he clasped her waist. "She can't sleep in an outhouse in November. She can share with Dinah."

"How long for?" She finished drying her eyes and looked at him, unsure of her own idea.

"She can come as second maid if you like—for a trial; if she doesn't suit she can leave. She'll find a new position more easily when she's had the baby than now and I'll give her references."

"I don't know. There'll be terrible gossip."

"I'm not interested in gossip. 'Though I speak with the tongues of men and of angels, and have not charity. . .'"

Laura settled herself more comfortably on his knees; sitting here in the firelight with him, spitefulness did seem too far away to touch her. She was filled with tenderness for the good in this man she did not love and a sudden, yearning ache to be worthy of him.

For years she had acted flirtation until she thought herself a flirt; could she not act love until she were a lover? Always when he looked at her she saw pride in his eyes, but it was pride in her beauty and in an illusion of what she really was; she longed for the pride to be for a quality of character she did not yet possess.

She had imagined that marriage meant ease and an end to endeavour; she saw, instead, that she had come to a meeting of two paths—one she could walk as a child with the grass soft beneath her feet and Richard, his love drifting into tolerance, protecting her from stony ground; the other was hard and winding and must be climbed as a woman beside her husband so that she could put out her hand to help him if he stumbled. She did not doubt that if she chose the latter she would often fail, often long for the green way, and perhaps never achieve the still waters that were natural to Richard; and yet, with the first germ of self-discipline, courage and consideration for others moving within her, she did choose the latter. Today she had seen injustice. She could, if she wished, ignore the responsibility that all men have for their neighbour; she did not wish it. None of her sympathy for Rachel had left her as they talked, and in this secure, sheltered evening bringing her into their home seemed the perfect way to care for her and to show Richard that he had a compassionate wife.

"Very well," she said, "bring her—but I don't know what Mamma will say."

Chapter Ten

Laura was sitting at her dressing-table cleaning her hair with eau-de-Cologne when the sickness struck. She stumbled to the washstand, knocking over her stool, and retched violently into the bowl. Snatching off the beaded muslin from the jug she rinsed her mouth with warm water, the heavy, aromatic scent of the Brown Windsor making her gag, and spat it into the bowl, then lowered herself shuddering on to the bed. Holding the rails she leant her forehead against the cold brass and drew breath.

"Oh, God," she whispered. "Not yet, not so soon."

She didn't have to wonder what was wrong. She was four weeks late and now she was sure her fears were confirmed—she was pregnant. No doubt, she thought bitterly, everyone will be delighted, Richard will be congratulated and Mamma will send me custards I can't eat. I shall be expected to give up enjoying myself for good. She laughed at herself for having ever been so innocent as to have thought a child could be the result of simply being in love. She had been shown a full store-room and been too blind to see that it could only be opened with a key. She had picked up her knowledge of pregnancy because the women around her had had too many children for it to be glossed over, and she did not like what she had learned. It seemed to her a horrific mixture of pain and danger. She felt that she would willingly have faced death if she was with James and marriage had been as passionless as she expected, but James was parading his new wife around the county and she was alone in her room on a January morning.

It was hateful to think that soon she would be so big and ungainly that her state would be obvious to everyone. It seemed to be flaunting an activity she would have preferred to keep secret. She had heard that the queen called this the shadow side of life and as she clutched the bedpost Laura thought it a close description.

The wave of nausea past, she lay back tentatively on the pillows and wrapped the quilt around her. It was warm in the room, but her skin felt clammy; she could have rung for Dinah to put more coal on the fire, but she did not feel equal to being seen.

A fire in the bedroom was one of the new luxuries in her life. At the farm they had only had fires when there was illness in the house; yet here it was lit every night and again in the early morning. It was delicious to lie in bed when you woke to the rain spattering the window-panes, or the wind rushing in the trees, and have your maid bring you tea and hang your clothes over the fireguard so that everything should be glowing when you chose to get up. Richard had had the railings put round the hearth when he had seen her skirts almost sweep into the flames the night he brought her home. It was wonderful how he cosseted her, she thought, smoothing the linen with her cheeks; she only hoped he would continue now that she was changing from a girl to a matron. Would he feel the same about the woman with no waist and six children as he had felt about the girl he had followed into the garden at Sherborne House?

She realised with reluctance that more than her pride would be hurt if he did not. She had tried to stifle the resentment she had suffered in those early weeks, and so much of her anger had been channelled towards Samuel that she had found herself adjusting to her experience of Richard. Fondness for her husband was creeping over her against her will. She had not met James since her wedding, but the esteem in which Richard was held by the villagers told her that the parson might stand very well in comparison with the lawyer and this opinion had been important to her; she wanted to be sure that everyone would see that she had won a prize. And they had been drawn together by the trouble over Rachel. Richard blamed Samuel as vehemently as she did herself and she found that not only did this seem to vindicate her new distrust of men, but that Richard's own embrace was less unwelcome when they had spent the evening defending their ward. Life never used to be so contradictory.

Nevertheless expecting her to lose her figure was asking a great deal. She knew she was vain, but every looking-glass told her she had reason. She had always taken first place because she was beautiful and fear of losing her claim on the world was growing within her like a canker. She told herself that she had had to marry, she had *had* to, she couldn't let Grace triumph over her, but she had forgotten that to marry was to leave the stage. No one would strive for her now; she had put herself out of reach.

She turned on her side and shut her eyes to keep out her nightmare, but it would not release her. She wished she had never mentioned taking Rachel in. It was true that shame kept her out of her mistress's path, but when Laura did see her the sight of the girl's bulging stomach gave her a feeling of revulsion; it had been an unrelenting reminder of what might happen to herself and a symbol of her loss of faith in Samuel. She was uneasy about having her own nephew or niece born to her servant in her own home and now that she too was to have a child the situation could not go on; the two could not be brought up together.

If only Rachel were more difficult she would have an excuse to persuade Richard to put her out, but she made no trouble at all. She was quiet and unobtrusive, she did not play on her relationship with Samuel, demand special favours or even leave the house and expose herself to gossip. No, thought Laura, it's me who has to bear that and I've done nothing. It's me who has to suffer being stared at in the street and knowing that I'm whispered about as soon as I'm past. Everyone who talks to me looks as if they're being choked by not mentioning Rachel, and Richard's noticed it too. Twice he had been compelled to preach on the subject and although he had not named names the texts he had chosen—the stoning of the adulteress and "I was a stranger and you did not shelter me"—had left none of the guilty in doubt that their behaviour had been seen and condemned.

How was she to make him turn the girl out? She knew him well enough to know he would do what he believed to be right whatever the cost. The only way to move him would be a direct appeal to do it for her sake and how could she do that when Rachel was so near her time? And then there was the decision she had taken to be a helpmate to Richard, not a burden; having agreed to give sanctuary she could not go back on her word. She felt herself failing as she had feared she might and yet she would not quite let go. How annoyed she was that Samuel should have put them in such a position.

He had made life more difficult and unpleasant for everyone concerned with the farm. The easy relations at Limekiln had been shattered by Rachel's fall and Samuel was suffering a more isolated existence than had ever before been his lot. Both Mr. and Mrs. Delaford were cold and distant towards him. They disapproved of his affair, but their anger was almost as much from its having been carried out on their own land with their own girl as from the harm that had been done to Rachel. Though they agreed with their son-in-law over the moral issue, they accepted that young men will sow wild oats and had not reacted as strongly as if one of their own daughters had become pregnant. If Samuel had taken the trouble to find his pleasures twenty miles away he would have escaped most of the ill-feeling that was being showered upon him, but his lack of foresight had removed his mother's most capable dairy-hand and soured his father's most valued labourers at one move. Since the revelation had followed so soon after Pack Monday there were no experienced maids to be had and Mrs. Delaford had had to return to the dairy herself to teach a young replacement.

It was Mrs. Delaford who was so against Richard's rescue of the unfortunate girl. Samuel and his father had both wished simply to have Rachel removed from the farm as quickly as possible and lodging at the Vicarage had seemed a reasonable stop-gap; it was, after all, quite usual for clergymen to shelter Magdalenes. But Mrs. Delaford had thought it a public advertisement of Samuel's behaviour and his family's involvement, and an invitation for ridicule.

Determined that an abandoned mother-to-be who was hardly more than a child herself should not be forced to spend a single winter's night in an outhouse, Richard had driven over to collect her as soon as Laura had agreed. Laura did not accompany him. She wanted it to be clear to Rachel that however much she was to be pitied they were not equals. To attain this she wanted to meet the new Rachel not on the old ground where they had been reared but as mistress and servant of the house, and therefore, pleading that the trap would not hold three and she was too tired to ride or drive, she had retired to her room and shut out the world. Richard had been glad to go alone, for Mrs. Delaford had put her views so forcibly that he was sure Laura would have been persuaded against her decision. He, however, had been determined on his course, suggesting to Mrs. Delaford that the following day the news would have spread throughout the town and people would begin calling just in the hope of glimpsing the wretched victim.

Now, two months later, Laura was fully aware of her mother's opinion of her idea and heartily wished it had triumphed. She and Samuel had always been close, but he had not visited her at Bradford Abbas since Rachel's arrival and she was lonely without his friendship. She did not worship him as the perfect elder brother any longer and it irritated her to see him so little abashed by the trouble he had caused—but still she missed him.

At least Christmas had gleamed out in the tangled months since her wedding. She had hoped to spend the day at Limekiln and have Richard join her for dinner, but he had wanted her to be with him to celebrate his first Christmas at St. Mary's and she sympathised, for she understood her duty as wife and parson's wife to Richard and the parish. She had stayed expecting everything to be tiresome and found it an oasis of admiration and compliment: the warm, comforting bath of flattery that she had known before with the added importance that a married woman has over even an eldest daughter.

Balancing dangerously on chairs and sitting amongst piles of evergreens, she and the ladies of the village had decorated the church and she had had the enjoyment of having her judgement deferred to because she was Mrs. Webster. She had had charge of a great boiling and baking, and stood at the kitchen door surrounded by gratitude as soup and bread were given to the labourers' wives and tickets handed in for coal and blankets.

She and Richard had been very merry on Christmas Eve as they hung scarlet-berried holly all over the house and loaded her first Christmas tree with gingerbread and sugared fruit. There had been one moment when Richard had pinned the mistletoe above the drawing-room door and there, in the warmth of the room with the curtains drawn against the night and the logs crackling in the grate, he had drawn her into his shirt-sleeved arms and she had felt the first stirrings of desire from his kiss. . . . But, as they had stood clasped together, rapt by their sudden closeness, the carol singers had rung the bell and the moment was lost.

She had imagined herself very adult and independent serving them punch and mince-pies in her own hall and withdrawing to dress for the service as they sang, but it was nothing compared with what followed.

She had sat as elegant as a fashion-plate in the front pew, with her feet resting on a hassock so that she could admire the square toes of her new morocco boots and a daringly modern hat setting off her coiled plaits and pearl earrings, feeling the interest of the congregation burn behind her, knowing that tomorrow the young girls would be plaguing their mothers for hats because "if Mrs. Webster wears one it must be proper." She had clenched her fists to keep back her delight in Richard—the man who took precedence over all this gathering—being *hers* and had walked demurely through the candle-light to the altar, second only to the Thornhills. She had met Richard's eyes over the chalice and suspected that he saw through her charade and loved her for it.

Taking her place beside him in the porch to wish their people good-night, she had had her hand touched by Old Mrs. Thornhill. Awesome in black satin, the old woman had leant on her son's arm examining Laura, then bent her head and said, "God keep you, Mistress"—and the seal of approval had been set. Then Keating, who liked this pretty little wife of his friend, had slipped her a small box tied with ribbon. When she opened it in the privacy of the drawing-room she found a gold bracelet and a packet of golden hair-powder called "Eugenie". Richard had said no empress could look as well as she and, laughing at her exultant face and filled with his own excitement, had swung her off her feet and whirled her about the room until they fell panting into a chair.

The next evening there had been a hard frost. The roads had been stark and furrowed as they drove to the farm and the metal shoes of the cob rang out as if striking iron. The wheels had crackled across ice between the ridges and the air was so cold that the veil Laura had worn was stiff with frozen breath when she tried to remove it. The stars had been clear and bright in the dark sky above them, and Richard had told her of his first night there and how he had never dreamed he would have such a wife beside him on his first Christmas. This was romance enough and for a day she had given no thought to another man.

They should not have gone to Sherborne, she saw that now, they should have dined alone and kept the spell unbroken. There had been nothing calamitous said at the farm, but there was undeniably more reserve than in other years; Laura had not been with them all day and had been missed, Richard was a newcomer and responsible for taking her away and Samuel—what need be said of Samuel? And Rachel who had been used to serve them was, of course, absent; and although no one had mentioned her, Laura felt she had haunted them like the ghost of Banquo at the feast.

Altogether, she thought petulantly, easing herself upright when the sickness did not return, life was very dissatisfying and this new development, this repulsive evidence of pregnancy so inconsistent with the fascinating creature she wished herself to be, was unbearable. She had known that babies follow a wedding as night follows day, but somehow she had not expected it to happen to her. She looked on herself as a young girl who could dress smartly with a tight, cinched waist, who liked to dance and ride and pamper herself—not as a staid matron. She felt that this was the first step towards middle-age and she did not want to take it; the cares and worries of motherhood were too much of a burden.

She got up and bathed her face, hanging a towel over the incriminating bowl, then rightened the stool and sat again at the dressing-table to put up her hair. She felt enclosed and stuffy. She needed someone to talk with, but who could help her? She must leave the house; if she stayed she would meet Richard and be forced to explain her paleness—or, worse, she might see her future in Rachel. Most of her close friends were unmarried and therefore out of the question, and she could not face the fuss and embarrassment of telling Mamma. Then she remembered Patience Page at Home Farm. She paused, her hands to her head and hairpins in her mouth, and looked in the mirror to consider her choice.

Patience was still young—just in her late twenties—and had five children of her own. Laura thought back to the day in June when they had walked away from the meeting of the Literary Society together and Patience had hinted that marriage was not the idyll it was made out to be. In that time of innocence she had not understood her friend, thinking only that she was tired and weak with carrying the new child, but now she saw that Patience must be as little enchanted with these matters as herself and her words had been a faint displaying of rebellion. She might be willing to talk discreetly and with a family of five would be experienced enough to answer any question.

Guiltily she clipped herself into her stays and took out her riding-habit. She knew both these things were wrong, but she yearned for one more day of freedom before they were set aside. Slipping into the stable-yard, as if anyone who saw her would guess her condition and forbid her to leave, she saddled the mare she had brought with her from Limekiln and trotted out through the village on to the Bradford road.

The air was exhilarating—warmer than December, but with a nip to bring colour to her cheeks and wind enough to whip at her skirts. The mare, skittish from her winter oats, pranced and side-stepped through the lanes, and when they had left all sight of buildings behind them Laura heeled her up on to the verge and gave her her head, leaving her to pound past the hedgerows and over the ditches as she willed. For this one last morning she would not be sensible Mrs. Webster, she would be Laura Delaford with all her life before her and nothing to fear.

She checked the horse as she reached the town and took the long way to Home Farm—up Green Hill, along Newland and past the Castle—to avoid being seen by any of her family. She tied Tansy by the mounting-block and, dry-lipped from the ride, knocked at the door of the farmhouse. It was a few moments before it was answered—and then by a girl who was smoothing down her cuffs as if her sleeves had been rolled up for heavy work. Hearing through an open doorway who had come, Patience called out for Laura to be brought into the kitchen and, knowing her way, the visitor preceded the maid through the hall.

The large kitchen was as clean and scrubbed as always, but to Laura's fastidious eyes it seemed all bustle and commotion. The four older children were playing or crawling on the floor, there was a lamb on wheels almost beneath her feet, an upturned wooden steam engine by the dresser, alphabet bricks everywhere, and Patience was standing by the long table in a plain, cotton dress with tendrils of hair already escaping from their knot, bathing her youngest in a great basin. Laura looked at her aghast. This, she thought, this is how I'll be in a few months' time, and, suddenly dizzy, she sat down before she was asked.

That night she did not tell Richard of her pregnancy and when she woke early the next morning, dreading a repetition of the previous day, she still felt no inclination to share the news. Let him wait, she thought, looking at his dark head on the pillow beside her. Why should he be happy when I'm suffering? It aggravated her to see him sleeping so peacefully when she was as irritably awake, and yet she had wished for this all the time they had been married. It was one of her minor grievances against him, one of the smaller offences that had risen up to justify her long ill-humour, that he was a bad sleeper. He was invariably awake when she fell asleep and awake again when she opened her eyes. She had always shared a bed with Naomi, so the presence of another was not new to her, but a man who could see her every night asleep and off guard was quite different from a sister; she could not protect her unblemishable image against this surveillance. He could see her with her hair every way, with her mouth open—but now that she was the watcher and he defenceless he was again in the wrong.

She pulled the sheets primly over her shoulders and wondered if this was how it was to be for seven months. She had not been encouraged by her talk with Patience. Considering the earliness of the hour and the strangeness of her visitor's look—glittering, frightened eyes in a drained face—Patience had known at once that she was not paying a social call and had left her work and children to hear confidences in the parlour. When she discovered that Laura was enduring the customary disquiet of a bride she tried to give her consolation, but she was the wrong woman to whom to turn. Bowed down as she was by too large a family too soon she could find little of comfort to say. She had unbuttoned her gown as they talked and fed her baby, and when Laura had asked if she hadn't thought of having a wet-nurse Patience had replied, "Yes, it would be a relief—but they do say that the longer you feed the longer before your next. It hasn't seemed to make any difference with me, but what else can you do? You can't refuse . . ."

This morning Laura, who could easily refuse, let the blame for Patience's burden rest on Richard and he went downstairs alone. He was always the first to leave the room, but today she did not join him at the breakfast-table and when he had eaten he returned. She was lying stolidly in bed, her tea untouched.

"I came to see where you were," he said. "Aren't you well?"

"No." She stared at the ceiling.

He came round to her side of the bed and laid a cool hand on her forehead. "You don't feel hot. What's the matter, my love?"

"I feel sick."

"Sick?" Oh God, he thought. Oh my God. "Why?"

Laura knocked his hand away and sat up. "For pity's sake," she asked angrily, "why would I be feeling sick?"

She would have gone on, she would have liked to pour forth the general baseness of mankind, but it is hard to make speeches when you are being kissed with such vehemence and it was some time before she was free. Then he was holding her gently in his hands as if she would fall and she didn't want to curse him any more. He didn't seem to expect her to rejoice and she was grateful. On their wedding-night he had looked at her and reminded her of Samuel, but now there was nothing of Samuel in his eyes, there was only the gaze of Richard who loved her, who adored her, who was proud that she was his; Richard who would always care for her and never forsake her; Richard who could already have caused her death. She clutched at his shoulders and he lowered her back on to the pillow and told her to sleep.

Richard filled his pocket with sovereigns and left the house, dazed by the turbulence that one woman could arouse in him. Laura had not listened to his words upstairs—and, indeed, they were the incoherencies of a proud lover, meaningless when said to one who could not return them—and now he was going into Yeovil to buy her a gift that would persuade her of his fondness. He knew that something with which to adorn herself would please her more than anything he could say.

He chose to walk the three miles into the town. There was more solitude to be had on foot and he wanted to indulge himself. This day would never come again, there would never again be a shy, apprehensive figure lying in his bed angry with him because she could not see that behind his joy was a fear greater than her own. He loved her and all her ways, the house had come alive to him since he had brought her home and he loved to see her playing at being its severe mistress. But more than that he loved to see her asleep, looking so young and in need of his protection—and here was something from which he could not protect her. If all went well he would lay the credit with her; if it did not he would blame himself and Keating would not be alone in his torment.

He wondered if he had done all that he could for her comfort. He knew that he couldn't expect her to change from the reticence of courtship to the openness of marriage at once, but still she was not as easy in her affection as he had hoped and sometimes a flicker of doubt about her happiness would rise in him. She seemed to have lost her homesickness but there was the problem of Rachel. The more she adjusted to their own relations the less she appeared to sympathise with Rachel, and he could not tell if this was because she now suspected the girl had been a willing participant and so "deserved her fate" or simply because of the awkwardness of sheltering her. He did not know if he had done the right thing in taking her in—but Laura had been so distraught and Rachel so helpless, what else could he have done? He could not have foreseen that Samuel would be so tardy in finding her another home.

It's all very well for me, he thought, taking the steep footpath that led downhill through the gorge to Yeovil. If I hadn't been plummeted into a crusade I'd have sought one out, but Laura can be hurt by spiteful tongues.

He was exasperated by Samuel's laziness in leaving Rachel with them for so long. He himself had made what enquiries he could with no success, but Samuel whose responsibility Rachel was had done nothing whatever. He was naively puzzled by what Samuel had done to the girl. He understood the longing—God knows he had felt it often enough himself—but not the doing. Had Samuel's desire been so great that it had blinded him to the consequences, or had he simply not cared that he could ruin her life—and that of his child? Surely if it had been the former he would have shown concern for her since, but he had ignored her. Was he then so callous that he truly gave her no thought? How could he be so hard? Condemn the sin, Webster, he reminded himself treading carefully on the wet ivy, but love the sinner. That too was hard.

He returned to the Vicarage carrying a flat box frivolously wrapped in blue-striped paper. It is a pleasant thing to shop for a beautiful wife: you have only to be recognised as prey and a bentwood chair will be produced and a flutter of assistants will unroll a silken opulence at your feet; prices are disguised with smiles, your suit is lighter without your gold and your only worry need be over your knowledge of fashions.

He entered their room expecting to find her lying down, but she was standing before the fire in her chemise pulling on her petti-coats. She turned her back when he appeared and wrapped herself in her dressing-gown; only her cheek was offered when he tried to greet her. She busied herself with her hair.

"Shouldn't you be in bed?" he asked.

Laura paused in her hundred strokes. "I'm not an invalid yet," she said pettishly.

"But you must take care. Look—I've been into Yeovil to collect something."

She turned without interest and noticed the box; she could not deny its attraction. "I didn't hear the trap," she said, putting down the brush.

"No, I walked. Here, my love, open it."

She took the box from him and carried it to the bed. The very feel of the wrapping shouted extravagance and in spite of herself her pretended indifference was touched. Richard watched her child-like seriousness as she discovered its perfections. She untied the ribbons, smoothed back the outer covering with the tips of her fingers and lifted the lid. Inside was the shimmer of crimson tissue-paper and in its folds, with the rich, heavy scent of patchouli rising from it, lay a Kashmir shawl. She lifted it from the box as if it were cut glass, and neither spoke as the East enfolded them and she stroked the length of its soft fineness. Here was splendour, here was magnificence, here was reason to have married. It was gorgeously expensive, vastly generous. She laid her face against it and breathed in the warm fragrance. Why must he do this? she thought. I try to resent him but he always foils me. He could have driven into town tomorrow and placed a cold order at a jeweller's —but no, he walks in today and picks me this. To go to all that trouble to find what I'd like! You measure men by things like this; would James have done it? Inexplicably she wanted to cry and for the first time it was not the cost of the gift that was important.

Chapter Eleven

Spring came early that year and the borders of the fields were white with blackthorn before the Delafords finished hedging. On a Friday in mid-April Samuel went alone to the small meadow by Honeycombe Wood to lay what was left to be done. Carrying a billhook over his shoulder and a stone jug in his hand, he walked uphill through the budding cowslips with the purposeful leisureliness of the countryman at peace with his life. There had been a shower in the early morning and now that the sun was drawing the water from the earth there was a pale, sharp zest to the air that belonged to the new season. The sap was moving and the land burgeoning; there would be a new tupping, a new sowing, a new hay-mow, a new harvest. In the orchard the plums and damsons were in blossom and the pears and apples waiting to bloom. The damp, low-lying meadows by the river were mauve with lady's-smock and as he climbed beside the trees Samuel could smell the thin, woodland scent of bluebells.

He worked quickly and well in fingerless gauntlets of hard leather and an old corduroy jacket that could bear the thorns; a solitary, skilful figure on the hillside. There was no sound but the rustle of leaves, the sudden, crying challenges of pheasants and the chunk of his blade against wood. With one stroke he cut upwards slicing the sapling through, with the next he cut down half-severing the stem so that it lay loosely on the ground. At the end of ten yards he would go back and weave these plashes in and out of the uprights, coaxing the branches into place until the hedge was solid and full.

It was work that he liked and, except to throw down his jacket and loosen his waistcoat, he did not stop until the row was complete and he was satisfied. He stood back to survey it and pushed the hair from his face with his glove. His hands were tanned by years of sun and there were lines of white skin on his fingers from old scars. He saw small smears of blood where the thorns had caught him but his skin was too hard to have been hurt. Farmer's hands. He looked at his watch; it wanted twenty minutes to the time when he was to meet his father to prepare the ram for the ewes. He squatted down by the cider and took the stopper out of the jug. He hooked two fingers into the handle, lifted it so that its body rested on the back of his hand and drank deeply, balancing on his heels.

When his thirst was quenched he left the jug with his hook and jacket and climbed the stile into the wood to gather the year's first bluebells for his mother. It was cool and damp beneath the trees and the moss on the path was spongy underfoot. He had entered from a higher point than the one he had used to meet Rachel, but even so the memory of her entered his mind and he felt a faint resentment for the trouble that had followed. He barely thought of her now—she was last year's amusement—but as the evenings began to lengthen he found himself regretting her loss and he did not care to linger here. Most of the bluebells were not yet out, but their buds had formed enough to open in water and he snapped off a sheaf as thick as his arm to take home.

Returning to the hedge he secured the flowers through his belt and collected his belongings. It was warm in the sun and the walk down the hillside and into the lane seemed pleasantly idle. He carried his jacket slung over his shoulder and daydreamed. He was looking forward to going to the Gentlemen's Debating Society that night with James; it lent that intellectual stimulus that could be missing from so much manual labour. He would go early and drink tea with the dashing Mrs. Sanderson. There was more to Grace, he considered, than met the eye. She might not be a beauty, but she did have style; she had a way of looking at you with those dark, almond eyes that made your skin shiver and she could be more provocative in dropping sugar into your cup than most women were half-dressed. Being with Grace made him wonder if he shouldn't look for a suitable lady to be his wife before the summer drew him into a new entanglement; it would be an advantage to be licensed to love.

The ram was enclosed in a stone-walled pen in the meadow opposite the farmhouse; Samuel leant on the gate and looked at him as he waited for his father to come. It was a Dorset Horn, as were all their sheep, small, finely-made animals, hardy enough to survive winters on the hilltops and still lamb twice a year. If the ewes took this week as they planned there would be a second crop of young in mid-September. This ram, King Dorset, was a compact, swaggering creature who stood four-square on the trodden earth and eyed Samuel belligerently. Delaford came up behind his son carrying a bucket of dye and put his hand on his shoulder. Samuel glanced round.

"Well," said his father, "what do you think? Is he ready?"

Samuel laughed. "Ready? If we don't set him to work he'll be climbing the walls."

"Let's look him over, then."

They entered the pen and approached the ram. He stamped as they neared him, rolling his eyes and butting with his curled horns, but neither took notice of his threats. Samuel grasped the fleece at the back of his neck and pulled back his head to examine the eyes and teeth. The ram made a token struggle, but finding himself ignored quietened and stood stoically in his master's hold. Samuel ran his hands down the legs, then searched through the oily fleece for parasites. All was well.

"If they all grow wool like this we'll have more than four pounds from each this summer," he said.

"We should have good prices anyway with all the liver-rot in the wet districts."

"They got the rot; we got a marriage." He peered closely into the "King's" ears.

"You think that's what did it, then? Laura going to him in the rain?"

"Oh, there's nothing like a maiden in distress for Richard. He probably felt obliged to marry her; they did have tea alone."

The comment that could have been made hung in the air between them. Samuel stood up, still gripping the fleece. "Do you want to paint him now?"

Delaford took a brush from the pail. "Yes—yes, he'll do." He wiped the excess dye on the rim.

Samuel straddled the beast and slipping his arms under its front legs lifted them high off the ground. Delaford squatted before him and began stroking the ram's underbelly with the sticky red dye that would mark out the ewes he had served. He broke the silence.

"The Garveys are crossing theirs with Leicesters this year, so Adams told me."

The ram kicked; Samuel wrestled it back on to balance. "Well, it'll give them more weight but they won't have the sweetness in the meat."

"That's what I thought. Who's this coming?"

They looked up from their work and saw Barratt, Richard's stableman, coming towards them with a letter in his hand.

"God," said Delaford. "I hope it's not Laura; your mamma's worried already."

The ram bucked and twisted as they dropped it, pushing its head down between its front legs to sniff the dye, and they went to the wall to meet Barratt. The note was addressed to Samuel; he broke the seal and read what was written: "Rachel brought to bed at three this morning. The child is not yet come. I would be obliged by your presence, R. Webster." Handing the paper to his father he was irritated and strangely embarrassed. The ill-feeling towards him from his family had largely disappeared; except for Samuel paying her maintenance—insisted upon but not legally established by Richard—they had not been troubled by sight or mention of Rachel, and Samuel had been deliberately practising his charm on them. Much folly can be forgiven an eldest son with such eyes and such knowledge of stock. It was true that Laura was given to waspish remarks about "this condition" not being easy for a woman and the complications of her own situation being the result of his lack of continence and self-restraint, but the interest of the family had so centred upon her that Rachel had been eclipsed. He himself had not seen the girl since November and the consequences of his actions not being plainly before him, he had hardly felt himself involved.

And now this interfering parson ridiculed him with this request as clearly as if he had published an account of those warm nights on the bank with Rachel's loving eyes and soft, passive body. How dare he call me to her bedside as if she were my wife and not some country slut? But would he have sent for me unless it was going badly? What if I refuse and she dies? There's Laura to think of . . . He felt a heat rising in his face and strove to seem collected.

Delaford gave back the note. "You must go," he said distantly. "Things must be amiss. I'll tell her father for you."

He rode over to the village with the humiliation rankling within him and at the house the tense silence where he had expected screaming fuelled his annoyance. He used his impatience as a protection; he had become increasingly convinced that a dying woman was asking for him and he was sorrowing for her. He did not want Rachel's death on his conscience; he had liked her before she crossed him and he had never wanted to do her hurt; it had always seemed natural that he should have whatever he wished and he had not seen the magnitude of the harm he was doing to her.

He let himself into the hall and found Richard in his study; there was a coiled aggressive air about him that Samuel had never known before. He was drinking sherry, but did not offer any to his guest.

"How is she?" Samuel asked.

"Well enough. It won't be long now."

Why the hell did you send for me, then? thought Samuel. Why me? Why not a midwife? He went to the decanter and poured himself a glass. He felt he needed a seat and took a chair.

"Is the doctor here?"

"She wouldn't have him. Mrs. Houghton and Dinah are with her. I said I'd send for him if he was needed, but I don't think he will be."

"Is Laura upstairs?"

"No, I took her to Mrs. Vaughan. It was upsetting her; she's not strong herself, she isn't sleeping." Richard put his glass on the hearth and poked the fire viciously. Samuel noticed the lines under his eyes, the strain around his mouth.

"We don't need a fire on a day like this," Richard said, "but it seemed empty without one. Laura feels the cold these days."

The room filled with silence; there was no sound from above and none with them but the hollow ticking of the clock. Ten minutes passed, fifteen, twenty.

Samuel picked up his whip from the floor. "If nothing's happening I'll go back to the farm. I've work to do." Still he could not connect this with himself.

Richard looked at his brother-in-law coldly. "Stay," he said. "This is your woman, your child. You've work enough here."

As if he did not hear Samuel made a motion to stand, but

Richard rose before him, put a hand on his breast and pushed him inexorably back. "Sit down," he said. "This is your child."

Samuel stared at him in surprise and saw not the vague sentimentalist, the besotted lover of his sister, the knight who saw princesses in peasants' clothes, but the curate who had gone into ale-houses on pay-nights and dragged out drunken men, emptying what was left in their pockets for their wives; the parson who was prepared to spoil his standing with his equals for the sake of giving comfort to one ruined girl. He sat back; he believed that if he resisted there would be violence, yet it was not fear that held him but shock—shock that before he had not seen the whole man and shock that he should feel the first sense of the meanness of what he had done.

He shrugged. "You're too much the parson," he said.

"And you're too much the farmer: you sow broadcast."

Like two dogs they bristled at each other.

"Well, have you a text to improve me?"

"'The lips of a strange woman drop as a honeycomb, and her mouth is smoother than oil—lust not after her beauty in thine heart.'"

"You're a little late with your advice," Samuel gestured up-stairs with his thumb.

"It will serve you next time."

"You have me measured," Samuel's voice was sour. He turned his head and gazed into the flames. His presence in the house was reviving memories of Rachel and because he remembered their friendship, their fondness as children, because he had given her tea to lighten her mornings and sugar-mice to hear her laugh, he was angry with Richard and himself. Richard sat down but immediately leant forward in agitation. For months he had striven to understand what had made this man cast off such a girl; he had continually told himself that it was not for him to judge, and when this seemed to fail he reminded himself of the bond between Laura and her brother and held his tongue, but he could not be patient forever. He watched Samuel sit seeming so bored by the silence that hurt the room around them and could barely control his passion.

"How can you take it so lightly?" he asked. "You've shown no guilt at all."

"I won't be told I'm wrong."

"Surely you must feel some sorrow? Didn't you care for her at all?"

"She entertained me," Samuel looked back at his companion, wanting to hurt and knowing how. "It was the contrast—demure as a mouse all day, then at night . . ."

"I don't want to hear."

Samuel smiled and put his heels on the fender, legs out-stretched. "You take too serious a view," he said.

This—with Rachel at her time above them—was too much for Richard. "You don't see the results as I do," he burst out, hands clenched upon his knees. "For you it's a moment's pleasure; it's me who finds women weeping in the church because they're to have another child, it's me who goes into the cottages and finds the floor covered with naked children and the mother desperate because she can't feed them, it's me who buries them when the last child proves too much."

"These are fine words considering Laura's condition."

"Yes—but I won't risk her again unless she wishes it."

Samuel looked startled. "Do you mean you'll be celibate?"

"Yes—what else is there to do?"

"But, God, man—what's a wife for?"

"Companionship."

Samuel was unbelieving.

"Well," demanded Richard, "wouldn't you give up your pleasures to save Laura from harm?"

"I would for Laura but I wouldn't for a wife. You have a novel view of marriage."

"I see that you should marry Rachel."

"How the devil can I marry a girl like that?"

"She's only what you made her."

"She's a labouring woman."

He rose and refilled his glass, banging down the decanter at the appropriateness of his words, standing rigid at the table holding its edge. "Look at you," he said, his tone loud and harsh. "You think you're so holy. You wear that damned collar to show how holy you are."

Richard turned to face him. "No," he protested. "You have me wrong. I don't think I'm worthy of my work—no one who thinks he is should even be in the priesthood. I wear it as a reminder to myself of the teachings I follow, not to say 'Look at me—a parson'. When I'm listening to some fat squire with a port-and-stilton face who's never done a day's toil in his life telling me that men without employ are too idle to work, or that children must be let starve to discourage surplus population, this collar stops me breaking his neck for him and makes me speak softly upon what the Gospels tell him he should do."

"Really?" said Samuel. "And that's better is it?"

"It works. Don't you see it works?" Richard stood up. "They're cruel here because of ignorance and you can't break cruelty with violence. You must persuade and tease until they think reform is their own idea and not a backing-down. You know that; you're always talking about education. And the collar works again; it marks me as their equal. I'm the parson, the figurehead of the religion they say rules their lives, my family is as good as theirs, we're man to man."

"If this", Samuel tapped on his glass, "is you meek and mild, what are you like without the collar? How does it work with these poor you raise Cain about?"

"I give them food, fuel, blankets, clothing, medicine. Not enough, but all I can. I pay their rent arrears so they're not thrown on to the street, I argue with their masters and sometimes make changes, I write letters to relatives they haven't seen for years, I give them references, I find their daughters respectable places when they go into service, I'm trying to get them all allotments and pigs. They trust me. If I wore a stocking around my neck they'd come to me. . . . But don't you understand, it's not me who does these things, it's the Father through me; I do them in His name not my own. What does it matter that I'm weak-spirited if I can stop typhus by persuading a farmer to make his men dig themselves cesspits—or dig them myself if it's necessary?"

"Perhaps that's what I needed with Rachel—a few cesspits to take my mind off being a man, a few good works to . . ."

Richard rounded on him, his voice tired and bitter. "You don't believe me. I was innocent when I married your sister so I can't have normal longings; I must be a hypocrite. If only I'd had the chance to seduce and betray I'd be singing a different tune. Well, I've had desires, I've had temptations. You forget my position.

Even before my promotion a curate with prospect was a catch. I've sat trapped alone in drawing-rooms with daughters, always somehow showing their legs, until their mothers thought I couldn't possibly not have compromised myself; I've been called late at night to the sick-beds of very healthy young ladies in need of spiritual comfort with just enough breast showing to encourage me. Laura married me because she returned my love, but she could easily have wanted me for my rank and income. I married her because I love her, but there's many another I could have bedded if I hadn't had the sense to see the injury I'd do them."

He halted, his throat dry, angry with himself for having gone so far.

"You exhaust me," said Samuel, "with your self-control."

For a moment they stared at one another in enmity, the atmosphere proud and tense; then into their isolation came the domestic sound of the housekeeper's footsteps on the stair and Richard crossed the room to ask for news.

He could not have opened the door at a more fortuitous or dramatic instant for he met a low, deep-throated roar of anguish from above, a single desolate, gasping cry made the more terrible to its listeners by the silence that surrounded it. It seemed to echo and vibrate around them, ringing against their tautened nerves, and Samuel felt the sharp pricking of sweat beneath his arms.

He had heard this moan before. He had been six years old; his mamma had gone to bed in the afternoon, something he had never known before, the doctor had been sent for—and in the night the child had been awakened by this same sound that was now awakening the man. He had jumped from his bed to go to her but his door had been locked, and when it was opened in the morning his sister Naomi had lain in the crib in his parents' room.

He sat weakly in Richard's chair. For the first time he realised that women were not divided into ladies and maids; the suffering of one was the suffering of the other. He remembered the bluebells he had picked for his mother in the wood—he had resented Rachel as he gathered them, but now he pictured those evening walks under the trees and saw that the love and trust that had awaited him had been the same love and trust that his mamma gave his father. Like Laura he had never seen beyond the pleasures of his attraction; in his way he had revelled in his appearance as ignorantly as she had in hers. Just as her wedding-night had awoken her to the responsibilities of enticement, so did this cry awaken him and a pang of the loneliness and fear Rachel had felt invaded him.

Neither man had the presence of mind to stop the housekeeper as she repassed them with her arms full of towels, and they were left with only a nod for comfort. Richard took a pipe from the rack on the mantelpiece and handed a spare to Samuel. Like two old men who cannot face the weather they sat by the fire and filled their bowls with slightly shaking hands, each nervous for a different woman—Samuel for the girl who could have been his mother and Richard for the girl who could have been his wife.

They did not hear the first wail of the child—only an increase of bustle upstairs, hurried feet on wooden floors, women's muffled voices—and when Mrs. Houghton entered to tell them that Rachel had had a son and both were well it seemed a surprise, as if the ending to a story had been wrong.

Richard left the house to collect Laura, and Samuel sat on alone until he was allowed upstairs to see Rachel. He opened the door to the back-bedroom more tentatively than he had ever approached her before. The room was close and stuffy with the window sealed shut and a coal fire burning slumberously in the grate. Rachel was lying in the double-bedstead that she shared with Dinah watching her visitor. She lay half-sitting against a mound of pillows, dressed in a cheap, white cotton gown warm from the clothes-rail, and in her arms she held a still, swaddled bundle. Her face was flushed and her plaited hair damp and clinging in tendrils to the edges of her brow.

Samuel stood in the doorway expecting the familiar look of dependency in her eyes, but it was gone, replaced by indifference, and she answered his gaze with neither hostility nor welcome.

"You can't stay long," she said. "I must sleep."

"I don't want to tire you." For the first time he was on the defensive, not master of their meeting. He saw that there was a difference in her and though he felt its sharp edges, even his new awareness could not see its profundity. He saw her as she was: not as the body that had sated him and then brought needless aggravation but as a girl—the age of his sisters—who had loved and given freely, been used, betrayed and cast off, suffered agonies of panic and desolation; who had been forced to take refuge where she was known and been scorned by her neighbours—all for something that had barely touched his life.

And because he now saw her as a whole woman with the feelings of any other the latent romance in him was released. Before today he would not have considered that there could be love between him and a girl of her class, but now he remembered the early morning rendezvous as she cushed the cows with the dew on her skirts, the secret glances and nods in company that had said so much, her steadfastness in going against her family's teachings to risk her future for him, the zest it had given to a day to know that they would be together that night, and suddenly these things did not seem trivial or sordid or contemptible.

Even so he did not love her; he was filled only with renewed liking, with admiration and pity for her and shame for himself —yet love rose in him to give, and as she uncovered her child for him to see it flowed out and found its object.

He went over to the bed falteringly and looked down into the shawl. The tiny face was very pink, very wrinkled and its eyes were tightly shut. Softly he touched its dark hair with a fingertip. This, he thought, is my son, my son.

"I didn't realise they came so small," he said.

Chapter Twelve

"You should never have sent for him, Richard; he's shown no interest in her since she came to us; he won't have thanked you for fetching him today."

"No, I wouldn't say he thanked me."

Laura stopped in the lane leading to the Vicarage from her refuge at the Mill and faced her husband fretfully. "Oh, you haven't been arguing? Don't we have enough trouble in the house?"

Richard took her gloved hand and drew it back to its place on his arm. "We've been peaceful these two hours, my love. He was quite—concussed when I left him." Laura's face lit with horror. "Metaphorically speaking," he explained. She turned abruptly away and they continued their walk.

Laura was not feeling very affectionate towards Samuel after her visit to the Old Mill. She could not deny that Mrs. Vaughan had been welcoming, but the reason for her appearance—Laura's maid giving birth to Laura's brother's child in Laura's home —had loomed so large as a forbidden subject of conversation that it had been hard to talk at all. She had been suffering this affliction since half-past ten that morning when Richard had judged her too alarmed to stay in the house. To Richard's relief, the irritations of her difficult day and the summoning of her brother against her wishes meant that instead of being supported pale and trembling, she was placing her feet with a firmness that would have been temper in one less beautiful.

"There was no cause for it," she went on, "no cause at all. He'll have thought the whole thing a charade. And naturally now everyone will be certain who the father was."

"There was no doubt before."

She glanced at him savagely. "And whose fault was that?"

"Originally," he said blandly. "it was Samuel's."

A few months ago she would have coloured; today she ignored him and he was amused despite himself. He leant round her to push open their front door and she preceded him into the hall. Her back was towards him as she untied her bonnet strings and he stood and watched her tenderly. From this view no one could have guessed that she expected her own confinement in four months; as she bent her head to pat her hair into shape she looked as small and fragile as when he had first seen her. He crossed the floor and put his arms about her in protection. She stopped in her unrobing and rested against him, her rosemary-scented hair pressed into his shoulder, her fingers clinging to the cloth of his jacket. There was a different air in the house: it was as still and silent as the morning, but it was no longer predatory, the waiting was over, all was well and for a moment they paused together, content to lay aside the fears and difficulties that surrounded them.

A door clicked upstairs, a man's footsteps came on to the landing and they drew themselves apart with reluctance, Laura busying herself with the buttons on her gloves, Richard lingering to wait for her. They heard Samuel coming down from the top floor with none of the usual authority or arrogance in his walk. He was taking each step with the slow deliberation of a dreamer, running the flat of his palm down the bannister and looking ahead with such a rapt, contemplative expression that Laura forgot herself a little.

"I can't congratulate you, Samuel," she said, "but I'll make you tea if you'd like it."

He wanted nothing; he kissed his sister's cheek, nodded vaguely at Richard and drifted past them into the brightness of early afternoon. All was dazzle and fragrance and colour. He wandered to the stable-yard where his hunter was tied and reached to pull down his stirrup, but as his hand closed on the iron the thin, newborn cry of his son wailed from the window above him and the rush of feeling it induced held him fast. He laid his cheek against the cold leather of the saddle and closed his eyes.

At twenty-five he was experiencing the enveloping strength of first love, not, as he had always imagined, for a woman, but for the child whose coming he had refused to acknowledge. He could barely stand upright under the desire to run to the possessor of this high, insistent voice and snatch it to him. Above him, out of his sight, Rachel cradled her baby and the crying faded; he raised his head in yearning towards the bedroom and his face was met by the flash of the sun on the water-butt, blinding, piercing his eyes. For a while he stood without seeing, waiting for some sound from his son, and presently when none came he gathered himself into the saddle and made his way out of the yard.

He was surprised by his own paternalism. He had avoided Rachel so thoroughly in the past months that he had hardly imagined that a baby would follow, any more than he had thought of its mother as a real woman. He had looked on her pregnancy simply as another annoying female ailment; the child that would result had been nothing to him, nothing—but now, because he had a brother-in-law who was scrupulous and romantic, he had awoken. He was dazed and stricken and exalted.

He rode home slowly, floating on this new and strange response, and at Honeycombe Wood he reined in to look at the land. He sat easily on the fidgeting gelding, one hand on his thigh, and smelt the air that was fresh and green and growing. It was here, hidden among the trees, that his son had been conceived. A girl had met him beneath their branches when the leaves were hanging full and today it was a new spring and they had a son.

He gazed around: he was surrounded on all sides by Delaford land—and, as clearly as if they walked before him, he saw himself as one of a continuing procession of fathers and sons passing their inheritance from generation to generation. He had always loved the land; before this moment there had been nothing in his life to equal it, but now there was a different reason to give it care. It was for him to cultivate and cherish, to raise the yield and enrich the soil so that his son might take it after him. His son—he hadn't even given him a name—what should it be? Edward Delaford? Ralph Delaford? And then a coldness broke on him, a physical sensation that began at his heart and spread round and out until he shivered with the blow to his self-regard. It wouldn't be Delaford, would it? It would be Cooper: the name of the men his father hired.

Over the next days his rapture increased. It was an emotion fostered in difficult conditions. In odd moments, when the memory of the small face was engulfed by the knowledge that it was not a Delaford, Samuel struggled against this alien passion, but it would not give way and he grew more determined that the child was *his* and he would have it.

He had no one at the farm in whom to confide; his family had been pleased neither by his news nor his attitude towards it, and the atmosphere which had warmed since November froze once again. His parents had been quietly hoping that the baby would be either still-born or female: if the first the mistake could be buried, Rachel sent away and the matter forgotten; if the second it would be unimportant and could be hidden with its mother until old enough to go into service itself. A boy, as Samuel's first-born son, would have a more sentimental hold on him—and was exercising it already, Mrs. Delaford told her husband, as anyone who watched Samuel could see. He should never, she said, have been called to Bradford Abbas.

Rachel was churched on the following Friday. Silently rebellious she thanked God for having delivered her from "the great pain and peril of childbirth" but there was no sincerity in her words. She believed in her heart that it would have been better for her and her son to have died. Since she had come to the Vicarage she had kept to herself, taking refuge in the mute brooding of a pregnant woman, rarely leaving the house to expose herself to sneers, but now the swelling of her dress had turned into a crying child who would draw contempt upon his mother with every sound. She would never be able to walk in the street; he would never be able to play out of doors without being despised by everyone who passed. The wrong of their existence would be as plain as if it were branded into their skin. She loved her child—whom she had not yet named —but she felt she had nothing to offer him and already his demands were wearing her out; she saw nothing ahead except hard work, loneliness and notoriety.

An inappropriate mixture of gratitude to the Websters and bitterness towards her father and brother made her allow the ceremony. She had come to the Vicarage in despair, glad to have been saved from the Workhouse for a little longer, but expecting to have it made clear to her that she was a sinner; instead she had found compassion: both Mr. and Mrs. Webster had run counter to the popular belief and placed all blame on Samuel, the house-keeper who could have made her life so hard had put her condition down to the foolishness of Dissent, and Dinah had simply accepted it as a natural pitfall of living. Her stay had been so untraumatic that she was doubly afraid of the future. She knew that sooner or later she would have to leave and that the world outside would be as cold and unforgiving as her own family.

There had been no reconciliation between herself and her father, and he had seen that she was cut by her Connection. She did not realise that his actions were directed more by his own temperament than by his faith and, wounded by her religion, she was ready to follow where Richard led. She had loved her Methodism and never questioned the choice of church—Anglicanism was for the gentry, Nonconformity for commerce and labour—but now, cloistered and safe as she was at St. Mary's and shamed by her chapel, she lost sight of its merits and saw only its harshness and hell-fire. Labourer as she was, she could not imagine the squalor and poverty that had driven her grandparents to raise themselves through Wesley; she could not understand the glory and dignity of their experience, the freedom for those used to the cheap back-pews of standing together under a sky owned by no landlord, listening to one of their own people preach from a farm cart.

She was weighed down with what she had been taught was sin, yet she could not accept that all the suffering and guilt should be hers alone. She had done only what tens of thousands of other girls would do that year—she had trusted and yielded where she loved—and she could not see why Samuel's treachery should be unreproached. As the weeks had drawn by with no message from him she had gradually shed her humble adoration, and when, in the week after the birth, he had called twice to visit her she had adamantly refused to see him. She had seen the effect the sight of the baby had had on him and was angered. Why should she have had to struggle alone all these months only to have him take pleasure in her son? She had neither forgotten nor forgiven his rejection of her.

The second time Samuel called he had brought her a posy of shop-bought flowers, and when Rachel's door remained closed to him he had given them to Laura to pass to her. Laura, wanting to see what had changed him so, had taken them to Rachel herself and, although she could see nothing remarkable about the child, had dutifully acted as Samuel's envoy. Had she decided on a name? Laura had asked standing at the bedside with hands folded. No? Then Mr. Delaford begged her to consider "Ralph". Not being traditional to the family it was a name Laura was prepared to advocate. She stood over the girl, bearing down Rachel's obvious irritation at Samuel's presumption with her own status as mistress of the house, until Rachel, knowing that Laura could turn her out for any resistance to her wishes and too tired to name the child herself, had found herself thinking of the baby as Ralph.

The christening was more of a problem than the churching. Her roots were too deep for her to want her son made an Anglican, but gentle pressure from Richard, who, despite his tolerance of other sects, thought them misguided, and Laura, who could not face even an illegitimate nephew being Methodist, persuaded her.

"Godparents," Richard said to his wife three days before the event was to take place. "Godparents are the devil."

She shook out the tiny robe she was embroidering and looked up at him as he leant distractedly against the mantelpiece. "Don't ask me," she said. "Don't even ask me. I'll have nothing to do with a natural child."

He returned her gaze sorrowfully and saw she was not to be moved. "I didn't think you would," he replied, and began searching the shelf for pipe, tobacco and matches, "so I sounded Mrs. Houghton. She agreed to do it; she's grown fond of the girl."

There was a mixture of brazenness and hesitation in his attitude that told her he had once again done something he believed to be right that would displease her, and a suspicion appeared in her mind. She put down her scissors on the round work-table he had bought for her before their wedding.

"You've offered to be one of the godfathers, haven't you?"

"Yes, I have."

"And the other?"

He pressed a wad of dark, deep-smelling cavendish into his bowl and wedged it with his thumb. "I met Samuel in the lane; he said he'd been here with flowers." He raised his eyebrows and she nodded in reply. "He said he wanted to be one. I thought it was a good notion, it shows he's taking some responsibility at last."

"You know very well I don't want us to be tied to a fallen woman."

Richard glanced across at her, a faint expression of detached humour in his eyes, as if he had set a flame to the touch-paper and was waiting for the flare. He held out a hand pacifically, "Now, don't start on me. It was Samuel's idea. He said to me, 'For God's sake don't tell Laura!' But I didn't see how we could keep it from you."

"But it wasn't his idea that you should volunteer?"

"No; I admit that was my doing." He relaxed as he saw that she would not take offence. "I'm sorry, my love, but I don't see what else is to be done."

Laura returned to her needle. "Well," she said with all the charity of a parson's wife, "if you insist on going through with it I refuse to attend," and another stitch was added to the robe.

The baptism took place quietly, between services, on Sunday, 6th May—a complicated ceremony with both the officiating priest and the unmarried father acting as godparents. Despite her threat, Laura was overcome by curiosity as to how such a strange assembly would be managed and she remained in her seat as a spectator.

The only other member of the congregation was Dinah, who sat alone some rows back from her mistress and watched Samuel. He was standing bareheaded at the font in the cool light of the North Aisle, with the starched housekeeper between himself and the pale Rachel, gazing at his son with a possessive hunger; yet she knew that for all his absorption, for all the seriousness with which he spoke his answers, he was conscious of her and that consciousness was making him uncomfortable. He felt that she was laughing at him and he was right—but she was also laughing at herself.

She had made such plans on the night of the Fair. She had known of Samuel Delaford all her life—his father's lands stretched almost to her home in Thornford—and when he had returned from Oxford, grown and seductive she had been as drawn to him as any other girl within his reach. That Pack Monday, however, had offered them their first chance of being alone and, had she been younger, she would have taken advantage of it, but already her years as a servant had taught her to ask for more. She was determined not to spend her life scrubbing other people's floors, and for the few weeks he had shown his interest in her she had dreamt of leading him on into marriage. To her it seemed a practical resolution of her life. His want of her had seemed so strong that she could not understand why he did not follow her to Bradford Abbas—until the thin-faced girl, fingering her dark hair as she watched her baby clutch at Richard's vestments, had been brought to share her room. It had not hurt her to fold away her dream; she had calmly turned to the books Richard lent her for another escape—but a mischievous relish in seeing this hungry man rendered so harmless by a new-born child spiced her observation of him.

It seemed to Richard that the gossip would never end. After the christening he had hoped they might gather together over a glass of sherry and seal their differences at the start of this new life, but Laura, who had thought they were becoming too much of a family party, had put her foot down and he, feeling that he had pushed her far enough, acquiesced. He felt he had not considered her enough since November; he had wanted to make her life perfect —instead she was harried by problems she had never had to notice before. For months she had had to bear the idle prating of neighbours, who were prepared to condemn the humanity of the Websters while thinking no worse of Samuel, and today he had heard what she could not be told.

He stood in the empty vestry the day after the baptism with his fists clenched inside his pockets and a silent rage billowing within him. One of his parishioners, an embarrassed, gentle-mannered man, had passed on the rumour that Samuel Delaford was not the father of Rachel's child, that only the true father would have cared for the girl so readily, that only the true father would have been eager to be a godparent to a bastard. He had heard it, he said, before it was known that Mr. Delaford was to take part in the ceremony, and no doubt his presence would have put an end to such talk—but he felt that the parson should know.

Behind his initial anger Richard was not surprised; it was a suspicion he should have expected and he felt no concern for himself. He knew that there was nothing serious in the idea—it was no more than a bubble of scandal that had floated up from a malicious conversation, passing from mouth to mouth, being enjoyed and forgotten—but to Laura it would be violently painful.

For the sake of their own child he must clear their house of anyone who could cause her such distress.

He was loth to tell Rachel to go. At that moment he had in his jacket a letter from the bishop, asking him to explain his position regarding the girl. Was he condoning immoral behaviour? it enquired. Since women are the weaker vessels, should he not be encouraging them to uphold their purity by casting out sinners? Why should they value their chastity if they were not to suffer at its loss? It was the wrong approach to one as sentimental as Richard. If he had had only himself to think of, he would have written that it was his duty to give shelter as long as it was needed and shown Rachel no hint that life would be easier for him without her—but there was Laura.

He stared at the blank walls of the vestry and found no comfort. He knew that Rachel must leave. However hard it was for him to move her, it must be done. The longer she stayed now that her son was born, the more afraid she would grow of the world outside the Vicarage and the more Laura would grieve at having left the farm. There was no other way left to him: he must find Rachel another home and she must leave.

Chapter Thirteen

It was Dinah who solved his problem. She had what was, in this case, the advantage of parents who were both poor and intelligent. Neither had been educated to the least degree and could write no more than their names, but, unlike their neighbours, they had ardently encouraged their children to snatch what little learning they could in order to better themselves. Her father had risen through perseverance to second horseman—a position scorned by bank clerks and admired by Samuel. Her mother had struggled with poverty and narrowly defeated it, bringing up their children in all possible cleanliness, godliness, nutrition and ambition. Already their eldest daughter was maid to a parson who lent her his books. But for all their efforts, they made no pretence of gentility and saw Rachel's position as a common misfortune not a moral outrage; so when the cottage beside theirs became vacant they told Dinah—who duly told Richard—who generously and gratefully paid a year's rent in advance.

Increasingly he found himself liking this surprising maid. When he had first seen her the sweet prettiness of her face had made his heart fall. He imagined a vacuous nature and a stream of clodhopping suitors, and thought he would soon be hustling her to a wedding—but none of these things had appeared. She applied herself to her work, giving the impression that she did it well because it was hers to do but that her mind was elsewhere. Once he had discovered her standing at his bookcase, with a duster under her arm, deep in *The Pickwick Papers*, and he had offered her the freedom of his library.

In bed by the light of a candle she read voraciously—novels, poetry, history and political economy. She read Dickens, George Eliot—she had a particular fondness for this lady—Mrs. Gaskell, Wilkie Collins, Jane Austen and Sterne; she waded through Carlyle and Harriet Martineau, revelled in Tennyson, despaired

at "The Shepherd of Salisbury Plain" and, with false starts, drank
in John Stuart Mill. She read *The Times* and *All The Year Round*
when her master and mistress had cast them off, and continued
with her own copies of the *News of the World*. She began to wonder
why her father and brothers did not have a vote; she was heard to
say that teaching as a profession for women was an admirable
thing. It occurred to Richard that he was out of the frying-pan and
into the fire.

It was a dreary May. The promise of April was not fulfilled and
Rachel looked out of her tiny windows to a world of grey skies and
squalling rain. She had never felt so lonely and she could see no
way of changing things. Locked in four small badly-furnished
rooms she stared at her future and tried to find an escape. She had
saved her wages from Richard, and with this to keep her, and the
allowance from Samuel, she could afford to live without working
for a few weeks while she recovered and came to a decision. The
rent for her cottage was paid for twelve months, but she thought
she would prefer to move to where she was unknown and begin a
new life as a "widow". But what could she do? She could not take
work in a dairy without putting Ralph in the hands of a child-
minder, and her love of being with him and fear of his being
quietened with just too much laudanum determined her against it.
For the same reason she could not go back into service or enter a
factory or a shop or nursing. She was neither well-educated nor
respectable enough to be a governess. She needed a trade she could
do with a child at her skirts. She could make lace and plait straw,
but neither fast enough to earn a living. All that seemed open to
her were washing and dressmaking, and in both competition was
cruel.

Richard had told her that she could come to him if she needed
money, but he had already given her so much that she could not
turn to him. She knew that now Samuel had seen his son she could
apply to him, but this again was no answer. She had no warm
thoughts of Samuel and could not even take refuge in memories;
what had once seemed rich and glowing was now shabby and
mean, and the trust she had shown him mocked her. She remembered how one morning when she was in the Vicarage kitchen she
had stumbled and almost fallen; Richard had put out his hand to

save her but quickly changed the movement to reaching for his paper, and with her new experience she understood that this was how it would always be—the Reverend Websters would think twice before touching her innocently, the Samuel Delafords would reach out the sooner.

One evening, between showers, desperation drew her to wrap Ralph in her shawl and return to her father's house.

Between hedges of dripping hawthorn she walked the muddy lane to Sherborne at late dusk, with the black shadow of the hills brooding above her. The same hills that had watched her birth and growing, her first and only love and her numbing flight in Richard's trap, desperate and ruined, now saw a changed woman carrying the son that had been conceived at their feet. Her tragedy had not been the first they had seen, nor would it be the last.

Night had fallen as she entered the garden of the cottage where she had been born. She stood for a moment at the gate timid and anxious, longing for her family's friendship. Now that she was so close to them, the consciousness of her shame in their eyes rushed back upon her and Ralph's christening loomed above their meeting like a megalith. With uncertain steps of her pattened feet she went on until, through the window, she could see her father and brother seated in the parlour reading the Old Testament. Terribly afraid of her reception after six months of bitter withdrawal and forgetting her rebellious thought that Samuel was more to blame than she, she lingered outside pressed back against a lilac bush, too apprehensive to go to the door and knock, the bedraggled blooms swaying and shaking around her in the breeze. Inside the room her father rose to close the curtains, and as he reached the window she moved forward into the square of lamplight that fell on to the ground.

With arms outstretched to pull the draperies that she had sewn and laundered, Cooper stared through the glass at the image of sin that was his daughter. Together they stood motionless, her eyes beseeching, his fiercely cold and then, with nervous fingers, she opened the shawl to show her child. As if the blood were being sucked inward to leave a waxen death-mask, hatred and disgust crawled across her father's face. He lifted his head as he did in the pulpit and began to speak. The rising wind that whipped her hair carried away the sound of his words before she could hear them, but unmistakably she saw his thin lips form "Jezebel". In a biblical gesture he drew the curtains and she was in darkness.

She waited in the garden, her breath painful in her chest, hoping that Malachi would come out to her, and when he did not she turned back to the lane. She could not bring herself to go back to Thornford, to the house that was not a home, and she was weary with a tiredness of the mind that would not carry her to Richard; she did not dare intrude upon the Delafords; she could not trust herself to repass the torment of the woods where she had used to meet Samuel. There was nowhere to welcome her. Hardly knowing what she did, she found her way down to the river, over the bridge by Darkhole Farm, on to the Common and there she sat all night nursing her despair.

She did not sleep or think—her mind was too choked to serve her—but as the hours went by the blankness that had brought her to desperation faded and the need to survive began to return. Country girl that she was, when the sun began to rise above the hills could not help her spirits lifting with it. She was stiff and cramped from her vigil, and her hands and feet were frozen, but her lap was warm where Ralph was sleeping and she was again alive enough to worry about him.

Cradling the child she sat in the shelter of the dry-stone wall and saw the pale dawn flow down the hillside to the Common. There had been a heavy dew and the cobwebs spun between the grasses glinted with the lightness of pearl and silver, with bright and soft whites, violet, dove-grey, clear blues and greens—as impressionable and lovely as she had been herself, and as easily destroyed. She heard the new dairymaid at Limekiln cushing the cows with a louder, more strident voice than her own, and her whole body filled with a longing for the days she had lost. Then Ralph, who had slept peacefully in her arms, began to whimper and in the cold morning she drew her shawl around them and rocked and suckled him, clutching him to her with her milk spilling over his chin.

The new Grace Sanderson was in that rare and happy state of possessing everything she wished to have. Marriage suited her: she had always been earthily attractive, but the past months had given her a bloom like a damson. She liked James, she liked the freedom he had given her, the house he had taken for them, the society of his friends. Perhaps an open carriage would have added to her enjoyment of life, but it was not a desire that kept her awake.

In the afternoon of the day Rachel gave up the hope of rejoining her family Grace was combining marvellously the roles of coquette and gardener. She was helped in this by Samuel, who appreciated women and cultivation equally. He had come to her home in Newlands to ask James a point of law, but when he was told that the master was out he was quite content to wander through to the garden and dally with Grace. He found her dressed in a wide straw hat and smock-like wrapper building what he took to be a very amateurish shed. There were ten denuded fir saplings thrust into the earth supporting the framework of a circular roof and between their trunks she was nailing horizontal laths very close together. As he approached her over the lawn he could see her dip into her pocket for a nail, tap at either end of the rod and step backwards to admire her work.

"Mrs. Sanderson," he said over her shoulder, "Carpenter Extraordinary."

She turned, pleasantly flushed with achievement, her green ribbons fluttering. "I'm making a moss-house," she explained. "The odd-job man put in the pillars for me and is going to thatch the roof."

"And what of the sides? You haven't made them watertight." He ran his finger along a groove between two laths. He thought she was looking extremely pretty.

"It will be. You see, I fasten these all round the sides like so . . ." she walked her fingers along the wood until they almost met his, "then I collect as many different coloured mosses as I can find and I wedge them into the cracks to make a pattern. I'm going to do an arabesque design like a Persian carpet. I draw it on first with chalk."

"Then you sit inside and eat strawberries?"

"Exactly—or rather I sit and admire my new garden."

"Are you going to change it?" Samuel surveyed the lake-like expanse of lawn with its border of shrubs. "What's wrong with it as it is?"

"It looks like a field—but I daresay you approve of that?"

"Tell me what you will do."

Grace gazed around with a serious face and began to point with her hammer. "At the foot of the terrace I shall have a border of geraniums and heart's-ease and tulips and carnations all set about with standard roses and edged with box, then I shall leave enough plain grass for a croquet lawn—do you play croquet?" Samuel nodded. "Beyond that a little rockwork planted with alpines, and then assorted beds between paths and walks before the green-houses at the end.

"I've a plan here for the beds; I copied it from a magazine." She took a folded paper from her pocket and smoothed it as best she could in the breeze. Samuel held one side as its edges curled and flapped. "They give you the shapes, you see, and you colour them in as you please. The first will be a Cone garden: you begin with a clump of very tall flowers—eight or nine feet—then surround them with a circle of shorter ones of a different shade, then shorter still and shorter still until you reach the ground. Then this one", she tapped an oval on the plan, "will be rose-bushes enclosed by a lattice fence with an arch of a climber from one side to the other, so that when it's in bloom it looks like a giant basket.

"This round one's the most difficult. It's going to be a clock bed. I divide the dial into sections with plants that open at different times of the day. Here are their names written at the side, look, from hawkweed, which opens at six in the morning, to cranesbill, which takes you to six in the evening. Do you see the idea?"

Samuel bore this horrendous picture stoically. "I do," he said, "but I don't think you'll find plants co-operate so easily."

"Neither do husbands," Grace returned the plan to her pocket. "I want to send to Stroud for a mowing machine to give James some exercise, but he won't hear of it."

"I don't blame him; if you want a good finish you must use a scythe." He bent his knees and swung his arms in the familiar low-cutting slide.

"Ah, but that would be too hard for a lawyer's hands. Let me feel yours." He gave her his right hand; she took off her glove and ran her fingers over his palm. "You see," she said, lightly touching the calluses, "such a difference." He knew that they were playing a formal game that would come to nothing, but the brush of her skin against his reminded him that he had been celibate for a long time and that summer was coming. James had the pleasure of coming home each day to a wife—he could do the same and the attraction of the thought gave fuel to the notion that had brought him there. He looked at Grace's soft, white hands and thought of Rachel.

Grace was examining a graze on his thumb. "Have you hurt yourself? What have you been doing?"

"I was ploughing between the beet this morning to kill the weeds. You only use the share for that and I got my thumb jammed taking the breast off. It's better now."

She folded his hand into a fist and released it. "I should know better than to show off my gardening to you, shouldn't I?"

He smiled. "I'm more of a wheat and barley man, myself. Do you want me to help you with these laths?"

"No," she stirred the pile of rods with the toe of her boot. "I've done enough for today and I'm thirsty. Let's go indoors and have tea." Together they walked back across the lawn that was soon to be carved into modernity.

"Did you come to see James?" she asked.

"Why would I call on married ladies if not to see their husbands?"

"I don't know what time he'll be back. Will you wait?"

"Long enough for you to feed and water me; I've been working since seven this morning." He offered his arm as they climbed the terrace steps.

"How is Laura? I keep meaning to visit but I'm so busy."

"She's not going about just now."

"Yes, but how is she? I haven't seen her since her wedding; she wasn't well enough to come with Mr. Webster to mine."

There was no suspicion or triumph in her voice, and Samuel, who would always protect his sister, was reassured that no one but he knew why she had not watched James promise himself to this girl nor called upon the bride.

"Her condition isn't agreeing with her," he said. "Physically there isn't anything really wrong, but she's got no strength at all and she's lost her serenity. I expect she'll recover after her confinement but—oh, I don't know, I don't like to see her this way. Of course, I haven't been with her as much as I would in other circumstances."

"No."

"Things will be easier for her now that Rachel's gone. I talk freely to you, Grace, because I know you don't gossip."

He followed her into the hall through the small conservatory, having begun he felt a need to confide in her. He waited in her upholstered drawing-room with its round, cloth-draped tea-table as she went to order tea and take off her smock. He stood in the window with his hands clasped behind him under his jacket watching the milk-woman lead her donkey cart slowly up the street, filling the jugs of her customers from a tap on her keg. He was impatient for Grace to return; he could talk to no one at home about Ralph, but he felt at ease here and he knew she would listen without criticism.

Tiring of the view and caught up in his thoughts, he wandered around the cluttered room until Grace appeared with her maid and the tray was set; then he sat familiarly on the chaise-longue with his feet resting on its plush.

"If you're going to lie on that," said Grace, "put a napkin under your boots; it's designed for people in slippers."

He lifted his legs obligingly and she spread a white damask square beneath his heels. Filling a plate for a ploughman's appetite she passed it to him through the curling steam of the tea-pot, and to relieve his tension and her curiosity she asked, "And how is Rachel?"

"Well enough. I haven't seen her since she left Bradford Abbas, but my brother-in-law visits her."

"And the baby?" She lifted the lid of the pot and looked inside, letting a cloud into the air between them.

"He's thriving." She could hear the difference in his voice as he spoke—a pride and tenderness he was half-ashamed to reveal. He went on, "I haven't been to see him because—well, I thought what I feel for him would wear off. I thought it would be 'out of sight, out of mind', but it's been 'out of sight, into the heart'."

"You have a heart, then?"

Out of habit, he glanced at her with deliberately shadowed eyes. "Can you doubt me?" he asked, but he could not keep the mood, he was drawn back to Ralph and, watching the changing patterns the swaying lace curtains threw on to the wall, he told her of his love for his son. She had never heard him talk this way before, there had always been a hint of humour or mockery in his speech, and she saw that what she and James had suspected had been right.

She said quietly, "You know that even if you married her he still wouldn't be legitimate."

This time his eyes were sharp. "How did you know I would ask that?"

"It was easy to guess, anyone can see how you've changed. You've been blind to the world these last few weeks; you still are."

"Did James tell you? It's what I came to ask."

"I'm sorry but he did."

For a moment he said nothing and she was afraid to intrude on his disappointment. She wished she had waited for James—for weeks he had been prepared to break this news and now she had let it fall without him. She knew she had nothing to fear from Samuel, but his stillness unsettled her. She felt she would say anything to end the silence. At last she said, "Don't take this amiss, Samuel, but you're not married to the girl and he's not the son you would have from a wife of your own position. A lady would have you and you could have proper sons."

It was a clumsy sentiment, badly said, but he was generous enough not to be angry. He sat upright and faced her. "You haven't seen him," he told her as gently as if explaining to a child, "if you had you wouldn't say that." He was hurt that he could not undo the damage he had done, but perversely the knowledge made him more determined to carry out his plan. Legally Ralph would always be a bastard—very well, he would fight to make the world regard him as a Delaford. He would marry Rachel—the quiet, loving Rachel who would make such a perfect farmer's wife—he would change Ralph's name, he would make a will leaving the land to him just as though he were legitimate. Seeing him grow up with a respectable mother and a monied father people would learn to accept him and when he was a man there need be no memory of his birth. "God," he said bitterly, "why didn't I marry her before?" He saw the discomfort on Grace's face as she watched him reach this unorthodox decision and a little of his usual manner began to return.

"And if I married her," he asked, "would I still be welcomed by you? Would the peasant's husband be invited to tea?" He bit into a scone.

"Naturally he would."

"And the peasant?"

She busied herself with unnecessary adjustments to the tray. "We should have to see," she said—and laughed with him at herself.

That same afternoon he rode to Thornford through the fields and lanes that had been made more precious to him by his son. The sky was gathering to dusk and the breeze that had ruffled Grace's paper was growing gusty, but he was warmed by his confidence. As he rode he imagined Ralph beside him with legs hardly straddling his first pony, and when he could turn his mind from this he pictured himself as a Good Samaritan. That Rachel should give him anything but a grateful acceptance did not occur to him. It was inconceivable that she would not clutch the opportunity that would give her the man she loved, the father of her child and a comfortable life with one word. Once again he was assuming that she would not act independently of his desires. He forgot that he had injured her too deeply for her love to have survived and that poverty was nothing new to her. He could not know that she had walked that road in the early morning believing that she need no longer be afraid because she could fall no further.

There was nowhere safe to tie his horse outside Rachel's cottage and he beckoned a boy on his way home from stone gathering to hold the reins for sixpence. A white-faced Rachel, with clothes creased as if she had been lying down, answered his knock and his assurance took him past her into the darkened room that held his son.

Outside the boy sat on the verge and let Samuel's hunter tear at the grass beside him with a clinking of harness. He had been at work on the exposed hillside since dawn and would have been glad of his own kitchen, but a sixpence was too welcome to be refused and his mother would be interested in Mr. Delaford visiting here—the girl's presence was already a scandal and talking-point although she hid herself from them; if she had returned to her old ways what a subject that would be. He rolled on to his stomach on the sloping bank and gazed over the broken wall at the cottage window. There was no light inside and he could see nothing, but as he waited he could hear an angry murmur of voices rise into violence.

"He is my son," he heard Rachel protesting. He pulled himself further up the grass by the elbows so that every word could be carried back to his mother.

"He is mine," Samuel was shouting, "mine. I am his father."

"How can you say that to me now?"

There was a pause as though Samuel was striving to master himself and then he broke out, "What's wrong with you? I'm offering to make you decent again. You can be the wife of a gentleman or stay a slut; which is it to be?"—and to the delight of his mother the boy heard Rachel's bleak reply that whatever she was she would stay.

There was no relief from the rain. For three days it fell continuously and Rachel stayed within doors. She did not want to leave the house. In her four rooms she had no contact with anyone but her neighbours, the Hillyards, and she could persuade herself that the answer she had given Samuel had been right and no one would think the worse of her for it. She tended Ralph, moved slowly at her work and allowed herself to look forward no further than Dinah's visit.

Knowing how lonely the young mother must be, Richard had persuaded his wife to allow Dinah an evening a week above her usual allowance to go to Thornford and Rachel. He imagined that they merely sat and sewed as they talked, but Dinah's new vision of learning reminded her that her friend came from a family where literacy was practised and asked for help with her writing. Together the two girls would sit at the scoured table, their heads shining bronze and gold in the firelight, and with cheap paper and ink tried to curb Dinah's round, childish hand into neat copperplate.

Tonight, when Dinah came in the shelter of the carrier's cart, the atmosphere of the room became suddenly a haven. The drumming of the rain in the night beyond the door, the candle flame throwing their faces into relief, the breathing of the sleeping baby, blended into comfort and they talked of what was close to their hearts.

Rachel told of Samuel's proposal and Dinah generously—for she would still have taken him herself—advised her to accept him. She understood and sympathised with Rachel's feelings of rebellion, but she was more worldly-wise and she saw that if Rachel continued unmarried her life would never improve, it would always be harsh, solitary and painful; if she took a rich husband she would have ease, respect and a name for the son who would otherwise go through the world despised.

She was sitting with her arm outstretched on the table and her head resting upon it, idly picking at the grains of the paper with her nib. Thinking of what Rachel had turned down she asked her what life she would choose for herself if she could have anything she wished. Rachel clasped her hands before her and let her friend into the dream that had supported her for years. "I would have a man who loved me," she said, gazing at her interlocking fingers. "A farmer. I'd have a solid house with wide windows to let in the sun, dark oak floors and furniture that had been cared for by my man's mother and grandmother before me. My rooms would smell of beeswax and my linen of lavender. I'd have a kitchen with a stone-flagged floor and an oven where I could roast meat every day. I'd have a still-room where I'd make herb beers and wines from the flowers and fruits on my own lands.

"Then I'd have my own dairy with white marble shelves and bowls of green and white—everything clean and cool—and a window of stained glass so that in winter the colours would fall in the milk like a fire . . . But in the summer I'd leave the door open so that when it was still I could stand in the quietness and look out over my own cider orchard—where the daffodils and snowdrops had been—to the hills and then the sky, I'd have an old dog sleeping on the doorstep and the scent of the honeysuckle and the hum of my bees would drift in to me . . ."

Her voice had dropped as she spoke of her naive desires and now it stopped altogether.

Dinah said, "You could have had all that," and Rachel straightened her hands and looked ruefully at their ringless condition. "No," she said, "I couldn't have the first and the rest is worthless without that. Anyway, it's just make-believe. In real life there would be wasps in the apples and mud on my floors and the butter wouldn't always come for all my coloured windows."

She leant back out of the candle-light so that her face was shaded and tipped her chair on its hindlegs until she could see that Ralph was drowsing. "Well?" she asked. "What would you have if dreams came true?"

For the first time Dinah seemed shy. "Don't laugh at me."

"I won't."

"I'd like to be a teacher." She dipped her pen in the ink and began drawing languidly on the pock-marked sheet to cover her embarrassment. "I've been reading a good deal lately and I remember what I've read. I'm sure I could pass it on; I know I could. Mr. Webster's been talking of a church school—if I could have charge of the girls—if I was trained . . ."

"Trained?"

"Yes, there are colleges now—there have been for fifteen years or more."

"But the pupils—aren't they gentry? Would they take you?"

"I don't know. I hardly know anything. You might have to write Greek or pass an examination—but before you go to a Training College you have to be apprenticed, so if Mr. Webster did start a school he would have to have a teacher and then perhaps I could go there."

They were silent: Dinah yearning and anxious, Rachel marvelling that her friend could aim so high. Ralph stirred and the creak of the wicker basket that served as a crib roused them.

Dinah stretched her cramped arms. "But," she said, "as you say it's make-believe. I'm not enough of a scholar."

"You could be. Ask Mr. Webster; he'd help you."

Dinah agreed that he would probably offer to coach her, but privately she thought that being closeted so soon with another servant girl would harm his reputation; she replied, "I will, but I'll wait until after the mistress's confinement; he has enough to worry over." She sat forward, elbows on the table. "I must get away from this," she said vehemently, glancing at the poverty that surrounded her; "I must. Look at my parents: they've worked so hard all their lives—so very hard—and for what? There are nine of them in four rooms next door and my mother is expecting another in the autumn—if she doesn't lose this one like the last for want of money to pay a doctor. They don't see meat from one week's end to the next. They've got earth floors and the rain comes in through the thatch, but they're still expected to curtsy or take off their hats when the landlord goes by. I can't bear to live like that, Rachel, I'd go mad."

"But you're working for the Websters."

"Yes, and they treat me well. I only had two half-days a month with Dr. Knapton and lower wages—but every ounce of strength I put into my work is for their home not mine. Either I spend my life a spinster cleaning someone else's dishes or I marry and be like my poor mother. What kind of choice is that? There must be another way. And think of this: Ralph and Mrs. Webster's baby are first cousins, you and she grew up not a hundred yards away from each other. Which of you has worked harder in those years? Which can give their child a better life? Oh, Rachel, for pity's sake don't miss your chance; if he asks you again—take him."

The following day Rachel left Ralph with Mrs. Hillyard and walked into the village to the shop. She had been unable to sleep for thinking of Dinah's words and having a craving for sweet things to comfort herself she had wanted to buy sugar. It was another grey, windy day and shreds of dark cloud were being driven westwards across the sky as she picked her way into the main street.

She walked lost in her thoughts, with her fingers tight on the handle of her basket and her eyes downcast, not looking in windows for fear of an answering stare. Dinah's comparison of Laura's child and Ralph had been preying on her until she was deep in guilt for her son's sake. She believed now that she should not have refused Samuel; she had had no right to hurt Ralph's future because of her pride—if her life was to be un-happy, better it should be unhappy and rich than unhappy and poor.

She climbed the iron-railed steps to the shop and went in. She had chosen the wrong time. This small general dealer's—once the front room of a moderate cottage—was the women's equivalent of their husbands' ale-house. Here amidst the sacks of flour and hanging poultry, with the scent of oatmeal, candles, tobacco and treacle, they gathered to order their pennyworth of this and sixpennyworth of that and to gossip.

Today as the bell jangled Rachel's arrival and brought her luckless figure amongst them, five of her neighbours were listening to the drab-gowned Mrs. Morrison's account of how her son had heard "that woman" turn Mr. Delaford away. It was no coinci-dence that Rachel should have come upon them; the story had already spread throughout the village and every group she could have met was talking of the same.

They stopped in their conversation as she entered and gazed at her in silence. She stood patiently in the dim light of the shop, the ridges of trampled sawdust painful beneath her soles, neither joining the company nor holding herself aloof, and the women saw their opening for sport. They turned from her and continued to speak as if she was not there. There was a blind, malicious pleasure in what they did as of tying a cat to a dog's tail or baiting a bear. Every one of them lived in squalor and would have given their right hand to be the wife of a man like Samuel. Rachel's rejection of him puzzled them. They could not understand what had made her refuse a wealth they longed for and they were shocked that she would choose to stay disgraced when she could have married. They wanted to punish her for both these things and they turned to the only explanation they had. Perhaps, they said with sly glances at the passive girl in the shadows, perhaps she wouldn't have him because she wasn't sure that he *was* the father, perhaps there could have been others—look what goes on at harvest. In their grand-mothers' day, they agreed, she would have been whipped at the church gates not protected by the parson and a ripple of laughter went through them as they asked—why *did* Mr. Webster take her in?

She did not stay to hear more. She walked painfully out of the shop and when she was beyond the sight of its door she leant her back against a wall to get her breath, as shaken as if she had been attacked. Was this the beginning then? Was this how it was to be? It hurt that Richard should be defamed because of her. She did not share his sanguine attitude towards the accusation and could not see that in a week or month it would disappear.

Her pulse was pounding. She rested her head against the stone and her eyes fell on a cluster of yellow and crimson wallflowers —the one bright, gaudy vision of her day. She stood quite still as if surprised by them, seeing that their clinging roots preserved their crumbling hosts but not that their spreading had first caused the ruin, and then she gathered herself and returned to her home —where Samuel, with a sprig of broom in his button-hole and determination on his face, was waiting to offer her his name.

Chapter Fourteen

The August sunlight shining full and warm on the vinery of Abbotsbury House turned its glass to sheets of molten amber. Inside, with their backs to the brilliance, Richard and Keating whiled away an hour of the hypnotic afternoon in idle companionship.

Keating moved among the vines securing tendrils, clipping yellowing leaves, pausing to feed the jays through the bars of their hanging cages—fastidiously offering them biscuits with a pair of brass pincers. Richard sat long-legged in a garden chair, the cast-iron fern-leaf on its back imprinting itself on his alpaca, sipping a glass of strawberry cordial. The luminous gold-green light that filtered through the plants and submerged the floor gave an opaque lustre to the black of his boots, like the bloom on the dark grapes around him. He looked worn. Beneath his eyes the shadows that had used to be half-circles were now straight, wide-angled lines into his cheeks. He had come for respite to this quiet, studious man who sympathised with fears he would not express before Laura. He was saying: "I don't know if I did right in bringing the girl home. I was angry with the way she was being treated; I couldn't think what else to do at the time; I didn't anticipate her being with us so long—not that I would have minded for myself, of course, but it hasn't only been me who has suffered."

Keating looked over his shoulder. "You shouldn't be so harsh on yourself. It was one of those actions that was socially unwise but morally correct."

His friend sighed and set down his glass. "Morally correct. Why does that have such a priggish ring to it? I don't know—I grow more pompous every day, I feel it covering me like a shell. I wonder whether I wasn't raised from curate too early."

"You'll be surprised how your imaginary shell falls away when your wife is safely delivered. There'll be a sun in the sky again."

"Perhaps—but I should never have been put in charge of a parish of souls; I can't even treat Laura properly."

"How so?"

"From the beginning I've never shown consideration for her feelings; never valued her sensitivity. I thrust her into marriage, forced her brother's concubine into her house, gave her this present discomfort to endure . . ."

He paused and Keating saw the misery of his own youth before him. Richard's pretty little wife reminded him so much of his own short season of content that now, as her time drew on, he was rarely free of the memory of Anne's face pale in death, the pathetic bundle of their child in her arms inside the coffin. He knew his own life to have been unbalanced by this one wretched, morbid accident and so he petted Laura, soothed Richard and held his peace.

"If I remember," he said, "it was first Mrs. Webster's idea that her childhood companion should take refuge with her."

"A notion, nothing more."

"And indeed she must have been eager for the duties of a wife or she would not have requested such a short engagement."

Again Richard sighed. Although not loving her less he could see Laura's weaknesses more clearly than when he had been the ingenuous lover. "I think she may have wanted a wedding more than a marriage," he said.

"An innocent failing, surely? Common to all the sex. It bodes no ill—come, water these pots for me."

He held a can of pond water towards the chair. Richard stood and stretched and pulled at the rear of his jacket. "How much do I give them?"

"Just a taste—that's right; perfect. Now follow me and I will give you something to take back to my favourite lady."

Together they left the vinery and walked through a glass passageway, scarlet and purple with fuchsias, to the corresponding wing that made the orchid house. Inside the heavy, humid air lay like a tropical night on the flowers. Keating went to the window and opened two small sections. "My problem", he said, "is to provide exactly the correct conditions. It must be moist, d'you see, and warm, but on the other hand there must be a frequent moving of air. Like all beauties they're temperamental." He caressed one immaculate white bloom with a manicured finger.

"How do you keep it so hot?" Richard moved to stand in what little draught now entered. "Is there artificial heat?"

"Steam. I have a boiler in a room beneath which feeds these pipes." With his toe Keating tapped a metal tube which ran along the floor.

"My brother-in-law would be interested to see it. Any such apparatus draws him like a dog to meat."

"You surprise me. I thought he was absorbed in land."

"The younger—Jonathan."

Keating took out his pocket-knife and with a slight, deft nick severed a pale-green stem. He held the orchid up into the light and turned it from side to side. "There," he said, "*Cattleya crispa*; four flowers on one stem—not a great number but excellent—excellent —in its way." He took a small trug from a recessed cupboard, packed its base with damp moss, laid the plant upon it and bound paper across to form a lid. He handed the prize to Richard.

"Tell Mrs. Webster that my wrapping does not do her justice; for a christening gift I will give her a Wardian case and she may have her own greenhouse in her drawing-room."

After the magnification of the vinery the outdoor heat of the somnolent afternoon was deceptively fresh. Richard walked out of his friend's grounds into the lane that led to the village. At either side towered green banks, topped to his right by dense pines, to his left with the old stone-built tithe-barn, and the sunlight fell only in thin, diagonal bars. In fifty yards he saw the silhouette of a young man holding two cropping horses. In the brightness of a gateway, where the banks sloped down to the level of the lane, the figure was standing gazing out over the heady barley crop within. It stooped, caught up a handful of earth from the field, crumbled it and dropped it back, brushing its hands on a kerchief; Richard saw that it was Samuel.

He approached silently over the thick, white summer dust of the road and touched Samuel's arm in greeting. Startled Samuel turned, then relaxed.

"I've been waiting for you," he said. "I rode over with a parcel of fallals the girls have been sewing for Laura. Your maid told me you were here. Laura's resting."

"Have I kept you long? Of course, I didn't know . . ."

"Just long enough to see what a splendid farmer I am." He gestured at the field with his free arm. "Look at that—more poppy than corn. There's been the same grain in there for three years to my knowledge. If I'd had the ordering of it I would have put in turnips this season to give it a rest. Is it yours?"

"No, the glebe farm is at the other side; down by Smith's Bridge."

"The Old Mill."

"Yes."

"I know it. More pasture than cropping." Samuel turned back to the barley. "'Fifty-four," he remarked reminiscently, "now there was a harvest. I was—what—nineteen and down from Oxford for the long vacation. I was Harvest King and I rode in on the last wain all silver with moonlight . . ."

"There'll be a different sight in there next year," said Richard; "I've finally been granted some of it for my allotments."

"Have you?" Samuel looked at him with interest. "How did you do that? I thought everyone was against you."

"Providence. I discovered I owned the only lady's fingers for fifteen miles and the Vaughans always have them for their cider; so at the Parish Meeting I confessed I felt myself forced to sacrifice the orchard and make over the field to the New Zealand scheme —in two days I had my land. Trust in the Lord . . ."

"And would you have pulled them down?" One of the horses nuzzled him and Samuel pulled its ear affectionately.

"Certainly not—the pears are 'Stinking Bishop'; how could I lose those? But I would have given the ground under them to the labourers if nothing had appeared; it would have been better than none—which reminds me," he held out his hands, "I'm collecting for the pig fund." He snapped his fingers.

Samuel searched in his pocket and dropped a shilling in small coins into the outstretched palm. Richard left his hand open and chinked the money; Samuel added a sovereign.

"I trust you've given something yourself," he said.

"Twice Laura's last dressmaking bill."

Her brother raised his eyebrows admiringly. "This is for the allotment holders, I take it?"

"Yes, old Mrs. Thornhill's been most generous. We had quite a discussion on the subject the first day I was here. She advised me to buy Gloucester Black Spots, but I can't tell one pig from another."

"Well, tell me when you want them and I'll look them over for you." Samuel motioned towards his horses who were tearing at the grass. "And talking of livestock, I brought this one over for you; I know you're looking for a hack."

"Which?" Richard stared with suspicion at the nearest; a fine-boned black mare with angry eyes and flattened ears and green-stained froth at the corners of her mouth. She shook her head as Samuel drew her closer and the dry earth was spattered with flecked saliva. Samuel laughed. "Not this one," he said. "This is my new hunter, Angel—a questionable name."

"Call her Vashti; she wouldn't do as she was bid."

"I might." He persuaded his mare out into the centre of the lane and stood between her and the second. "I bought this one from the Burtons at Cerne Abbas on the chance you would take him. He's sound, I promise you that, six years old, sixteen hands, a gelding, as you see, quiet and a good stayer. Try him."

Richard came to their heads and laid his hand softly on the grey Roman nose of the gelding; it gazed back at him through its dark, white-fringed eyes with an oddly serious expression, as if it had mislaid its spectacles. It was an air that appealed to Richard. He said, "I intended to call in along Back Lane on my way home; we could ride that way."

He had forgotten what a pleasure it was to him to ride; in the past months of worry and doubt he had forgotten almost all his pleasures; yet, as he accommodated himself to the low, swinging stride and felt himself rocked by the lazy movement, he found that he was not thinking of his haunting responsibilities but only remembering that he was, after all, still young. Samuel watched him as they ambled uphill, seeing that this action came easily to him, and he was surprised—as Laura had been surprised that her lover had proved such a graceful dancer. Somehow they did not expect physical accomplishments in him—but when the two horses shied and wheeled away from a sudden scream of laughter it was Richard who first regained control.

"My God!" said Samuel, as his mare fought to plunge herself against the hedge. "What's that? Should we go in?" He turned his face towards the cottage they had passed; an agonised moaning and weeping came to them from an upper room. Richard stayed him as he leant forward to dismount.

"It's no matter," he said: "the aunt in that family is mad; the warm weather makes her restless."

"Can nothing be done?"

"What can, is. I go to her every two or three days to talk and read aloud, it seems to calm her—and I've supplied her with paints to amuse herself. I got the idea from the asylum near Dorchester; occupational remedy is applied to great effect amongst their lunatics."

Samuel shivered. "Rather you than me."

"Oh," Richard kicked the gelding on and Samuel followed, "she's rarely vicious. She's allowed nothing with which to do injury."

Samuel considered the back of his earnest, artless relation. "You get what you want, don't you?" he said. "You wanted a country living and you got it; you wanted Laura—you got her; you wanted allotments—you have them; you wanted me to see my son—I did. What do you have for us next?"

An hour before, Richard had told Keating that he could put no heart into plans for the future—he lived only from day to day—now he could not be so frank. "I've various small charities in mind," he said: "a prize of five shillings to the mother who knits the best worsted stocking—and by the bye," he looked at Samuel who had drawn parallel with him, "as Laura nears her confinement her additions to the parish lying-in box are becoming more and more extravagant, best tea, port wine, raisins—she'll be the ruin of me—but the subject I think on most is a school; reading, writing, numbering, scripture knowledge, needlework, baking—I'll root ignorance out of my parish if I must try till I'm ninety. And here," he went on, pointing at a decaying cottage in front of them, "we have a family who will age me before my time. I must go in. I'll be but a moment."

He slid to the ground. Samuel took his reins and reached to fasten Keating's gift more securely to the saddle as Richard approached the open door. Thick, warm wafts of fetid air drifted towards them and mingled with the dry scent of harvest and the smell of heated horseflesh. A half-clothed child ran into the hovel and a frowsy woman drying her hands on sacking appeared in the doorway. Richard stepped over the rain-board and disappeared into the gloom. Samuel sat idly flicking away the flies that hovered above the shifting horses and listened to the conversation that took place.

A child was sickening again—and little wonder, thought Samuel, turning his head from the stench—there was an exchange of questions and answers on her illness, then Richard asked to open the back door. No, was the reply, there was wood leaning against it. He said that he would go around through the garden but made no move, and there was a discomforted silence until he spoke again—"You've been emptying your slops there again, haven't you? How much sickness do you need before you will learn?" "It's my man, sir, he's so tired when he comes home he can't dig what you said." "I hear from the midwife that he's not too tired to put you in the family way again." "No, sir, my seventh." "Then tell him to have the pit dug by Sunday week or I'll come and do it myself. I'll send you chloride of lime and carbolic acid for cleansing tomorrow. Now mind what I said or you'll all be down with the fever."

He emerged from the darkness and remounted, a pungent sourness clinging to his clothes. Amused Samuel asked, "Is this how you spend your days, then? Pigs, maniacs and sewers?"

"It is. I wonder I don't become a medical officer and have done." He put his hands on the pommel and arched his back to stretch away the tensions that had returned. "How much do you want for this hack?"

"Are you thinking of taking him?"

"Yes."

"I'll let him go for forty guineas."

"Oh? That's very cheap. He must be worth at least eighty."

"He is."

"Brotherly love?"

"Look on it as a bribe." Samuel took an envelope from his breast pocket and passed it to Richard. He did not watch as the priest unfolded it and took out a licence to marry him to Rachel Cooper. He was half-ashamed of Rachel; after the wedding he was prepared to put a bold front on his action for the sake of his son, but he could not pretend that she could take part in the society he had expected for his wife. He knew that the clamour that would arise when his marriage to a farm girl was announced would dwarf the gossip caused by her pregnancy. She could be by his side in their domestic life, but not all the world were Richards and he could never take her into the company of his equals. Her place would be confined to their farm and here he would take pride in the skills she practised. He was quite prepared to drink milk drawn by Rachel while her detractors drank theirs blue with bought water, eat bread baked by Rachel from flour ground from their own wheat, not poisoned by alum, spread butter newly churned by Rachel, not rancid from its ride to the wholesalers—but for all this she must not stray beyond the limits he set her.

Richard, too, sat without speaking. He understood that Samuel's reason for bringing a licence must be to prevent the banns being read. He must believe himself to be diminished by the match and wish to hide his intentions until the act was done. What hope could this bring for Rachel's happiness? But what hope had she or the child without him? He knew that he would marry them, yet it had come too late for him to be impressed by Samuel's chivalry.

"Will you do it?" his brother-in-law's voice was defensively hard.

"Yes. I think you're marrying her at the wrong time for the wrong reasons, but yes, I'll take the service."

"The delay wasn't entirely my fault; she wouldn't agree to a day."

He thought back to his second proposal and Rachel's weary acceptance of it. It had not been the eager acquiescence he had wished, but it had been enough. He had posed the question in softer terms than the first, reminding her of their old friendship and the prospects he could give to Ralph; although she had given in, her coldness had been such that he dared not touch her and always she had drawn back from a date.

"I had a previous delay in mind. However, I'm glad you've decided in her favour."

"Have a care with your lectures—or I may make my escape."

"When do you want the ceremony?"

"Tomorrow—early."

"Will your family be there?"

"No; and I'd be obliged if you didn't tell Laura—she'll only warn my father and he'll try to stop me. Since I am not to be stopped it would be wasted trouble."

"Have you considered that you might be disinherited?"

Samuel looked unconcerned. "I've considered that people will expect it, but he won't. He'd no more leave the land away from me than I'd leave it away from Ralph."

"He has two sons."

"Sooner or later Jonathan will break loose and go to build engines. He knows that."

"Well—the tenants at the glebe will be moving back to Devon in eighteen months. I'll need a new manager; remember it."

Samuel inclined his head and twisted a strand of mane between his fingers.

Richard went on, "How old is Rachel now? Is she of age?"

"Climbing nineteen—but I have her father's permission."

"Are you sure? I gathered he wouldn't even talk of her."

"He says he has no daughter; I say it's unwise to cross your future employer. Better to be a father-in-law than on the parish. He saw my argument."

The following morning, before the dew had risen from the meadows, Samuel Edward Haverly Delaford and Rachel Ruth Cooper came quietly to the church to be married. Jonathan Delaford was groomsman, Dinah Hillyard attended Rachel; both were promised to silence.

Rachel had come in a new gown of her own choice—a blue muslin in a plain design—a straw bonnet and her first silk stockings. She carried a sheaf of barley, wheat, poppies and cornflowers picked from his fields by Samuel. Her face was passive, but in her heart was a sense of overwhelming relief and resentment. She did not deceive herself that if her child had been still-born or female Samuel would have returned to her. He married her solely to have possession of her son. She still could not think of his deception without pain; and though she swore to love and honour him she knew she could not do it. For a fleeting moment in the service she held her fingers closed before he could put on the ring, and when they emerged from the porch to be met with the news that Laura had reached her time, she was not surprised that Samuel should turn at once from his wife to his sister.

Chapter Fifteen

It had seemed a long time coming. For an instant after the housekeeper told him the news that he had dreaded for so many months, Richard paused. It was a pause so short that none of the wedding-party noticed him hesitate, but in it he saw himself as though from a window, standing alone in the churchyard, the black and white of his vestments distinct against the slab-like shadows of the yews, a thrush singing in the wet branches above him, and he thought that if he could only turn and go back into the safety of the church he would again be the new arrival, with Keating by his side pointing out the painting on the beams; there would have been no vision of Laura coming last into her parents' drawing-room, no rain to make her take shelter with him, no breathless, tender evening at a country ball, no Samuel, no Rachel, no dragging fear that Laura's love did not equal his . . . he would walk back into the June afternoon of the year before and all would be calmness and confidence. It was a temptation of gentle, sighing seduction.

He said to Samuel, "Will you ride for Dr. Langland? I'd go myself but I'd rather stay."

Samuel turned to his younger brother. "Drive Rachel back in the gig, will you? I'll take your horse." He did not glance at his bride as she stood fingering the flowers he had picked her that morning, nor stop to wonder if she compared his present concern with that he had shown her at Ralph's birth. His most precious sister had need of him and there was no room in his thoughts for his wife.

Richard reached across and took Rachel's cold hand between his own. "Mrs. Delaford," he said—and saw her eyes first dull then warm, "forgive me for taking your husband from you so soon. My only excuse is selfishness."

She did not know how to reply; she had never before been talked to as an equal by such men, even in her contact with Richard she had always been conscious that he was a master and she a servant; now they were of the same family and his wife was her sister, yet she could not think what to call them. She wanted only that he take his kindness from her and the conversation be at an end. Forcing herself against a lifetime of restraint she pressed his hand. "You must go to Mrs. Webster," she said.

He found Laura in the dining-room arranging roses. She was dressed in a morning robe and her hair was loose. She stood at the table selecting single blooms from the tumbled pile of teas and bourbons on a silver tray and fitting them into a china vase. Her fingers shook as she moved the flowers and drops of water and fragile petals fell on to the waxed surface of the mahogany.

Richard came up beside her and put his arm gently around her shoulders. She went on choosing her roses; he saw her pick up a *Gloire de Dijon* and twist off the lower leaves as he had done before he had sent them to her fourteen months before, hoping she had taken no harm from the rain. He stayed her wrists. "My love, let me help you to bed."

"I have the flowers to finish." Her voice was distant and it made him afraid for her. He held her more tenderly.

"They'll wait, dearest. Come, let me take you upstairs."

She moved her head and looked at him as if she did not understand. "I'm quite well," she said.

He knew she was not. He had been told that her pains had begun almost as soon as he had left the house, but that she had refused to let either himself or the doctor be called and had insisted she come down. She put a hand to the hair that had fallen about her neck—it was the first time he had seen it loose outside their bedroom. "Where's Dinah?" she asked. "I wanted her to put up my plaits." A light sweat began to prick at her brows; for a moment she closed her eyes and held tightly to the table edge; then the pain was gone. "I'm going to the Vaughans' this afternoon," she said. "They've news of their sister in Boston. She's been helping the Abolitionists; you'd be interested, Richard." One by one the roses were placed in the bowl—lemon scented *Mme Hardy*, full, delicate *Sombreuil*, *Souvenir de la Malmaison*, pale as the hands that touched them—each stem carried with an increasingly stiff motion until at last she slowed and was still, standing in the filtered morning light frozen and defeated by her fear.

Behind her Richard dropped his surplice and cassock over a chair and took her in his arms again. She leant her cheek against the linen of his shirt. "I don't want to go, Richard," she said quietly.

"No, my love," he tried to tell himself that this was a scene enacted once in every marriage, but this was Laura and different. "No, I don't want to make you but you must, and in a few hours all will be over." He bent and lifted her and took her from the room.

He could do nothing for her. Afterwards he thought that he should have asked Rachel to stay. She with her restful, competent nature and her scrupulous, dairy cleanliness could have prevented all the pain that was to follow, but he had remembered only Laura's dislike of her presence and let her be sent away. The doctor was to come, her mother would be sure to follow, there were women in the house, all that there was for him to do was to lay her gently on her bed, allow her to order him out of the sight of her suffering and wait, helpless and guilty, as she was delivered up to nightmare.

All would have been well if the doctor had only been longer delayed. In an hour Samuel returned with his mother, as she discarded her gloves and went sedately to her crying daughter, he pulled Richard aside. "I've been God knows where after that blasted doctor," he said; "I was round the town twice before I found him." He paused to draw breath, his coat was hanging open and clinging to his back, there was dust from the road on his face and neck. "He's at another confinement in Greenhill; he says he'll come when it's ended. He says it will have finished shortly but that Laura's won't come before noon—first child and all. I said he must come to us directly he can; he could have one of our horses if he needed it . . . Jesus, will you listen to that!"

Upstairs Mrs. Delaford opened the door to Laura's room and for a moment they heard a muted, whimpering weeping, a cry of "Mamma, Mamma!" and the mother's "Hush, hush now, my dear" before the sound was cut off. It was not the single agonised moan that had awakened Samuel to the knowledge that Rachel was a woman like any other, but in its very dissimilarity it was as heartrending, showing as it did how unprepared Laura was to face this most common trouble.

The two men, for whom she was the epitome of what a wife and sister should be, stood dry-lipped at the foot of the stairs, aching for there to be some feat for them to perform to keep her from danger—some midnight dash across the snows, some wolf to drive away. Her own unhappiness in the last weeks had infected them with a pessimism for her safety. She was young, she was healthy, yet each one felt her marked down for death and each regretted every part they had played in her wretchedness; Samuel would have given up his son to have saved her, Richard would have renounced his marriage—but these were modern times and there were no gallant acts to ward off evil, nothing for them but to sit impotently by and wait for the all-powerful doctor.

Dr. Langland was not a man to be hurried by agitated brothers; nor was he one to be disturbed by doubting his own talent, being serenely confident that if illness was not to be frightened out of existence by the appearance of his florid bulk—mightily adorned by top-boots and riding-whip—entering the sick-room, then it was not to be defeated at all. He had trained in Dublin, where he had paid the ailing poor to let him use the knife, qualifying as a surgeon–apothecary in 1837, twenty-one years before the registration of doctors, and since then had forgotten much and learnt nothing except that relief of pain brought custom. Overgenerous as he was in his prescription of laudanum and spirits, his patients were grateful to learn that where Dr. Langland made an entrance, pain took its exit. That life often followed it was not surprising to an age that expected little of medical science and rarely dreamt of cure. It was enough that they should be ushered through their trials in a haze of opium.

The Delafords, who had always been robust in health, had never had occasion to test his skills by calling him in for anything that even he could make fatal. Richard had wanted Laura to have the new, younger doctor in Yeovil, but she had insisted that if she have a man at all it must be the one she had known from a child, not a stranger; and as her parents agreed and Sherborne thought well of Dr. Langland, he was engaged. The patients who could have complained of their treatment were housed in the church-yard; there was no one to speak against him.

Richard, like the Reverend Osbourne and his fellow parsons, was more acquainted with sanitary reform than was the man he had hired to tend his wife. He was familiar with Osbourne's theory of the causes of cholera and his experiments showing the presence of "countless masses of animated, active bodies" in decaying matter, and he pursued cleanliness in his own parish relentlessly. It did not occur to him that a doctor—who must surely have known of Semmelweis's work—would dismiss the contagious-ness of puerperal fever, that scourge of Victorian brides. He himself was better suited to delivering his child in safety than was Dr. Langland; indeed, had he gone out into the village and brought the first passer-by to Laura's bedside, he could not have chosen a more dangerous midwife than the man who was riding towards the Vicarage with the promise of death drying on his hands.

Lying in her overheated room with the curtains drawn, Laura did not care who came to her if only it would end her torment. All her life she turned away from what little pain she had encountered, refusing to accept that any unpleasantness could touch her, until she had spent the last years of spinsterhood believing that nothing she did not wish to happen to her could happen to her. The shock of her wedding-night had shaken her conviction, but even now, with the labour upon her, she could not break her habit and she would not help herself. It was unthinkable to her that she should increase her pain by pushing—and so she would not push. She would bear what was unavoidable, but she would not deliberately add to her agony.

After two hours the chance to hurry her suffering to an end was gone: she was too weak with terror to struggle for the child—and the child was no longer positioned to be expelled. If she could have rested a little to recover her strength, if her mother who never handled disease could have kept full charge of her, still all would have come right; but while she was at her lowest ebb the man who should have been her saviour swept down upon her—and she was lost.

Dr. Langland was well pleased with his day. It was true that the baby he had spent the morning delivering was born dead, but it had been obvious from the state of the body that it had been so for several days and no blame could be attached to him. He had no imagination that could make him share the parents' distress and was not visited by sentimentality over still-births; considering the fecund nature of women it was unlikely to be more than a few months before the unfortunate mother was his patient once again. Moreover, he preferred to interfere actively with whatever process was racking his victim, and the difficulty of this birth had given extended opportunity to wield the one-bladed forceps— an instrument with which he felt himself proficient.

He entered the bedroom in a bluster of self-satisfaction that he knew to inspire confidence and cast his hat and whip into Dinah's arms—another theatrical trick, implying an eager desire to have at the illness. He approached Laura—who was regarding him with animosity now that he was by her side and able to cause nameless humiliations—and, removing the wet cloth that was cooling her forehead, felt her temples. Fastidiously she tried to turn her face from his fingers, but feeling her head gripped fast she could only close her eyes.

He knew at once that here was an opportunity to repeat his morning's performance. He had been told by the white-faced husband that this girl was "in a bad way" and weakening. This was not so. True she was tired, frightened and excitable, true she was in pain, but she was not a desperate case. The child had not moved as much as he would have expected but, if left to itself, nature would eventually take its course; it would be a long and tedious process, however, and if he had judged Laura aright she would not be so consumed with motherly love that she would forget the passive part he had played in those hours; she would complain to Richard and he, poor fool—the doctor recognised the type—would go to any lengths to find her a physician she preferred. The fees for future confinements would therefore not reach his own pocket. On the other hand, if she was given the notion that her misery had been ended by the laudable intervention of himself, his charges would never be questioned. He smelt money and reached for the vectis.

There was dried matter clinging to it from the earlier delivery; he scraped half-heartedly at it with his thumbnail, rolled up his sleeve and returned to the bed.

It was with some effort on Dr. Langland's side and some endurance on Laura's that two daughters were brought to birth —small, weak, bloodstained creatures that could barely pule. There was silence from the adults in the room; Laura rested her wet, flushed cheek on the pillow and smiled to think that she could hear the stableman outside in the lane replenishing the straw that was meant to keep all sounds from her. Her mother looked at the smile and wondered what words were gentle enough to explain.

The doctor made a sign to Dinah, "Girl," he pointed at the babies who lay so still on the sheet, "take them down for baptism; they'll not last the night."

Laura lifted her head from its resting place and moved her lips, too tired to form words; her mother took her hand and held it in both of hers. Dr. Langland bent close, as if childbirth had rendered her deaf or an idiot. "Madam," he said, "your children will not live. Do you hear me, madam? Your children will not live."

She felt betrayed. She heard Dinah carry her daughters out of the room but she did not see it—her eyes were again closed against the world, which was not what she had thought it. She did not know what she had done wrong. She had been brought up with no aim but marriage and she had played her part. In innocence of its meaning she had flaunted and enticed and taken a husband, and where had it led her but to this foreign bed with the fetor of her blood in her throat? Where were the moonlit walks now? The bridal flowers? The clean, pink baby in the nurse's arms? Oh God, she thought, don't punish me any more. I didn't know what marriage meant. It isn't fair to hurt me for something I didn't know. Don't let this happen to me every year. Against the black and red of her eyelids she saw the face of the cousin whose pale skin she had admired so much—the cousin whose unlucky thirteenth had killed her—she saw Rachel so clumsy in climbing from Richard's trap the night he brought her from the farm, she saw herself in the Kashmir shawl that was not a shawl but a shroud —and the smell of blood was patchouli, and rose to smother the room.

She did not ask for her babies; she would not let herself think of them. She lay with veiled sight conscious only of the absence of pain and romance. She allowed coverlets to be put on and off, the fire to be banked, a slop of gruel and brandy to be given, a message to be sent to Richard that she would see him when she had slept—but she did not sleep; her torpor drifted into the loss of awareness that comes with a temperature. She did not notice the twilight closing into night, nor when a candle was lit did she notice the change from the sunlight. Instead of lying drowsy and comfortable, she became restless and could not settle: the sheets were twisted, the pillows too high or too low; at first she grew cold and more eiderdowns were fetched to stop the shivering and the chattering of her teeth, then there were too many blankets, always too many, and she was hot, too hot.

At three in the afternoon, when she had rested half an hour after the birth, her pulse was safely at eighty beats a minute, at 6.15 p.m. it had risen to ninety-five, at 7.40 p.m. it was a hundred and four, at 9.30 p.m. a hundred and eighteen, at 11.20 p.m. when her face was barely recognisable and she believed herself at the farm, it reached a hundred and thirty.

On Richard's insistence Dr. Langland had stayed to dine. Loaded as he was with grief for his two failing daughters, who had so torn at his heart at his improvised font, and with fear for his delicate wife, he had had no wish to eat a dinner with the doctor, but as it had been Langland's intention to return to Sherborne for his customary roast beef, it had seemed the only way to keep him in the house to attend to any decline. Thus he was at hand to pose magisterially in the bedroom as Laura's condition sank.

At midnight Richard was waiting alone in the drawing-room. No one had thought to draw the curtains and through the open windows he could hear the low cry of a barn owl as it sought its prey. There was death in the house and though it had not yet found its victim it hovered in the dark corners of the room. He lit a lamp and hid in the shelter of its light. He who had sat at the bedside of so many dying women, clutched at by their work-browned hands, was barred from Laura's; if he had been confident that she would be glad of his presence he would have gone to her, regardless of the protests of mother and doctor, but he could not feel that she would welcome him. Already he felt that she haunted him, that if he turned his head he would see her standing silent behind his chair.

He pushed a spill into the flame and moved about the tables and desk lighting every candle and lamp that he could find, a horror of night creeping over his skin. As he replaced the pink shade that stood by Laura's work-basket Dr. Langland returned, his shadow spectoral against the wall.

Richard blew out the spill and threw it into the fireplace.

"How is she?" he asked.

"It's as you feared. It's certainly the fever," the doctor took a rose from the bowl Laura had arranged that morning and held it to his nostrils to be rid of the smell of the sick-room. It was an irritating conclusion to the day; he was likely to lose a patient and without doubt this earnest young man would be difficult. "However," he continued, tucking the rose into his lapel and picking up a peach and fruit-knife, "don't be distressed—it's by no means always fatal."

"I've seen one woman recover; I've filled churchyards with the rest."

"Then let us pray your·wife will follow the good example. I've the treatment well in hand."

Richard watched him coldly. He did not like Dr. Langland; he did not like his loud confident manner nor his apparent indifference to Laura's suffering. He tried—as he always tried to excuse those he disliked—to put this down to a professional calm on the doctor's part and a desire to blame another for her pain on his own, but the pieces would not fit.

"What treatment?" he said.

The doctor engulfed a slice of peach and patted his lips with his handkerchief. "The progress of the sickness has been surprisingly severe. The rigor has come and gone; Mrs. Webster is in the second stage: there's a great heat in her body, a tiredness, an aching in the head and muscles, she thirsts but the water being passed is scant, she retches though her stomach is empty, her pulse and breathing fleet, she has no knowledge of time and place—my worry is that she will sink into the typhoid state and become comatose." He paused to underline the seriousness of his case.

Richard tapped the table-top with a forefinger; the atmosphere grew noticeably more frigid. "The treatment," he said.

"I've prescribed one grain of opium to five of calomel. The opium will bring out the sweat, deepen the breathing and calm the nerves, but it has a tendency to cause constipation—thus the mercurous chloride which will purge the bowels. I've also applied leeches to the abdomen to prevent congestion of the blood."

He talks of her as if she were a horse, thought Richard, and she is Laura. "And will she live?"

"I can't answer you; she may, she may not. It's in God's hands."

"Not entirely or I wouldn't have hired a doctor."

Dr. Langland levelled a practised stare at the offender, but finding it had no effect cast down the peach-stone and began to peel a pear. "Mrs. Delaford was asking for her son to fetch her husband."

"I've already sent him." She is to die then. And at her funeral will be Rachel Delaford. How will that end? I asked Samuel, what of his wife tonight?—and he told me he had forgotten he was married. Another tragedy. Lord, what have I done to this family?

"No one", said Dr. Langland, "is to visit the patient without my permission. There must be no exertion, no excitement, the heart is in a weakened condition and will not bear it."

The hall clock struck the quarter-hour. The doctor dropped the long, curling section of peel into the fruit dish and idly cleaned his nails with the point of the knife, smearing their contents on to the edge of the bowl. The silver gleamed and a thick, red substance clung to the glass. Richard watched the movements with revulsion. Blood? Was this man scraping Laura's blood from his hands? For a moment the room seemed to shift about him and bile rose to his mouth. The foulness of the taste reminded him that not an hour before he had heard his housekeeper telling Dinah that she had always said the cord should be bitten not cut. Why should she have been so vehement? An ugly suspicion came into his mind. He went nearer the dish; the redness was not blood, it was the wax that sealed medicine-bottles. A cool relief flooded his body, then retreated. If this was wax from the drugs the doctor had given Laura, he must have touched her since to administer them and yet not cleaned his nails. He had come straight from handling a putrefying disease to putting food into his mouth. What else had he fingered today? Why did his hands look so dark, so unwashed? If he was so reckless with himself, what risks would he take with a patient?

He said, "The other confinement you saw today? How did it go?"

"Interesting but unfortunate. The mother will do well, but the child was delivered a corpse." The lateness of the night and a desire to hurt this curt young husband drove Dr. Langland to expand his picture. "The foetus in itself would have been over-small, but it had swollen in its decay, the limbs were white and putrid, they . . ."

"I presume you washed in lime?"

"Ach!" the doctor removed a pip from between his teeth and examined it. "Fashionable nonsense."

"You didn't?" Shock and loathing were plain in Richard's voice.

"I did not; nor will I. I've seen women through their travails for twenty-five years—I won't turn Kraut now."

An empty, angry nausea rose to Richard's chest. The wilful, arrogant ignorance of this man, and his own naive belief that a doctor would have no vanity but in seeing his patients well, had killed Laura as surely and as cruelly as a garrotte. For all the light in the room the darkness seemed to press around him alive with whispers. The lamp between them sputtered; he reached to adjust the wick, but he had no touch and the flame died, shading them greyer.

Dr. Langland turned to leave the table. "I'll attend your wife," he said.

"No."

The doctor stopped and raised his eyebrows.

Richard spoke with a quiet, level ferocity, a tired determination that would not be broken. "I won't have you near her, nor in my house, nor on my grounds. Take up your instruments and go."

"And Mrs. Webster's drugs?"

"I have laudanum in my study; God knows I have chloride of lime—every home in the parish has been doused with it."

"You know nothing of medicine."

"It seems I'm not alone."

"You insult me, sir?"

"I do indeed. I am waiting for you to leave."

"This day I have delivered your wife of twins—I will not be thrown out like a beggar."

"I am a man of God, Dr. Langland," said Richard conversationally. "and I wish for the salvation of all—but with all my conviction I say be damned to you and your filthy knives and your butcher's tricks. Damn you for the fool you are. May you burn with me in Hell."

The handle of the bedroom door turned soundlessly and Dinah, heavy-eyed from watching by the bedside, rose and approached it as her master slid in. His face was grave-pale. "How is she?" he asked.

"Poorly, sir." She could say no other, there was no comfort to give.

He left her and went to the bed. He had seen nothing of Laura since he had carried her here from her roses; now he looked down upon a tortured stranger. The room was thickly hot and sour with sweat. On wet sheets lay his fastidious, delicate love with streaked hair clinging to her face and mouth open to catch the air that grated as she drew it to her lungs. She rolled rhythmically from side to side as if afloat on her pain, clutching and squeezing at her belly.

"Dinah," he said softly, and she came to his side. "Where's Mrs. Delaford?"

"Lying down, sir. I'm to call her in an hour or if . . ."

"This room is too hot. Damp down the fire and open a window."

"But the doctor said to . . ."

"I've sent him away."

In the half-light she looked her surprise.

"Do you think me a monster?" he asked.

"No, sir, a doctor can do no good," she indicated the writhing figure of her mistress. "This is how it is."

"Yes. Let's give her what relief we can while we can. Go you and cover the fire, then make up a solution of lime and put it on the landing—and bring up the roses; she was fond of the roses."

The night-breeze that fluttered the curtains stirred the smoke spiralling from the cigarette Richard lit. He held it in his left hand, grateful for Samuel's habits, and lifted away the sheet and Laura's gown with his right. On her white skin a dozen gorging leeches lolled and pulsed, threads of blood escaping their suckers. In her delirium Laura stretched down to tear them from her and he held her hands in one of his.

Dear God, he thought, was it for this she came down the aisle with such brilliance? To die worse than an animal in bringing life to children she never really wanted? Not even life—our daughters will die. Before her or after, I wonder. Lord, dear Lord, tell me where the justice is in this, the love, the mercy. Tell me for I can't see it for myself. I'm failing you, Lord, but I've failed Laura worse. I loved her so I put a cord around her neck and now I've drawn it tight. In a few hours her flesh will begin to turn cold and corrupt and this hand will stiffen in mine. I've killed her and everyone will be sorry for the killer.

And he sat in the silent, fear-ridden room with the shadow of death at his shoulder, burning off the worms that ate his wife, and all his heart cried murder.

Chapter Sixteen

The dawns that August were pale and cool, giving way to a rising heat that drew pearly, translucent mists from the ground. At St. Mary's House their beauty went unnoticed. From the higher windows which overlooked the churchyard the newest grave could be seen, and when the white-scarfed mourners had drifted away the lily-strewn mound lay to remind onlookers that life and death were cruel.

When the first of his daughters died Richard had had no doubt that her sister and mother would follow; but as the days passed and the silence in the house made the subtle change from the solid weight of anguish for those who will die to the fear for those who may, a hope began to grow within him and was answered. After her faltering start the second girl throve in the arms of a wet-nurse and, though she did not yet have strength or inclination to cry, in a week she was safe from the shroud.

He guarded Laura night and day, never leaving her room except to bury his child and to bathe, sleeping upright in an armchair, delegating his services to the Yetminster curate. He imagined he did this solely for his own comfort in being with Laura during what he believed to be her last hours, but she could not have had a more gentle nurse nor one more conscious of how neglect could injure her. Too late he had had his solution of lime put outside her door and everyone who entered was required to wash in it. Whoever was with him, it was always he who was first to tend her and, though she was too delirious to recognise him, below her distress in those tormented, furnace days she was aware of a solicitude that would hold her to life if it could.

On the fifth day after the birth her fever slackened and that night she slept. Early morning found Richard alone with her, seated in the chair between bed and window, pretending to himself that he was reading. Outside was the strange, ethereal dawn and the sun, reflected off the mists, threw a glowing snow-light into the room. He was tired, deadly tired, and there was a new loneliness in him. Night after night he had sat by her cooling her burning face, listening to broken, incoherent words, racking himself for proof that he had ever made her happy and then last evening she had held fast to his arm and called him "James". He told himself that a rested man would think nothing of it: she had called Dinah "Naomi", she had begged for Rachel to bring her milk from the dairy, if she had lost her sense of time she would not remember that she had even met himself, she would look for old friends, but still he thought of Samuel's warning that she was "sweet on Sanderson" and of her acceptance of him following so closely on James's engagement. He sat with a coldness in his chest that was not entirely unselfish and turned the pages until he was forced to close his eyes.

It was thus that Laura saw him when she awoke. For the first time in a week she recognised him as he sat, seemingly asleep, with a book on his lap and his head leaning against the wing. He was thinner than he had been and his face was strained and drawn; suspended between fever and health a tenderness for him came over her—a tenderness as for a favourite dog that was brave and true. She no longer wished to blame him for her suffering; the pettiness of her resentment had been burnt out by the horror of her experience. Fear of its repetition would return to her, but not the desire to punish the one man who she could be sure had not deliberately tried to harm her, nor taken his share of the burden lightly.

She put her tongue to wet her crusted lips and found it dry. The action made a curious, sticking sound and roused Richard. He looked at Laura and saw that the soul was back in her eyes; their sockets were sunken, her skin like paper, her hair lank, but to him she was again perfection. He dipped a cloth in barley water and wet her lips, then raised her cautiously upon her pillows until she could rest in the crook of his arm and drink. She drank two glasses with slow, painful swallows and lay back. She tried to speak and her voice came husky and low, "Oh, Richard," she said, "I had such dreams. I thought I was dead."

He stroked the hair from her forehead, feeling its new coolness. "No," he said softly, "nor anything like."

From their position they could hear the swell of bird-song welcoming the day and for a moment they stayed silent, soothing each other with their presence, then Laura said, "Is Mamma here?"

"She's asleep with Naomi. Do you want me to fetch her?"

"No. I just want her in the house."

"Your father and Samuel will be here soon. All your family are back and forth—I'm thinking of an omnibus." He smiled and she saw that there was no sting in his words. "Are you hungry?" he asked. "We've jellies and wines to feed an army. Everyone's been coming with this and that to tempt you."

"Later," she stirred in the bed, gazing at the ceiling. "Why is there this winter light in the room?"

"There's deep mist outside."

"Then, if you were to carry me to the window, I couldn't see the graves?"

"Only one grave, my love: we have a daughter living. She has your eyes."

"Living?" she lay puzzled, unable to believe. "But I was sure . . ."

He turned her face to his with gentle fingers. "She lives," he said, "and she will live; she's strong, she has a colour like a peach."

"Which? What have you called her?"

"Laura Rose."

She nodded. "And—the other?"

"Elizabeth Maud."

"When did she die? Was she baptised?"

"The day she was born: she died on the second night. All the village came to follow her."

She put her hand to his arm as she had done the evening before. "What text have you given her? For the stone?"

He touched his cheek to hers. "From Philippians," he said, "'I thank my God upon every remembrance of you.'"

On the morning of the sixteenth, when Laura had been safe for a week, Samuel visited his wife to tell her to begin wearing her ring. In the fortnight since their marriage he had seen her only twice. It was not deliberate unkindness that had made him turn his bride over to his brother on the church steps and forsake her for a further two weeks, it was merely that whatever had his love—whether son, sister or land—could absorb him by its need until he was blind to all else. It was obvious to him that while Laura was in danger he could not trouble his parents with a wife he knew would hurt them, and therefore his married life, like his courtship, must begin in concealment.

Today, now that they were no longer concerned for Laura's health, he had determined to tell them the news; and so that he could not slide into waiting another day he rode to Thornford to ensure his state was published. He had not yet made up his mind where he would be staying that night. His first hope had been to take Ralph and Rachel back to the farm. But Rachel had been adamant in her refusal to return to the place whose occupants had treated her so basely, and he could see that for all concerned it had been a foolish notion. He had a choice of either joining her in the cottage or continuing to live apart until he could find another more suitable house, an occupation he had given no thought to while Laura had been all his worry.

He found Rachel in the garden hanging her washing over the elder bushes and, scooping Ralph from the basket where he lay, he preceded her indoors. It was as shabby as it had always been. He sat on a stool and bounced his fat, smiling son on his knee. "Snail, snail," he chanted in time to the tapping of his foot, "Come out of your hole and I'll give you barleycorn."

Rachel lifted the baby from his hands and began nursing him, seating herself at the other side of the table.

"Do you still have the money I gave you?" Samuel asked. She nodded without looking up from the child. "You can start spending it now. Just get what comforts you can here; I'll take you into Dorchester for household things and clothes."

Now she did look up, glad that he was aware of the conditions he had brought them to in the long weeks before he had proposed. She remembered what he had not—that it was a year yesterday that she had told him of Ralph and he had rejected her. Her face was neutral, but inwardly she compared his concern for Laura with his treatment of herself and found him wanting. She saw why he had come and she did not want to live as husband and wife with all the intimacies and daily contact that it meant. She was resigned to her marriage, but she longed to have been able to give Ralph such a life without surrendering herself to Samuel—or to have been wed while her love was still untarnished.

"Will you be coming here tonight?"

"I don't know; we begin harvesting tomorrow so it would be more convenient to stay at the farm. I may come—otherwise I'll look about for somewhere decent for us to start."

Again she nodded and wiped milk from her breast as the baby opened his mouth too far. Samuel watched her with a possessive pride for the boy. He had hoped that she would be more eager, but he knew he could expect nothing and there was a certain attraction in the astringency that had replaced the soft compliance he had used to meet.

He rose to leave. "You can tell who you like," he said; "my family will know by this afternoon. Where's your ring?"

"In the jar on the mantelshelf."

"You can put it on."

She did not move. "It isn't usual for the wife to have to do that," she said.

He paused, then reached for the jar and shook out the ring. It gleamed gold in his palm. She sat and rocked Ralph, crooning to him as she stretched forward her left hand, not taking her eyes from the child. Samuel took her fingers and slid the ring over her knuckle; her skin was hard and tanned, unlike any hand he had expected to have joined to his. He folded it back around the suckling baby.

"Take care of my boy," he said.

He knew that his father would be in the estate-room at eleven and at a few moments before the hour, when he had returned his horse to its box, he went into the room to wait. He felt strangely ill at ease and younger than he had done for years. He was a man grown with a wife and a son, yet as he stood in that familiar place, smelling the leather of the bound day-books, the polish of the cabinet where the guns were locked, the dryness of the piles of sample grain on the desk, seeing the harsh August sunlight filtered through the old green linen curtains his father would not have changed, he felt like the child he had been when he first knew these things. Perhaps, he thought, I would have done better to have spoken to him outside where we're equal in our profession.

He dribbled kernels of wheat through his fingers. God, he wished he had love for Rachel to bolster him, then he could have led her by the hand and damned anyone who dared belittle her, but he was only too aware that he had married beneath him. Now he would never add to his lands by a judicious contract, nor have the satisfaction of introducing her as "daughter of—" and naming an old Dorset family, nor see her sitting in equality with his sisters. His wife would always be a shadow and it hurt that he, who had been so sought after, should have fallen so far—but there was Ralph. He opened his hand and gazed at the seed. Whatever he had lost would be made up for by Ralph. He would watch the boy grow and strengthen and in years to come, when his father and grandfather were dead, Ralph would stand in this room with corn in his hands and dream of harvest.

He brushed the grain dust from his palm as his father came in and began to search through a drawer in the map box. "Can you remember what I did with the chart of Home Lea at Darkhole the year they ploughed it over? I want to know what they sowed where; I'm sure we could get better weight off the headlands. Pour me a brandy, will you?"

"Sir," Samuel found his breath coming short to his lungs, "may I speak with you? I'm here for a reason."

Mr. Delaford turned from his rummaging and regarded his son. "You must be," he said; "I've never known you indoors the day before harvest. What is it?"

"I'm married," in the hole these words left he groped for something more to say, "I've taken a wife."

His father's eyes were like iron. "That is usual when you marry," he said. He slid the sketches he had taken from the drawer back into their bed and pushed it into place. Neither man was speaking, but the air was loud with recrimination and defence. Samuel felt the blood retreat from his face then surge back as he tried to be angry. At last Delaford said, "I presume this is our maid? Cooper's girl?"

Samuel inclined his head. "Yes, but now that she's Rachel Delaford I don't think we need remember her father."

"Do you not? We'll see if the county agrees with you." Again there was a silence, then, "Well, I can't tell you that you surprise me for you don't: I've seen this coming since April. I would have forbidden you, but I knew that if you came to your senses you would see how impossible it was and if you didn't I couldn't stop you. You obviously have no care for your family's position. You don't have my understanding and you certainly won't have your mother's."

"I have a son."

"I have two." They stared at each other coldly. "Have you considered that I might disinherit you?"

"I've thought of nothing else."

"And what would you say?"

"I don't have the words for it. You'd be tearing the heart out of me."

"Yet you'd risk it for your son?"

Samuel put his hand on the desk and leant towards his father. He said, "Because he *is* my son and a fit successor. I'll rear him till every inch of the land is his own flesh, till the seasons are his blood . . ." He halted embarrassed and urgent and Delaford turned from the sincerity and anguish that hurt in his son's voice, holding back his rage, forcing in himself a philosophical calmness over what had already been done.

"Why did you have to marry her?" he asked. "You could have overseen the child without that. If he meant so much to you we could have found him work on one of the farms. Couldn't you have been content with that?"

"No. He's my son, my boy, my first-born. What if his mother was a working woman? I am his father; he is mine and I won't shame him. Whatever I have must be his."

"Did you give no thought to anyone else? You've degraded us all. What kind of matches will your sisters make now that their brother is joined to a labourer? How is your mother to take pride in her family? There's never been anything but gentle blood in her line. She thinks of the girl as a harlot—everyone does—how is she to acknowledge her?"

Samuel said nothing; he had no argument.

Delaford went on, "She'll always be a drag on you. You can never bring her into the kind of life you could have had. And what of the farm you say you love so dearly? Where are we to find workmen of the Coopers' standard before the winter ploughing?"

"Why should we turn them off?"

"How can we keep them? It would be impossible. We must find them another place—or did they know? Rachel's under-age for a free wedding."

"They knew nothing. I told Richard I had her father's permission, but it was a lie."

"Richard married you?"

"Yes. Before Laura's lying-in."

Delaford rapped the table-top in irritation. "I needn't have asked; and does he intend to provide for you both if I disclaim you?"

"He's offered me the glebe farm when it's vacant."

"His bounty knows no ends." Delaford smoothed the papers by his side and shifted pens and measures as he thought. He was wounded by what Samuel had done. He had spent a lifetime building on the riches of his land that his family might progress proudly through the years and now, when he should have been looking for a prudent alliance, the son for whom he had planned, of whom he had always been proud—wild oats were nothing, after all—had ruined his prospect and tainted the stock. He had only two courses open to him: he could cast off his cherished son or he could accept the marriage and all it entailed. It was a bitter choice, knowing as he did that by assenting he must receive Ralph, for unless Samuel were to pass him over for a future son he could not keep the father without the child. Could he turn Samuel from him? Surely Samuel could have the better of his wife: she was a quiet, retiring girl; if she was kept in the background the children might be well enough.

Samuel stood stiff and severe, waiting for the word that would decide his life. Delaford put a hand on his son's shoulder and saw in the rigid face the eyes of the boy. "Come," he said, sorrowfully, "do you think I could do that? I have a first-born too. This land has been father to son for fifteen generations; how could I break that? I'd rather you'd got your children on a lady; it grieves me that your sons will be mongrels—and the first a bastard—but it's the father's blood that's important and, God, we're farmers, we ought to know an outsider can improve the breed. But don't expect us to meet her. I won't have your mamma subjected to more insult than can be avoided."

Samuel left the farm with what he needed for the night in his saddle-bags and money to care for a family. He was to return at dawn for the harvest, but there was a gulf between yesterday and tomorrow. In order to bring Limekiln to Ralph he was leaving it himself, perhaps never to sleep a night under its roof until his father died, and he felt that in this he was committing himself to Rachel more profoundly than he had done in church.

He met her before he reached the village. From half a mile distant he saw her standing straight and upright in the strong midday sun gathering kindling from the hedgerow, walking the lane slowly with the bundle on her hip. She was wearing a green gown that brought out the tawny of her skin and the russet of her hair where her shawl slipped from it. She had simplicity and dignity; she was her own mistress for all his possession of her and, to his credit, he did not see the slut his mother saw nor the labourer of his father, but a true-hearted woman skilled in all that he valued. He enjoyed the society that was barred to her by her birth; yet it was a peripheral, butterfly amusement that had no real worth to him. This girl and he might yet succeed.

He reined in when he drew close to her and she turned, shading her eyes. Vashti stamped in the heat. He said, "Come, give me your hand and ride with me."

"But my wood."

"Leave it in the ditch, I'll come back for it, but now I want no one to mistake that you're my wife."

He sat back in the saddle and held out his hand. She pressed the firewood into the long grasses of the verge and clasped his fingers, putting one foot on his, and he swung her up to sit sideways in front of him. His arm was strong and warm about her waist, but it woke no answer in her. She swayed as the horse began to move; he held her securely to him and together they rode towards their home.

Chapter Seventeen

Laura stretched languorously for her lemonade glass and the hammock rocked gently under her weight. Around her the scented air was murmurous with the lull of wood-pigeons and the droning of summer-heavy bees, the distant hills were hazy with heat and the stubble-fields shimmered pale gold. Attracted by the sugar, a butterfly settled on the rim of her glass and fearing it would be trapped she helped it away with her fingertip.

She was suspended above the lawn to the rear of the house between a stout, ivy-covered post driven in for the purpose and the smooth trunk of a lime; a book of love poems lay unread on her lap and, instead, she looked up through the mottled shade to the light that danced and shifted amongst the leaves. It was the first day of September and the first afternoon that she had ventured beyond the day-bed in the drawing-room. She was now under the supervision of Dr. Simmons, a recently qualified young man with the face of a compassionate bear, who had lately taken up practice in Yeovil and been interviewed within an inch of his sanity by Richard before being engaged. She enjoyed his visits; he would settle on the chair beside her bed, holding her wrist with ridged, scrubbed nails and gaze at her with round, brown eyes that invited confidence. "Hedonism, Mrs. Webster," he would say softly, "is a cure for all ills." It was he who had recommended that she should be placed in the garden while the sun shone and he who, knowing that there was no physical reason to bar it, had instructed her not to take the stairs but to let her husband carry her.

And so this afternoon she had been lifted from the sofa and brought to lie here, swaying comfortably in her white muslin dress with heliotrope pinned beneath her throat, intoxicating her with its drugging sweetness, giving herself up to pleasure and the knowledge that she was loved. Her illness had given a wan fragility, a sheen of transparency to her skin; no one who did not

189

know her would have guessed that she was a wife and mother, and aware of her look of delicate youth she played with the idea that life could again be good.

The sound of a door opening made her stir. She turned her head and saw Dinah approaching her along the lavender-edged path with Rose in a wicker basket. The girl reached her mistress and set down the crib on the grass beside the hammock; both women gazed at the baby who lay placidly sleeping under a light quilt, wearing a tucked and goffered bonnet of miraculous complexity.

"She's just been fed, ma'am," said Dinah; "she'll sleep for hours now. I thought you'd like her with you."

"Yes. Thank you, Dinah. Leave her here. Has the post come?"

"Yes, ma'am," Dinah took several letters from her pocket and handed them to Laura, "and Mr. Keating's man brought a pineapple with his master's compliments and said to say his carriage is available whenever you'd like an airing."

"How kind of him. That will be all, Dinah."

When the maid had gone Laura leant her cheek on one hand and looked idly down at her daughter who was sending small milk-laden sighs into the summer air. As Dr. Langland had suspected she had not been overwhelmed by maternal devotion, but she found herself more fond of her child as each week passed. They had really had very little to do with each other. It was Dinah and the wet-nurse who tended the baby's needs and, as she was not a crier, she did not declare her presence when her parents would rather have been oblivious of it in sleep. Thus Laura's affection was nourished by seeing Rose only when she was quiet and contented. She had had no wish to give up her young ease for the responsibility of a child, but because nothing was expected of her, because everyone thought "Laura must rest", she could spare time for her daughter without resentment. Perhaps because both her children had been so weak and near to death themselves, she did not blame them for her own danger; and though she did not mourn the one she had not seen, she was growing to love Rose.

Richard, of course, was completely besotted by what he called her delicious rotundity and was already talking of a donkey cart. Laura smiled at the recollection and lay back in the hammock, taking the letters from her side and holding them up to see who they were from.

She saw that one of the notes was in Grace Sanderson's hand and when she had broken the wax she read that her friend would call upon her that afternoon. The visit—though not the day—was expected and her heart did not jump with annoyance at meeting James's wife as it would have done weeks before. Although they had never been close, they had grown up together and it was natural that Laura's sickness should arouse Grace's concern. Their relationship had cooled after the announcement that Grace was to become Mrs. Sanderson—Laura had had no desire to be civil to the one who had taken the man she loved, Grace had been aggrieved by Laura's wedding overshadowing her own, both had been separated by Laura's removal to Bradford Abbas—but since Laura's confinement Grace had written twice, sending small gifts of fruit and flowers, and Laura had become more reconciled to the memory of her.

She liked to attribute this reconciliation to a philosophical acceptance of her position, but she knew it was not so. Before her wedding she had loved James as a young girl will, adoring him not as a man but an ideal. Though they were parted by only three miles, she had not seen him for almost a year and in that time he had changed for her from a romantic hero to a country lawyer. During her initial disillusionment with marriage, her resentment of her pregnancy, her pain and illness, she had tried to warm herself with memories of him and found she remembered only friendship. She realised that he had never encouraged her, never noticed what had seemed so plain, and now in her languid convalescence she did not regret either the lover she had lost or the one she had gained.

Through the days of heat and indolence she had dreamt new dreams; her mind rested gently on Richard. It was him she thought of when she wished for comfort; her trust lay in his devotion by her bedside, her romance in a parson too shy to wait for his dance. She was afraid of the future; no affection for husband or daughter could still her terror of what seemed the inescapable fate of women, but she did not reproach him for what had occurred and, had it not been for this one fear, she would have said she loved him.

At the moment that Laura thought of James he was within a mile of her. He had business to transact with the Thornhills of Clifton

Maybank and was using the opportunity to escort his wife to Bradford Abbas. He was mounted on the same grey gelding he had walked beside Grace the day they met Laura in the lane to Lenthay Common, and today Grace was again close to his side —this time not on foot but riding a safe, stocky pony and secured by a leading rein. She was clinging to the horn of her saddle with some bravado; it was only in the last few weeks that James had begun to teach her to ride and though she welcomed its promise of independence, she would have preferred her transport to have fewer legs and teeth. Her concentration on controlling the pony —which was so docile as to be almost unconscious—was such that she was not able to carry on a conversation and they progressed in companionable silence.

James did not intend to enter the village—his afternoon allowed only legal affairs—but his mind was occupied by Laura. He had been sincerely sorry to hear of her illness; he had always liked her and she had been the only one he had felt ready to confide in about his love for Grace. He had even begun to tell her, saying "Laura, love is so . . ." before they had been interrupted. He had occasionally wondered whether she might have misinterpreted this beginning, but her engagement to Webster had settled his doubts —not, he had told himself, that he need have worried that he had caused her distress—she had never shown any sign of love for him—but perhaps he had forced her to frame kind and ladylike refusals to an imagined proposal.

When he thought of her at all he missed her company and he determined that in future the Websters must be asked to dine; Laura was charming, Richard intelligent, they would make an agreeable enlargement to their social circle.

He halted at the junction above Smith's Bridge where the Bradford Abbas and Barwick roads diverged. Grace withdrew her attention from the pony's sedately forward-pointing ears and turned it upon her husband.

"This is where I leave you," he said. "Will you be all right from here?"

She wriggled insecurely in the saddle. "I think so; it's just around this corner."

"I can take you if you don't feel safe."

"No, no." She tightened her grip on the reins.

"Well, if you don't feel happy about going home by yourself, tell Webster and he'll send someone with you. I'll leave the leader on his neck." He leant and dropped it over the pony's mane. "Then come kiss me, sweet and twenty . . ."

"I can't—I daren't move."

"Just give me your hand, then."

She lifted it tentatively and he pressed her glove to his lips.

"Now," he said, "on with you—and straighten your back."

Grace arrived at the Vicarage with no alarms and, a little flushed with her courage, was led into the garden and seated in a basket-chair beside her friend's hammock. Laura was surprised by her own composure as she greeted Grace. It was Grace's act in taking James that had led to her recent communion with death and, even with her new attachments, she had expected to be disturbed; yet she could lie close to her with almost perfect equanimity. How strange that this should be.

For a while there was little said. Laura was too confused by her own calm, Grace was too intent on refreshing herself with lemonade to talk freely, both were inhibited by their long separation, but gradually little nothings were spoken over the baby—its health, its beauty, its good fortune in its parents—and the ice of convention began to melt back into the ease of familiarity. Grace flapped her flower-bordered handkerchief before her face, Laura offered her fan and advised that no one would be entering the garden to see her if she removed the jacket of her habit. She was interested and annoyed to see—as Grace draped the garment over the back of her chair and adjusted her sleeves—that her rival's waist was as slim as ever. She could not understand why there should be no sign of a child in a woman ten months married, nor why Grace should escape destiny when she herself had suffered—but it was warm, it was somnolent, the heliotrope overpowering—why waste your life in wishing?

"You've recovered so well," said Grace, "and you look so delicate. Convalescence suits you. But then I always did envy you your complexion."

"And I the colour of your lips," Laura looked at her graciously. "I bite mine and I rub them with geranium petals, but I can't get them so rich. You're lucky."

"Luck has nothing to do with it," Grace leant forward as a

conspirator. "I stain them with red ribbon dipped in gin. I keep the gin in an eau-de-Cologne bottle. It smells very like." She pulled a prim face and they giggled like the schoolgirls they had been.

"Does James know?" The name was easily said.

"Certainly not. Would you tell Mr. Webster?"

"No." Laura laughed at the thought and reached to tuck in the edge of Rose's quilt. A bee hovered about the lemon jug and they froze until it departed.

"Now Samuel's wife, she has a natural dark red—her face is so tanned though, perhaps that's why—oh, Laura, I'm sorry. Should I not have mentioned her?"

"Why not? I think everyone knows by now. You probably knew before I did; Samuel spends so much time with James."

"Do you mind?"

Laura played with the lace of her cuff. "I don't think I do. It doesn't seem real to me yet—Papa says he expected it, but I didn't—and I wasn't at the wedding and I haven't seen Rachel for weeks. . . . I don't know why, I haven't seemed to be worried by anything since the fever. I daresay it will hurt when I see them together, but as I don't intend to receive her that may never happen. Do you call on her?"

"Oh, no. Do your parents?"

"No. Mamma won't even hear her name—won't even think of her."

"She's hardly of a class we need think about. James says she should have been left to find her true level—these working girls always do."

Laura let her hammock rock gently as she considered; for someone who had announced her intention to cut her sister-in-law she found the comment curiously unpleasant. She did not know what to say.

Grace went on, "What about your father? Is the land still to be Samuel's?"

"Yes. Samuel says Papa was quite collected about it when he heard. Sam went expecting to be thoroughly cursed—he said it made him feel more guilty than if there'd been a real argument."

Grace refilled their glasses. "Your husband visits though, doesn't he?"

"Naturally. He looks on her as a lame dog, he simply can't see her for what she is."

"Oh? And what is she?"

"For want of a more expressive description," said Laura, her eyes fixed safely on the pip that swirled in the vortex of her drink, "she's a loose, scheming woman."

"Oh, come, mayn't she just have been caught out? You can't expect girls of her class to be as careful as we were—and, I mean no disrespect to your brother, but men are not always angels; could he not have had a hand in the persuading?"

"I thought that at first, I didn't even believe that she was willing, but it's grown clear to me that from the start she intended to use a child to lure him into marriage. The affair had been continuing for some time, you know. Why else would she continually submit? It's not as if she was obliged to by being a wife."

Grace raised her eyebrows. "But it's so nice," she said.

There was a sudden, surprised silence as Laura stared at her friend, and Grace felt an uncomfortable sensation of vulgarity imposed upon her. She hurried to disperse it. "I know we're not supposed to speak of these things," she said, "I know there has to be such a secrecy when we're young, but we're both married now; there needn't be pretence."

"I'm not pretending."

Grace flushed. "It's different for you, of course, after what you've endured; it's bound to colour your picture of it all."

"My picture," said Laura, acidly, "was coloured in October last."

"Oh? Was it a shock for you?"

"Certainly. Wasn't your wedding-night the same?"

"Not exactly because I knew what to expect. It would have been if I hadn't been forewarned."

"You knew?" Laura almost sat in her hammock. "You knew and you still married?"

Grace plied her fan languidly. "It's what the knowledge is for, my dear. How are girls like myself to find a husband—and that's what we're brought up for, don't forget that—if we don't know when to give the right word, the right look? My mother told me when I was fifteen so that I could cultivate an attraction. I had to—I had to have a style. I'm not really pretty—though men don't

195

notice it now—and I had no dowry. I had to make a man want me as a wife. It so happened that I drew the one I loved. It was different for you, Laura, you're so beautiful, you always stood out from the rest of us. All the men wanted you; you could be innocent and pure and they'd still want you—I could only be pure."

That night Laura lay alone in a confusion of mind. She was secure, comfortable and free from pain, she should have been content, but the soft light of the single lamp shone on eyes that were troubled. For the first time she was afraid that she might have fallen short as a wife, that her cold resignation may not have been all that her husband had expected. Perhaps, for all her beauty, the favour she had granted had been less than she imagined. She wanted to change, but how could she now?

Every night it came to her that as her health returned this celibate life could not go on. One evening Richard would leave the bedroom he had used since her illness and the misery and fear of death would begin again. How she wished it need not be so. She liked Richard—more than liked, she loved him—and if they could share a life of friendship and good company she would be satisfied, but if Richard should take possession of her body—however considerately, however lovingly, however much the world would think him right and she obey because it was her duty—she knew that the anguish it would bring upon her would turn their marriage to bitterness.

She stirred restlessly against her pillows. When the doctor had told her not to walk but to let herself be carried by Richard she had dreaded his touch; now she welcomed it in this chaste and caring form. His affection gave her warmth; she could not bear that it should ever be withdrawn from her, but she could imagine no alchemy that would turn her appreciation of it into desire. How could she believe that Grace welcomed such things? Grace was as much at risk from pain and death as she and even James could not save her from it. And Rachel? Had it been love and not artifice that had led to Ralph?

Perhaps it was her own attitude that was at fault.

There was a click as the snib of the latch turned. She saw the door pushed gently open and Richard come into the dim light as if he would steal upon her. She held her breath. He never came to her so late. Surely her fears would not be realised so soon.

Seeing that her eyes were open, Richard entered more confidently. He was dressed only in trousers and a shirt, which was collarless and unbuttoned at the neck. "Did I startle you?" he asked. "I didn't knock because I thought you might be asleep."

Laura shook her head.

"I came for a collar," he went on. "I looked for a clean one for the morning but there weren't any. Dinah must have forgotten and put my things away here."

Laura let out her breath in what might have been a laugh.

"Can't you sleep?" he said. "Shall I stay and read to you?"

"No, I'll sleep in a while."

He came closer, concern plain on his face. "Are you quite well? You look pale."

All at once she felt the tears brimming. She bit her cheeks to keep them back as relief and uncertainty fought within her. The sound of his voice made her feel more shielded and protected than anyone's had ever done, yet all her good intentions became impossible when faced with the reality of further suffering, endless childbearing. The paradox of the shelter and danger he offered was too much for her.

He sat softly on the edge of the bed, as he had the night they were married, and smoothed her hair from her face. Alive with a renewed anxiety, he said, "Dearest, tell me what troubles you," but she could not answer; instead she took two bunches of his shirt into her hands and rested her forehead on his shoulder. He curved his arm about her and asked again, "Tell me what hurts you." There was the silence of one struggling to speak, then she said, "I thought . . . I can't face another confinement so soon."

She felt him gather her closer.

"Oh, my love, do you know me so little? Do you think I'm so heartless? I wouldn't come back to your bed before you wanted me to."

"And do you want to?" Her voice was muffled against him.

"Yes," he tried to lift her face, but she held it fast to his chest, "but you mustn't fear me; if I take your hand or touch your hair that's all it will be—no further."

She wanted to reverse her year of coldness, wanted to say to him,

"Then come back to me now," but the fear was too great for her. She asked, "What if I should always want separate rooms?"

"You should have them."

His tone of compassion made her start to cry softly and he, too, could hardly keep back tears of pity for her.

"Wouldn't you mind?" she said. "Would you be hurt?"

"I told you, I love you, I'll give you the life that you want." He paused then went on, "I want you, I won't pretend I don't want you, but I love you too much to risk you again."

Her fists were hard on the linen of his shirt and he could feel her tension increase. He said, "You don't believe me, do you?"

She shook her head. "How can I? Samuel was so desperate he couldn't even wait till he was married."

"We're not all Samuels," he said. This time a hint of bitterness in his voice told her that what he said was true and guilt for her past treatment of his love made her retreat.

"But my vows," she said. "Richard, you're a priest—am I doing wrong in refusing you?"

He stroked her cheek with the back of his fingers, a light, gentle touch. "My love," he said, "you can't refuse something that isn't asked. And as for the vows, the first is for the procreation of children and we have Rose, the second is a remedy against sin and you are not a sinner, and the third, the most important, is for mutual society and comfort and that isn't lost to us."

She rubbed her face against his hand in a small gesture of gratitude and he looked down on her hair with regret for the innocence of life he had caused her to lose.

"You didn't know what you were promising," he said. "It isn't right to send girls to the altar not knowing what they promise."

He wanted to hear from her that she would still accept him if they had their time again, but he dared not ask. He put his hands one on either side of her face, his fingers reaching to touch one another amongst her hair, his thumbs resting on her temples, and raised her to look at him. He said, "We didn't understand life, you and I, we both thought it was all romance."

"No," she said, and her eyes were earnest. "You don't know my guilt; you don't know how little romance there was for me, Richard," she took his hands and held them between hers. "When I married you I did it for reasons that were not just. I didn't know what you were; how much better than—than anything else I could have had. Even today I learnt—but, Richard, I wanted to say that I love you and will love you, and if it were not for my fear I would have you back now, at this moment, and never a regret."

For an hour after he had left her Richard stood in his unlit room watching the night through an open window. Outside hung a fat and buttery moon, a nursery-rhyme sight that had no part in his mood. Under its light he could see far across grey meadows and black, one-dimensional trees to the shadowed rise of the hills. So he had seen them the first evening of his life here, but it was not the peace and contentment he experienced then that had returned—it was the haze and glitter of first love, the golden, expectant days when the ground had pulsed beneath his feet.

He had thought himself despised and found there was no rejection. Always, even before she had learned of her pregnancy, even in the first signs of her warming to him, he had felt her to be measuring him against her ideal and finding him wanting. He had opened his heart to envies and imaginings that should have had no place in him. But, he thought, she is my wife and she does love me; it has only been fear of a real danger that has made her seem cold—and there has been no coldness since the fever, no word or look of blame; it is me she turns to in distress, me she talks to of her love.

He turned to look at the bedroom that offered as little comfort as a bachelor's home. There were no lace and silk garments dropped across chairs, no lingering, exhilarating scents of rose and lavender, no Laura sitting before the mirror talking idly to him as she prepared to sleep, but now there need be no loneliness for him in the scene. He had expected to be banished here, to live in seclusion, cut from her, as if he were her brother, instead he had been drawn into her confidence as he had never been before.

When he had found that he was not distasteful, encouraged by her willingness, he had told her that a curacy led to paths you could not reveal to a bishop. He had heard rumours that the choice was not between celibacy or endless childbearing; he had read of the illegal circulation of literature that told of the artificial control of births; he had seen families whose increase suddenly stopped without explanation or estrangement between the parents; he knew of his Church's opposition to a knowledge which allowed the limitation of children born to a couple—a limitation by mechanical means. He did not know what these means were nor where to find the knowledge, but he was a practical man and could see no depravity in the protection of women from suffering—if he could discover a method to prevent conception, would she accept him, would he be welcome in her bed? And she, who had not imagined that she could be offered a chance to love completely but without fear, had coloured and nodded and laughed at herself as she had not laughed since the evening they had met.

Now he stood at his window in gladness, an affectionate wife asleep in the room next to his, and he, a heretic in search of the obscene, smiling at his situation. It could bring him imprisonment and the loss of his vocation, but he would not draw back. She was his wife and he would not hurt her for the love of God—nor could he see divine glory either in her pain or their separation. He would search out this knowledge and they would return to each other as if there had been no shadow between them.

He longed to have her in his arms again. For all his romantic view of women he had never seen them as purely spiritual creatures, he had always recognised the call of the flesh, but he had underestimated the hunger that marriage would release. It was one thing to be celibate before taking a wife, another to be so after tasting the delight she could bring. When once you have bitten the apple there is no return to the unblemished fruit. He knew without question that he loved her too much to put her in terror of him—but if she could be protected from her fear? And if he could find nothing to guard her, why should he grieve? Was he so petty that desolation should come upon him because so small a thing was to be set aside? Not a month ago he had been sure that she would die and yet she was alive and his; with passion and truthfulness she had told him she loved him. Why chafe when there was this bond between them? Hold to the quiet pleasures and there would be joy.

Chapter Eighteen

Two days later Grace Sanderson again took to horse. On Saturday she had been led home by the Websters' man; tonight she wanted no attendant. She did not tell James of her going and when they had dined and he left the house for the Gentlemen's Debating Society, he had no idea that an hour would find the wife he thought at the piano venturing alone through the dusk to Bradford Abbas.

She waited for him to leave with a nervous expectancy and when, by watching his progress along the street through a crack in the curtains, she had ascertained that he would not turn back, she took an old newspaper from the rack and went upstairs to their bedroom. She knew that her staff were at their meal in the kitchen and there was no one to see her, yet as she mounted the stairs she felt that the eyes of the house were upon her and her mission plain to all.

With relief she entered her room and slid the bolt behind her. The curtains had been drawn earlier for her to dress and only one lamp left burning; she lit others and, taking her keys from her pocket, unlocked her bedside cabinet. Inside was a china bowl containing a round sponge attached to a ribbon and a small book wrapped in a piece of cloth. She knelt on the carpet undecided, her wide skirts puffing out around her, then lifted the cloth-bound parcel and took out the pamphlet. Now that it was in her lap the courage she needed almost left her. The book she held in her hand, the book given to her by her solicitor husband, could have him prosecuted for obscenity. He had told her to show it and speak of it to no one—and now she intended to put it in the charge of a parson.

She was not betraying James; it was kindness and generosity towards Laura that moved her. These pages had saved her from the worries and fears that afflicted youthful wives and she wanted only to share them with a friend who had suffered.

She smoothed the cover and opened the book. *To The Married in Genteel Life* it proclaimed and in it the admirable Francis Place, whom Grace had every cause to thank, promised the prevention of unwanted births by the use of the same ball-shaped sponge that lay before her. Accoucheurs of the first respectability, it said, and surgeons of great eminence have in some peculiar cases recommended this cleanly and not indelicate method.

She took the sponge from the dish and let it rest on the palm of her hand. Strange to think that such a simple thing could prevent her being driven into an untimely old age. This was something she had not guessed at until she married, and then how much more at peace she had been to learn that she could choose the number of her children and when to have them. Like Laura she had had relatives who had not survived their lying-in, like Laura she had seen friends grow tired and hag-ridden by what should have brought them happiness. It should be good to be young and married to the man you love. She had no reason to doubt that Laura loved Richard as she herself loved James and that, if her fear were lifted, the anger she had shown on Saturday would disappear. She thought as she looked at the ball how much happier Laura would have been had she married James, not because of the man but because of this single device.

Lifting the silk valance of the bedstead she drew out the wrapping-paper, scissors and paste-pot she had secreted there that afternoon and began carefully snipping separate letters out of the newsprint until she could glue "Rev. R. Webster" on to the paper. When the idea of delivering the book had first occurred to her in the late hours of Saturday night, as she lay awake pitying Laura, she could not think how to direct it. If she addressed it in her own hand she might be recognised and the law brought upon her; for the same reason she could not simply lend it—she must be disguised. Again, who should receive it? It was Laura she wished to save from distress; yet she realised that it was the husband who decided these matters and if Richard did not choose to utilise it Laura's opinion would be of no importance.

When the package was bound tight enough to discourage the curious she placed it on the counterpane and changed hurriedly into her habit, then, hiding the parcel in a travelling bag of leather, she descended the stairs and ordered her pony with a firmness that surprised the outdoor-man as much as herself.

It was a miserable ride. She was afraid to be alone in the night, afraid of the shadows that shifted by her sides, afraid of being apprehended and forced to explain herself, afraid that she would miss her way, afraid that she would be stranded by the pony beginning and refusing to cease to crop the verge, so that James would discover her gone and come to search for her before she could accomplish her design. But she was glad of the darkness that hid her from those who would notice that Mrs. Sanderson rode late and solitary.

She reached the village unaccosted and dropped from her mount at the church gates. She could see lights burning at the Vicarage, but could not know that inside, as bright as any lamp, burned a desire for the knowledge she carried. She dared not raise the servants' speculation by leaving so oddly addressed a package at its door. Instead she gathered her skirts in her hands and crept into the chill gloom of the church. It was black and melancholy but to her, in its deserted state, it was sanctuary. She stood quietly to let her eyes adjust, praying that her pony stay silent, then walked softly along the nave. Laura had told her that Richard slept badly and would often rise and come to the church long before Communion—please God that he should be the first tomorrow. With her heart beating to fill the stillness that stared at her audacity she stole into the vestry and there upon a surplice—where hours later a man, more husband than parson, found, read and gave thanks for it—she placed the book.

James and Samuel strolled up Hound Street through the midnight air. Between the patches of yellow-blue radiance thrown by the sibilant gas-lamps their way was lit only by the glow of their cigars. Both had spent an agreeable evening discussing temperance over the brandy-and-sodas; now they wandered aimlessly home, Samuel softly humming "Meet me by Moonlight", James occasionally providing an uncertain descant. It was the first debate Samuel had attended since his marriage became public and he had enjoyed the discomfort of his fellows, who had not known whether to comment. He had watched their difficulties with an aloof, cat-like smile, nurturing a perverse pride in the wife whose existence could so embarrass the conventions.

They had been talking idly of their wives as they meandered through the streets, and now James again broke their music-making. "So your family still won't call on Mrs. Delaford?" he asked.

"No," Samuel threw aside his stub and trod out its lustre —tobacco fumes rose as the crimson died, "only my brother-in-law—though I think Naomi would if she were allowed."

"Does Mrs. Webster not . . . ? But, of course, she isn't well enough yet; though Grace told me she seemed surprisingly recovered on Saturday."

"Surprisingly is true. I saw her on Sunday and she was quite sentimental over her 'dear Richard'; I thought I'd gone to the wrong house." He checked before he said too much and they fell into step, drifting through the artificial darkness and light of the town. A bat swooped from grey eaves and was gone.

I could have saved him, thought James. Knowing what I know, reading what I've read, I could have kept him from any need for misalliance, but I dared not. How can you tell how anyone will react? What if he should have revealed what I told? To be found passing such information in my profession—I still dare not.

Together they reached Newlands and divided their paths, James to his home, Samuel walking beneath the high walls of Sherborne House where Laura had learnt that life was not what it promised. He collected his hunter from the stables of the George and rode down the hill into open country. Out of the shadow of the houses the moon that had shone on Richard's gladness glimmered on the landscape, spreading a subtle shading over the woods and hills.

He left Vashti in the meadow he had rented beside their garden and let himself into the cottage. All was quiet but for the rustle of dying coals in the grate. He stood for a moment in the dimness of the room, savouring the home that was his and the complications that lay in it. He had made improvements in the three weeks he had been here: there were two Windsor chairs brought from the Chilterns, copper pans on hooks beside the hearth, good china, a ham suspended from the pantry ceiling, shelves of books.

It amused him to live in such confined surroundings, amongst people he thought so different from himself. But how different? He had come home on Thursday to find a Latin dictionary open upon the table and, on his mentioning it, Rachel had told him that its reader was Dinah. Dinah—a strange girl. What longings were there in her that made her read old languages and expect to be called Miss Hillyard? Was she another who would find herself a husband whose friends could not rejoice with him? Again he remembered his fellow debaters' unease, again he smiled his queer, panther smile and felt more kindly towards Rachel. With barbed pleasure he noticed the signs of her in the room: the neat cleanliness, the folded length of silk she was sewing for a gown, the squares of satin and velvet she was turning into a quilt, with the defiant embroidering of a tiny hand in its corner to remind him that she had been a mother when she married. He would have her mistress of a farmhouse yet.

He drew the bolt and climbed the narrow, bottle-lined stairs. In the bedroom Ralph and Rachel slept, the baby heavy-fed, the girl softly against white sheets. Here, too, there had been changes: a Turkey carpet was thick beneath his feet, new window-glass shut out the night, painted papier-mâché bed-panels gleamed at her head and feet. A wave of tender protectiveness rose over him for the sleeping girl who had brought him Ralph, the girl once so open and trusting, bringing him every small worry and fear, now so self-reliant, so sparing with knowledge of herself. A streak of moonlight fell across her hair, an ivory wash on russet. He undressed in silence and slid into bed beside her. She stirred without waking. He kissed her gently from her brow to the hollow of her throat and half-dreaming, half-aware she rolled into his arms.

By the afternoon of the following day an anticipatory autumn crispness had crept into the air. The pale sun was warm and mellow, but the breeze that brushed the leaves told of frosts to come. In Samuel's parlour the range had been banked high for baking and the windows laid open to catch the wind. All morning Rachel had stood at the table, hair bound back, sleeves rolled, kneading the dough with a slow, rhythmic motion of the heel of her hand. Now she had no need to mind Ralph for Samuel had come home unexpectedly to eat and to claim the boy for an hour. He had brought her chrysanthemums that gleamed golden in their jar; she had given him chine striped green with chives from their garden. It had been an oddly tranquil meal. He had drawn water for her and then, taking their son bundled in a shawl, had put his arm through hers and taken her out to savour the season.

She could not decide whether to please him. Last night, when he returned, she had been too drugged with sleep to restrain her natural response and today she was troubled by the complacency of their waking. What she had once given so freely, she now gave in smallest measure and took her satisfaction from knowing herself a cold lover; but though it was hard not to resent him, it was harder not to enjoy him, and when the candles were out and they were enclosed in nearness and darkness she would feel the old pull and despise herself for it.

She found her moods dipping and rising, changing with every moment. At one hour she would be light-headed with the joy of security and respectability, the next her heart would beat with the despair of being tied to a man who had so humiliated her. She could not deny that there were benefits apart from the very fact of being married. Samuel had promised her that when they had charge of a farm the egg and butter money should be entirely hers, and even now, when she relied completely upon his generosity, she enjoyed having money in her purse and being encouraged to spend it on luxuries of dress; she enjoyed the change of diet from the labourer's eternal potatoes and bacon to whatever Samuel willed for that evening. Working as she had in a dairy and feeding three people on farm-men's wages, she had had little experience of cookery, and it was a delight to her to have expensive meats delivered and to spend quiet afternoons learning step by step from the Eliza Acton Samuel had brought home.

She was surprised by how she feasted upon being called "Mrs. Delaford"; like Samuel she would relish the discomfort of the speaker, looking intently at the strained face as if striving to catch mumbled words. Newly offered friendships were nothing to her; she had given her coveted trade to the shops of Sherborne and she had found herself laughing inwardly as their delivery carts passed along the main street to her door. She loved the new affluence of her home and felt herself almost ready to manage the concerns of a farm, thus taking the first step towards giving Ralph pride in his mother.

But for all this, she could not destroy her defences and let herself love her husband—and he seemed neither to desire her love nor want her to take any further part in his life than caring for himself and his son. She did not want to meet his family or friends, but it hurt that he had not asked her to do so; and though she was lonely, she no longer looked to Samuel for tenderness; all the love that had once been poured upon him was now for her son alone and, with a silent inner ferocity, she cherished a determination that he should grow in the ways of living that she had been taught. He would be truthful, loyal and sober, diligent and responsible, loving innocent joys and never making light of a girl who had given him her heart. She had married his father to give him the advantage of wealthy, landed parents, but she would fight Samuel with a quiet, earnest strength if he tried to turn Ralph from the path she had chosen.

Outside the scene had made the change from summer oils to autumn water-colours. In the exhilaration that comes with the observed passing from one time to the next Samuel could neither work nor rest. He had carted seed-clover since six that morning, but at noon the hunger to show his family the dying of summer had taken him to Thornford and brought him out on to the hills, with a child in his arms and a girl's steps in time with his own. He walked back towards Sherborne along the deserted lane as far as Pitman's Leaze, then turned and climbed upwards to White Hill Wood until he could stand on the brow of the hill with the trees at his back. The road was dry and thick with dust, but he could taste that rain would fall and tomorrow would see showers. A scent of wood smoke drifted up the slope, but at the summit the air was clear and drenched with the expectation of a new year.

He sat down on the grass, spreading his jacket on the ground for Rachel, and she curled at his side, a little above him, resting her hand on his shoulder. He stayed silent, wrapped in well-being.

From here he had command of a rural panorama: in the valley a woman hung out washing that would soon be condemned to drip out winter on to earthen floors, a grey-blue heron, soft with distance, stood carven on the river-bank, nearer, at the wood's edge, a deer browsed the meadow until the breeze let her smell her watchers and she melted back into the brown-laced leaves. But more than this was in his mind; half the land within his sight was his, all his four farms lay beneath him, and the pasture on which he sat would fall to the Delafords before November was out.

He lifted his son and held him on his lap, strong fingers girdling a tiny waist. It was for this small child that he had risked all that he loved—and won; for him that he had taken a wife for no more reason than that she was the mother of his son. He smiled to recall the strange, prowling contentment that was growing within his marriage, a contentment that fed on having set his acquaintance askance and proved that he valued skill before ornament. He did not yet love Rachel nor she him, but they were bound by her past love and its consequence, by vows, by the sensuality that he would coax back to its first bloom—above all by their son. Together they would move to Darkhole and teach Ralph to revel in the growing of crops and the sweetness of the passing seasons, to despise those who believed that to be a gentleman meant overseeing the toil of others from a chair before the fire. Together they would plough and sow and reap and leave more land to Ralph at their deaths than would be left to them in their turn. Together they would work so that Delaford ground might run in a continuous line from Digby Park to Richard's glebe, and in that working love would come.

He looked with pride at the wife he had not wanted and there was understanding in her eyes.

"Ours," he said—and Rachel said, "Ours."